THE LIAR OF RED VALLEY

WALTER GOODWATER

T0127494

SOLARIS

This edition published 2022 by Solaris
an imprint of Rebellion Publishing Ltd,
Riverside House, Osney Mead,
Oxford, OX2 0ES, UK
www.solarisbooks.com

First published 2021 by Solaris

ISBN: 978-1-78618-532-7

A CIP catalogue record for this book is available from the
British Library.

Designed & typeset by Rebellion Publishing

Printed in Denmark

To my daughter,
who came into the world late
to give me time to finish writing this book

CHAPTER ONE

SADIE NEVER REALIZED just how full of shit her mom was until the day she died.

Of course she'd known her mom was a liar; her lies paid their bills. People would come from all over Red Valley to see her. They hated her—because she knew their secrets, because they needed her, because she hated *them*—but they still came, in beater trucks with rusted wheel wells or glossy Audis with no license plates, winding up the dirt road to knock on the Liar's door. And after a lifetime in Red Valley, her ledger was full of every dirty thing the people in town had ever tried to hide away.

When Sadie was younger and the customers came, her mom would say, "Why don't you go play outside for a few minutes?"

She'd go, but she peeked in through grimy windows enough times to know how it worked. The customer would tell her mom the Lie they wanted to be true, and she'd write it down in her ledger. Then they paid her, usually cash—the Liar didn't accept checks—but sometimes in barter: groceries, Lotto tickets, tuna casserole. Honest Bob, owner of Honest Bob's Used Automotives, must have had a real whopper he needed telling—and didn't want to touch his savings account—because he gave her mom the keys to the Mustang he'd driven up in. She'd kept it for a few months then sold it back to him, said she didn't like how the convertible top messed up her hair.

After her mom was satisfied with the offered payment, there was only one step left: they had to pay the Liar's Price. This was probably what her mom didn't want Sadie to see. She forgot that blood isn't as scary to kids as it is to grownups.

Her mom would take out her pocketknife, clean the blade, then make the customer hold out their hand, though some people preferred she made the cut somewhere less conspicuous. In the end, she only needed a few drops, enough to smear next to the Lie written in her ledger, to seal the deal.

People got out of there real fast after that. Maybe they didn't like the sight of their own blood. Or maybe they didn't want someone else to come down that dusty driveway and find them there. Sadie didn't care either way. After a while, watching the forbidden ritual became a bore, so instead she'd go off and play make-believe in the dry oak trees that surrounded the tiny blue house. She liked to climb up in the twisted branches and pretend she was invisible, pretend she could see the whole world but they couldn't see her. She'd sit up in the trees for hours and wonder what Lies she'd tell:

Everyone at school likes Sadie.

Sadie lives in a big house with a fireplace and a pool and a garden.

Sadie doesn't feel lonely all the time.

So Sadie always knew her mom was a liar.

But still, she never expected she'd lie to *her*.

"EXCUSE ME?"

Sadie blinked hard. Memories of gnarled oak branches and blood soaking into paper scuttled away, replaced in a flash by the diner's heavy air, greasy with French fry oil and floor cleaner. Sadie's head swam for a moment, like she'd fallen asleep on her feet and woke just before toppling over.

The frowning man at table six was waving irritably at her. Sadie let the afterimages fade and slipped on a cheery smile—the most important part of the waitress' uniform—as she came out from behind the counter.

"*Excuse* me," he said again. He sounded like he didn't much care for having to repeat himself. Calloused fingers drummed on the table. He glanced down at Sadie's nametag but didn't even bother to use her name. "I ordered that coffee ten minutes ago, sweetheart. I'm just wondering when I should expect it to arrive."

A coil deep in her chest tightened a little. The smile threatened to bail, but Sadie locked it back into place. Working in Red Valley, you got used to the assholes. Some entitled, some bitter, some just plain *mean*, but every shift had a least a couple. Sadie didn't know if the town drew them or bred them, but she'd learned to stop expecting better from people around here. Fake smiles, thick skin. Never look them in the eye, so you don't have to remember their stupid faces when trying to sleep at night.

"I'm sorry about that," Sadie said, her voice a little too sweet. "I'll go get that right now. I think we've got a fresh pot going."

He said something through his frown as she walked away, but she didn't listen. She could tell by the shape of the words that it would just make her want to pour the coffee on his lap instead of in a mug, and that wouldn't end well for either of them. So she got the coffee and returned to his table, her smile never fading.

"Finally," he said. "That wasn't so hard, was it?"

There's that irresistible Red Valley charm, Sadie thought, and cringed immediately. Now she sounded like her mom, and *that* was terrifying. The Liar could get away with casual disdain for everyone in town; Sadie, on the other hand, still worked for tips. Not that there was much hope for any this afternoon. Other than the cranky guy sucking coffee through his mustache, the diner was mostly empty, just a couple of the old-timers in the booth by the door, arguing about the drought and how the whole town was drying up under our feet like a raisin. Their tips usually came in the form of pocket-warmed pennies and dimes. The lunch rush had only been a couple hours ago, and she figured it must have been busy, but truthfully she could barely remember.

Someone in a hairnet stuck their head out the door from the kitchen and called to her. "Phone call!"

Sadie wiped her hands on her apron and frowned. No one called her, not at work.

She went through the flapping doors into the kitchen and was greeted by hot air scented with day-old bacon. The dishwashers were laughing in a corner while they broke down oily cardboard boxes, all except Javier, who had drawn the short straw again and was sweating over the grill, hoping to find some clean metal under all that old black grease. The chefs were seeing how many times they could flip their spatulas in the air before catching them—or dropping them with a clatter. Denise, the owner and head waitress, glared at the chefs and pointed Sadie toward the phone hanging on the wall in the back.

"Sounded serious, hon," was all she said.

"Hello?" Sadie said into the phone.

"Can you hear me? My name is Abagail, I'm a nurse down at St. Elizabeth's, and we've got your mom in here..." Sadie listened to the rest without hearing it, and somehow was able to repeat enough to Denise for her to tell her to take the night off and go see her mom.

"You need a ride out there?" Denise asked. "I can send Javier."

"No, that's fine," Sadie said. Her voice sounded like a stranger's. "If I go now, I can catch the bus."

She made it to the bus stop just before it pulled away. She took an empty spot by the front, the A/C frigid on her clammy skin. Toward the back, a couple of high school kids whispered sharply to each other while they stared at Sadie. She ignored them. An ageless woman with saggy, tanned skin sat across from her. Despite the blasting heat outside, she wore a heavy winter coat that was filthy at the cuffs and shiny on the elbows, and a massive garbage bag full of aluminum cans crinkled at her feet. Her eyes kept darting over to Sadie, but Sadie kept her gaze fixed on the window. She was used to the attention. People in Red Valley always noticed her—the daughter of the infamous Liar—but rarely spoke to her. Instead they stared and they whispered.

Luckily St. Elizabeth's Hospital wasn't far and was on the safe side of the River. Outside the bus, the dry dead hills around Red Valley seethed in summer heat. The few people she saw braving Main Street were flushed red and soaked in sweat. She didn't understand why they bothered; most of the shops were boarded up and empty, cracked-glass storefronts of buildings left to rot in the sun like overripe fruit, victims of the arrival of Walmart on the edge of town. Signs for the 4th of July picnic at the park still hung crooked on telephone poles, long past the celebration. Taped to dirty windows she saw election posters in red, white, and blue: ELECT UNDERSHERIFF DWIGHT HASSLER FOR COUNTY SHERIFF. FOR A SAFER RED VALLEY. The undersheriff's grim face and thick mustache stared back from every poster, watchful, unrelenting eyes on an empty street.

Sadie thought she could remember a time when there was some life here, but if that memory was even real, it was a long time ago. Maybe the old-timers were right: maybe the town was just drying up.

Her mom was in ICU. The room was dark except for the lights on the machines helping her to breathe. From the doorway all Sadie could see was a vaguely human shape propped up on pillows. Tubes sprouted from her nose, mouth, and arms. She nudged the door open further and the over-bright hallway light fell on her mom's pale face.

"I've never seen it come on so sudden," Nurse Abagail said with a careworn sigh. She was a broad woman with brown skin and a pink floral smock.

Her mom looked the same. After the phone call, Sadie hadn't been sure what to expect, but she looked exactly like she had this morning, just now hooked up to life support. "Seen what?"

"The cancer," the nurse said. When Sadie didn't move or reply, she made a clucking sound and said, "You knew about it, right?"

Cancer. *Fucking cancer*. "No," Sadie said. "She never said a thing."

"Oh, child," the nurse said. "I'm so sorry. I'm sure she had her reasons."

Reasons. Like there were any reasons that could possibly make this Lie okay. That's why she didn't look like a cancer patient. She'd written something in her ledger so she didn't have to. A fresh coat of paint on a rotting house. A Lie can do lots of things, but it can't make cancer go away.

The nurse seemed uncomfortable with Sadie's icy silence, so went on. "She's been a real fighter, your mom. Doing her best anyway. Been coming in for chemo for months. For a while we thought it was working, but then…"

"But then what?"

"Doctor told her a couple days ago it was back and had progressed to stage four—that's where it spreads all over her body," Nurse Abagail said, an apology in the way she said it. "Inoperable. Then today she comes in for a checkup, and then they found her in the chapel, passed out on the floor. Doctor did an x-ray and there's more cancer than woman in there now."

Sadie swallowed. The hallway fluorescent lights screamed overhead and the room began to spin. Beneath the hospital's sharp chemical odor, Sadie could smell something sour. "How long," she asked, "does she have?"

The nurse put a hand on her arm but she barely felt it. "That's why we called you, dear. We thought you'd want to be here when…" She trailed off again. Machines beeped and exhaled. A toilet nearby let out a muted flush. Down the hall, a gurney with a squeaky wheel creeped along. "And she still looks so healthy. What a shame. I'll be just outside. Let me know if you need anything," the nurse said before leaving to oversee someone else's tragedy in some other room.

Sadie had known her mom was the Liar of Red Valley all her life, but it wasn't until she was fourteen that she understood the Liar's Price. A little old widowed woman—Mrs. Bradford, with owl-eyed glasses and colorless hair dyed pink—had come to their house. Her son drove her, but he waited outside with the car. For the first time, Sadie's mom hadn't asked Sadie to leave, so she sat on the couch, legs hanging over the arm, bare feet dangling.

"I bet you never thought you'd see me here," Mrs. Bradford said in a creaky voice.

Sadie's mom motioned her to a chair and then sat across from her. "No, Mrs. Bradford," she said, "I did not. I didn't think you thought very highly of my services."

"I don't," the old woman said tartly, drawing her gaudy purse up in front of her like a shield. "It's the Devil's work, and that's the truth of it. Pastor Steve just gave a fine sermon on Sunday about the wickedness that goes on in this town, especially on the other side of the River. In fact, I brought you a copy of it." She rummaged in her purse and produced a white CD in a plastic sleeve. Sadie's mom took it, although they didn't even own a CD player.

"So," her mom said, "what can I do for you, then?"

Mrs. Bradford's face crumpled, wrinkles upon wrinkles. Her mouth opened and closed a few times without saying a word. With great force of will, she finally said, "I miss my Jack."

Sadie's mom leaned forward in her chair. "Would you like me to bring him back for you?"

Mrs. Bradford nodded.

Her mom produced her ledger, a simple blue notebook with a worn ribbon bookmark. She always had it with her, no matter what. She opened the book and pressed the pages flat.

"You know he won't really be back, right?" her mom said as she raised her pen.

"Yes, yes. But he'll seem like he is, won't he?"

"Yes," her mom said. "But you'll know he isn't."

"He'll be there when I get home?"

Sadie's mom nodded.

Mrs. Bradford dabbed a tear from a watery eye with an embroidered handkerchief. "I think I'll be willing to forget."

Her mom didn't start writing. She tapped the paper with the end of the pen instead. "And you're willing to pay the price?"

Mrs. Bradford scowled. Sadie only saw it out of the

corner of her eye, but that was enough to make her uncomfortable. She was used to people hating her mom, but this was an intensity she hadn't seen before. The old woman pulled an envelope full of cash out of her purse and tossed it on the table between them. "Oh, yes," she said. "I'd never expect charity from you."

Sadie's mom didn't reach for the money. She didn't even look at it. "That's not the price I meant, Mrs. Bradford."

"Oh," the old woman said. "Yes, well." The anger drained from her seamed face, though there was still a tightness in her lips as she pressed them together. "I know I don't have a lot of time left before the Lord calls me home, but... but whatever I have left, I'd rather not spend it alone."

"Okay," Sadie's mom said as she wrote into the ledger. "I'm going to need some of your blood."

When Mrs. Bradford was gone, Sadie twisted around in her perch on the couch to face her mom, who was counting the cash in the envelope. "What did you mean, about the price?" she asked.

Her mom tucked the envelope away. "Life, Sadie."

"I don't get it."

"The Lies these people want me to tell for them," her mom said, "come at a price. Time off of their lives."

Sadie sat up straight. "You steal days off their lives?"

"Hours, days, years," her mom said casually. "The bigger the Lie, the higher the price. So when Mrs. Bradford's idiot son came by last month and asked me to Lie about his receding hairline, that probably cost him six months. I'd guess Mrs. Bradford's Lie cost her a year. Hard to know." She pointed a finger at her daughter.

"But I'm not stealing anything. I don't get to keep that time. It just gets burned up."

"That's harsh."

"I don't make the rules. The King does."

Sadie thought about that for a long time. Mrs. Bradford didn't seem like she had much life left, yet she had just given away some of it because she was tired of being alone. That certainly seemed better than dying sooner so people didn't think you were going bald.

"At least she used it bringing her husband back," Sadie said. "That's romantic."

Her mom snorted a laugh. "That old bitch hated her husband. Jack was her dog."

Sadie saw an obituary for Mrs. Bradford about a year later. She'd shown it to her mom, but her mom had just shrugged.

As she sat now by her mother's bedside, Sadie thought about Mrs. Bradford, and about her son's thinning hair, and about every other person in Red Valley who'd driven up to see the Liar and put their blood in her book. What Lies could be worth it? Sadie remembered thinking about what Lies she'd tell if she could, about having more friends and living in a big house. But once she understood the Liar's Price, those dreams withered and blew away. Life was short enough already.

And yet her mom had paid the Liar's Price just to hide her cancer. The doctors had given her the diagnosis, and rather than come home and break the bad news to her daughter, she wrote down another Lie in her book and sealed it with her own blood. She'd given up hours—days? weeks?—together, and for what? To look pretty for one more day? So she didn't have to see her hair falling out because of the chemo? Or so she didn't have to have a hard conversation about death?

They'd fought that morning. They fought most mornings, about stupid shit: taking the garbage down their long driveway to the cans by the road, an unwashed coffee pot that had started to grow mold, or musty clothes scattered on the bathroom floor. Ever since Sadie had graduated from high school, their little house had felt even smaller and her mom less forgiving. *You don't like it, there's the door* was the unspoken threat under every argument.

A lot of her classmates had gone on to the state university in Paso Verde, the next town south, but Sadie's grades had doomed her to a life waiting tables at the diner, seeing the same faces every day, a little bit older and more worn out each time. She'd been miserable at first, but as the interchangeable weeks became interchangeable years, she'd gotten used to it, numb to it, like blistered skin finally growing a callus. She still hated Red Valley sometimes, with its lifeless streets and dead-end jobs, but mostly she couldn't bother to care. Red Valley had more than its share of strangeness: weird, unexplainable shit that might be the coolest thing you ever saw or the last, but the real power in this town was its ability to make sure nothing ever really changed.

Sadie watched her mom's raspy breaths. She did still look healthy, but there were signs, if you looked closely. There were new wrinkles deep around her eyes. Her fingers—usually bright with some awful polish Sadie secretly coveted—were colorless save for dried blood around broken nails. Her lips were cracked.

"You let me yell at you about the fucking cornflakes," Sadie whispered to the quiet room. She wanted to scream; she wanted to cry. Her heart was a dead weight in her chest and her whole world narrowed to a sliver of fluorescent light falling on a face she barely recognized.

CHAPTER TWO

HER MOM DIED around dinnertime. Sadie was holding her hand when it happened. She wouldn't have even noticed if the machines hadn't started putting up a racket; the change in her mom—from a person to a body—was subtle. Nurses came in, but they didn't seem to be in much of a hurry. They put up a bit of a fight, but Sadie knew it was mostly a performance, one last bit of dignity afforded to that poor woman and her stone-faced daughter.. Someone wrote the time down on a chart, someone else squeezed Sadie's arm, and Nurse Abagail turned off the machines. The room fell quiet. Even the old A/C unit shuddered and went still.

Sadie just made it to the toilet down the hall before she threw up. Her whole body jittered like she'd grabbed an electric fence and held on tight. The bathroom's tile floor was cold on her legs and her face felt like it was on fire. She sat there for a long time, afraid to even move, because once she did, she'd have to get up, and go back out into that hallway, and then outside into that heat that never let up, and then... where?

What the hell am I supposed to do now?

Nurse Abagail found her there and gently helped her to her feet. She kept talking the whole time in a soft, careful voice, like you would to a wild animal you didn't want to spook, saying how sorry she was, and how someone would call her about arrangements for the body, and how they'd pack up her mom's things and drop them by her house, and how Sadie ought to go home and get some rest, and how she could cry if she needed to. But Sadie didn't cry and didn't speak. Just stood in silence on numb legs that didn't know where to walk.

Someone was standing outside her mom's room talking to the nurses there. Sadie stared blankly at him until he noticed her. She recognized him then: Pastor Steve, the youth pastor from the First Church of the Risen Christ down on Walnut Avenue. Sadie had been to their meetings a few times over the years—her only friend in the world, Graciela, had wanted to check it out—but had never felt much during their singing or preaching. Graciela hadn't cared much for the sermons either, but she had liked the hot young pastor, with his trendy haircut and tattooed forearms. He was a little older now, but still cute, if anyone could be cute under whitewashed lights in an ICU.

"I'm so sorry," he said softly when he got closer. He had on faded jeans and a rumpled button-down shirt and had a well-worn bible tucked under one arm. "I was here doing my care visits, and the nurses just told me what happened. I'm just so sorry."

"Yeah," Sadie said.

"I've already called the church to activate the prayer chain," he said. "People all over town will be praying for you and your family."

Family. Her mom was all she had. Now she had nobody.

When she didn't reply, Pastor Steve went on in his smooth, soothing tone, "No matter how it feels right now, remember that you aren't alone in this time of trouble. We're all praying."

A short-lived anger rose up in her chest like the vomit that had carried her to the bathroom. *What good are your prayers now? She's already gone.* But Sadie didn't say anything. This was just another kind of asshole, like those at the diner. Fake smile, thick skin. She mustered the best smile she could and Pastor Steve didn't press further. He gave Sadie a hug, the bulk of his bible smacking hard on her back, and then left her there, alone. Really, truly, fucking alone.

She signed a few forms, absorbed a few more condolences, and then made her way outside. The doors slid open to another hot Red Valley summer night. No breeze moved. The sky was still a little pink along the horizon, but it was fading fast. Thick-bodied insects tick-ticked away at the street lights in the half-empty parking lot. A pair of male nurses in green scrubs crowded around a concrete ashtray and blew gray cigarette smoke into the air.

So, she thought. *What now?*

A car slowly drove into the lot, blinding her for a moment with its headlights. It pulled up along the red-painted curb and stopped. The nurses looked up, but when they recognized the car—a charcoal 1967 Cadillac lined in chrome—they quickly averted their eyes. It was parked illegally, but in Red Valley, the laws didn't apply to everybody the same.

The car's door swung open on creaky hinges. Sadie didn't move. She knew who this was; everyone in town knew who drove this car. You stood aside when you saw it coming, out of fear or deference; didn't matter, as long as you got the hell out of the way. Sadie had seen this car—and the others like it—plenty of times, cruising slowly down Main Street or Baker Road, passing easily through stop signs and traffic lights, always watching.

The driver stepped out. He was a tall, gaunt man with sandy hair. His clothes—a decade or two out of fashion—didn't fit quite right, including a brown leather jacket with a ripped sleeve. Sadie couldn't see his eyes through his large mirrored sunglasses.

Some people in town called men like this *mirroreyes*, because when you stared at them all you saw was yourself looking back at you. Everybody in town called them creepy but never when one could hear you, and you never knew when they could hear. Their official name, if they had such a thing, was the King's Men, and they were the King's voice and ears in Red Valley. You didn't want one of the King's Men looking at you, and you damn sure didn't want one of them talking to you. And you really, really didn't want to get into their car.

The King's Man was staring at Sadie.

"The King offers his sympathies," the King's Man said. His voice was flat, lifeless, like he was reading a prepared statement. His hands hung limp at his sides. The two nurses quickly crushed their cigarettes and retreated into the hospital.

"Excuse me?" Sadie said. Sweat was creeping steadily down her spine.

The King's Man said nothing at first. Instead he cocked his head slightly to the side, as if he was listening to something. Then he said, "The King wishes to express that he thought fondly of your mother and mourns her passing."

Mom knew the King? The Liar's power came from the King, but Sadie had never considered that her mom might have met him. Everyone knew *of* the King, but no one interacted with him. As far as Sadie knew, no one had ever even seen the King, though the effects he had on Red Valley were felt every day. Everything weird in Red Valley had some connection to the King; his presence had seeped into the hills, the forests, and the fields, and had altered the land forever.

"Thank you?" Sadie managed to reply eventually.

"The Liar is a vital part of Red Valley," the King's Man said. "It is an essential function."

Another car entered the parking lot. Behind the glare, Sadie could see a rack of lights mounted on the roof and a seven-pointed star painted on the door: a sheriff's car. It moved real slow toward the King's Man, almost reluctantly.

"Well she's gone now," Sadie said, maybe a little too sharply, considering who she was talking to. She knew she should be afraid and could feel the expected fear down deep in her gut, but every time it started to take over, she pictured her mom's still face and suddenly there just wasn't any room for fear in a head choked with grief and anger. "I guess we'll all have to make do."

The sheriff's car circled the lot, staying conspicuously far from the hospital entrance.

The King's Man raised one of his pale hands and traced the tip of a finger across his pale lips. It was a strange, foreign gesture, and she wasn't sure he was even aware he was doing it. "There's always been a Liar in Red Valley. There will always be a Liar in Red Valley. There must be."

"I don't know what you're trying to tell me."

Another pause. "Your mother had an arrangement with the King. Her mother did too. And her mother. And hers." The King's Man took a step closer, or at least she thought he did, but she didn't see him move. He was just suddenly only a few feet from her, the lights from inside the hospital glaring back at her from his mirrored eyes. "And now so do you."

"What?" Sadie backed up. "I'm not the Liar."

"You are," the King's Man said. "You will be."

The sheriff's car finally pulled up next to the Cadillac and turned on its lights. Pulsing red and blue filled the parking lot and flickered off the King's Man's glasses. A deputy got out of the cruiser and stood there behind the door like it was a barricade.

"You'll need to move your car," the deputy said. There was a forced strength in his voice, manufactured bravado. He had one hand on the car door, but Sadie couldn't see the other one. "This is a Red Zone. For emergency vehicles only."

The King's Man didn't react. He didn't look at the

deputy or even acknowledge his arrival. The muscles on his face were slack, his hands limp.

"Did you hear me?" the deputy said, louder now. He moved out from behind the car door and now Sadie could see his other hand resting on his pistol. "I said move the damn car."

The King's Man cocked his head again. Some brief, muted emotion played around his mouth. Surprise? Amusement? Then he turned toward the deputy.

"You have lived in Red Valley a long time, Deputy Jason Allen Johnson. You were born here, in this very hospital. You grew up here, played little league—third base—and watched fireworks over the River on the 4th of July. Your family lives here. You have roots in the community, Jason Allen Johnson." The King's Man turned his head to stare at the flashing lights for a long moment, then turned back to the deputy. "So you know better."

The deputy swallowed. His grip tightened on his gun. "Things change. Laws get enforced on everybody now," he said shakily. All that swagger had leaked out of his voice by now. "Orders of Undersheriff Hassler."

Sadie wanted to move back, move away, get out of any crossfire if this kid with a gun decided to man up and be a hero. But in that moment, her body decided the best thing it could do was not move even a muscle.

"Laws," the King's Man said. "The King has been in Red Valley long before your laws. The King was here long before there was a Red Valley, before there were hills, before there was sky. The King has always been here, blessing the land with his presence and bestowing boons upon his faithful. And you would interrupt the

King's business over a parking violation?"

The deputy looked at Sadie for the first time. His hand was still on his gun. Then he looked back at the King's Man. His fear was curdling into a new-found resolve and Sadie cringed.

"You need to move your car, sir," the deputy commanded. "Or I will have to arrest you."

The following silence thundered in Sadie's ears. She'd left her mother's deathbed only a few minutes ago, and walked into this?

The King's Man said nothing. Even after his customary pause, he remained motionless. The lights flashed in his mirrored glasses.

The deputy drew his gun.

Then the King's Man moved.

To Sadie, it was just a blur, backlit by blue and red. One moment, the King's Man was in front of her. Then he was gone. And then he was back.

And the deputy was screaming.

The deputy's gun was on the blacktop. He held up his hand, or what remained of his hand. Blood spattered the ground, his shoes, his pants. His eyes were white and wide, his skin already losing color.

"You'd best go inside," the King's Man said without looking at the deputy, "and get that looked at."

When he spoke, Sadie could see blood in his teeth. The deputy's blood.

Nurses rushed out of the sliding doors at the sound of screaming. They quickly and quietly ushered the deputy into the hospital, eyes carefully averted from the King's Man and Sadie.

The King's Man ignored them. "The King apologizes for that unfortunate spectacle."

Sadie struggled for a moment to get enough moisture on her tongue to reply. "Okay," she said.

"The ledgers," the King's Man said. "The Liars' books. They are yours now; not just your mother's ledger, but all of them. Others will covet them. With your mother gone, they will come looking for them. They do not respect the sanctity of secrets. They do not understand that some things deserve to be forgotten."

Sadie had no idea her mom had other ledgers, from her grandmother, and *her* grandmother. They didn't have many books in their little house, magical or otherwise. But where was her mom's ledger? She always had it with her, but Sadie hadn't seen it in the hospital room, though she had been distracted at the time.

"So all the King asks is that you keep the books safe," the King's Man said. "And you keep the books secret."

"Okay," Sadie said again, not trusting herself to say anything else.

"The King values one thing above all other things," the King's Man said. "Loyalty."

"You can trust me," Sadie said as she tried not to look at the puddle of black blood by the deputy's car. "I'll take care of the books."

"Good." The King's Man produced a crisp white card. Sadie took it. There was a phone number on it, nothing else. "For emergencies," he said.

"Thanks."

After a long, weird pause, the King's Man said, "Have a pleasant evening." And then he returned to his car, turned it on with a rumble, and drove slowly away, leaving Sadie alone in the deserted parking lot. No one came out from the hospital. Even the deputy's screams had died away. The only sounds now were the cicada hiss of insects and the distant murmur of traffic on the road. Sadie stared out into the growing dark and realized she had no idea how she was going to get home.

CHAPTER THREE

SADIE WAITED FOR almost two hours before she decided the bus wasn't coming. She wasn't used to riding it this late in the day—her mom usually picked her up from work—and hadn't had many opportunities to catch a ride from St. Elizabeth's, so maybe she got the schedule wrong. Or maybe it just decided not to bother. She couldn't blame it.

So she shoved her hands in her pockets and started walking. The sun was long gone, but it was still well into the 90s. Mosquitos buzzed around her head and gravel crunched under her shoes. A few cars passed her on the road, but they didn't slow down. She tried not to look at them, because when she did, she pictured the King's Man and his mirrored eyes staring back at her, drops of the deputy's blood quivering on his lips.

Yesterday, the world had made sense. It hadn't been kind or fair, but Sadie thought she'd understood it. Her life—uninspired as it was—had an order to it, a structure. Rules. And then one phone call and a few hours later, she didn't even have a ride home.

Bats flew overhead, chittering and flapping into the dark. Other things followed, bigger and meaner, with glinting granite eyes and hungry mouths, but they left Sadie alone. There was an order to Red Valley too, and at least that still held. The humans lived out their lives on one side of the River, and the other things mostly stayed on the other side. In reality, it wasn't that simple; plenty of people lived on the far side of the bridge—real estate sure was cheaper—and other things sometimes crossed over here as well. But even when they did, they didn't mess with the people of Red Valley, on the King's orders. The King's Peace, it was called.

And Red Valley had its rules, too. Every kid in town learned them from a young age, if they wanted to live to an older one. In a normal town—if there was such a thing—kids might learn not to run out in traffic, or play with fire. In Red Valley, the rules were simple:

Do not cross the King
Never, ever go in the River
Don't trust the Liar

Before tonight, Sadie had never interacted with any of the King's Men, let alone the King himself, so had never had reason to get on his bad side. And of course she'd never gone into the black waters of the River, because if you did that, you didn't come back. But as tears began stinging the backs of her eyes, she realized she'd broken the third rule: she'd trusted her mother. Trusted her not to lie to her.

Trusted her not to leave her.

The stars winked at her, leering and sharp. The moon barely made an appearance. Sweat ran down her spine. She'd kill for a breeze, anything to blunt the heat, but she knew better than to hope for any relief. Not here. Not in Red Valley.

Sadie's best—and only—friend Graciela lived with her family on a tree-shaded street a mile or two from the hospital. As Sadie walked up the driveway to the front door, light and sound spilled out to greet her. Laughter, voices, the drone of the TV, the clink of dishes getting washed: it was all so vivid, so alive, and it hit Sadie like a punch in the chest. Her house had never sounded like this, not with just her and her mother. At times, their home barely felt lived in, and on any other night, Sadie would have welcomed the jarring contrast, but not tonight. Because tonight she had to go back to her home, and no lights would be on. No voices would ever come out to welcome her.

She almost turned around and kept on walking, but that would be stupid. Sadie lived nearly ten miles outside of town and her legs were already barely holding her up.

Javier opened the door when she knocked.

"¿Graciela está aquí?" Sadie asked. Javier blinked at her, then pointed down the hall. Sadie came inside, instantly grateful for the chill of a functioning A/C. She could hear Graciela's parents talking loudly in the kitchen. It sounded like they were scolding someone, probably one of her older brothers. Sadie thanked Javier and he shrugged and wandered off.

She found Graciela in the living room at the end of the

hall. Ashleigh, her girlfriend, was there too. Graciela was laying across her legs on the tattered couch, both their faces illuminated by the colorless glow of the television.

"Hey," Sadie said over the white noise of a commercial for allergy medicine.

Graciela jumped up. Her dark hair was pulled back in a tight ponytail and she still had on the faded polo shirt and khakis she wore as a cashier at Walmart. Large silver hoops dangled from both ears. "Finally, some life to this party!" She hugged Sadie before flopping back to the couch next to Ashleigh. "You want a beer or something?"

Sadie said no and sat down in an overstuffed arm chair across from the couch. It felt good not to be standing.

"Ash," Graciela said, grabbing a Cheeto from a half-crumpled bag on the carpet, "tell our girl here what you were telling me earlier. You're going to love this."

Ashleigh flashed a wicked smile. She was pretty, Sadie thought. Straight blonde hair framed her pale face, always painted with perfect makeup. Sadie had kind of hated her when they were younger—she'd seemed like every other stupid high school girl, interchangeably vapid and cruel—but after they'd graduated and she'd started dating Graciela, a more interesting version had emerged.

"So last week my mom and I were running around town, picking up crap for my little brother's birthday party," Ashleigh began. Sadie just sat and listened, focusing intently, trying to hear the words over the roaring in her head. "And we were driving down Sycamore Avenue, you know, where the Planned Parenthood is?"

"Oh, man," Graciela said, kicking her feet in the air. "This is so good."

"Quiet, sweetie," Ashleigh said. "I'm telling a story."

"Not fast enough."

"You want to tell it?"

Their banter was like music, like a favorite song. But the key was wrong, the notes all twisting up in Sadie's ears, and instead of wanting to dance, it made her want to cry.

"Where was I?" Ashleigh said, giving Graciela a playful shove. "So as we're driving by, who do we see walking out but Courtney Barber." The name was said with appropriate gravity.

"That's right!" Graciela said, cackling. "The same self-righteous Courtney Barber who stood on the street and yelled 'slut!' at the other girls going inside Planned Parenthood. The same bitch who straight-up told me to my face I was going to hell because I was dating a girl. President of the Bible Club, sweet little youth group leader Courtney."

Some distant part of Sadie's mind remembered her. She went to Pastor Steve's church and had been nice to Sadie when they visited, but then never spoke to her again after they didn't come back.

"I wonder who knocked her up," Ashleigh said. "She was dating that skater punk Danny for a while. Trying to win him over for Jesus with her feminine wiles."

"Hey," Graciela said, snapping her fingers in front of Sadie's face. "Why aren't you laughing? We boring you?"

They both looked so happy. Young and beautiful and happy. Why had she come here, to ruin their night with her pain? There were only a few feet separating them, but she suddenly felt like they were on different planets, different planes of existence, like their lives were on separate and separating tracks.

"Mom died tonight," Sadie said, her tears racing the words and winning.

Graciela's face went blank. "Wait, what? No."

Sadie just nodded and wiped away the tears before they dripped from her chin.

"Oh, honey," Graciela said.

Sadie sat with them a long time, crying and telling them in halting bursts about what had happened, with her mom and with the King's Man in the hospital parking lot. Even as she was telling it, it all felt so unreal, like if she hurried home she might still get there before her mom went to bed. She couldn't really be gone, could she?

Graciela's mom brought in some leftover pork tortas and they picked at the food in heavy silence. Sometimes life didn't really leave much to say.

Eventually, Ashleigh said, "I can't believe one of the King's Men talked to you."

Sadie was grateful for the distraction. As freaky as the encounter had been, talking about that was preferable to remembering the smell of the hospital room or the weight of her dead mother's hand.

"Beto said he saw one of them kill a dude once," Graciela said. Her eldest brother had always scared Sadie more than a little bit. "Just some guy, walking down the street, and then one of those old cars drives up and this mirroreyes gets out and says something to him. The dude tries to run, and then he's just dead. Splat. A smear on the sidewalk."

Ashleigh gave Graciela a sharp look that said, *Talk*

about something else, you insensitive dipshit. "What are you going to do?" Ashleigh asked. "About these books the King wants kept safe."

"I don't know," Sadie said. "I didn't know my mom had them. She never told me anything about her job."

"I wonder what the King wants to stay hidden," Graciela said.

"What do you mean?" Sadie said.

"The books," she said. "He doesn't want anyone to read them. Must have something juicy in there, something real good."

"Don't," Ashleigh said firmly.

"What?" Graciela said. "We're all thinking it. The Liar keeps everybody's secrets, maybe even the King's. He's got to have some too."

"That's the King of Red Valley you're talking about. The *King*."

"So? He can't hear me."

"What about the whispers?"

"Don't give me that bullshit," Graciela said. "The whispers aren't real. That's just something parents tell their kids to scare them."

"Are you so sure?"

"If you'd seen him," Sadie said, her voice sounding far away in her head, "if you'd seen what he did to that cop, just like that. If you'd seen that, you wouldn't talk like that. Not anywhere in Red Valley you wouldn't."

That shut them up. Sadie hadn't meant to, not really; the conversation was the only thing keeping her from losing her mind. But she kept replaying that moment over in her head: the gun, the blur of movement, the screaming, the blood on the pavement, in his teeth. Maybe she'd already lost her mind.

Ashleigh put a soft hand on Sadie's. "I think it's best if you do what the King asked. I think you want to stay on his good side. I know he's supposed to be our protector and all that, but he doesn't seem very… forgiving."

"It'll be fine," Graciela said. "No one's going to come after those books. Everybody may not love the King, but they're all scared of him. And probably scared of you too, now that you're the Liar and all that."

But she wasn't, not really. She didn't know the first thing about using the Liar's magic, even if it was in her veins. And the thought of becoming the Liar gave her little enough comfort. While the town had hated her mother, people sometimes had at least shown Sadie some measure of pity. Not anymore.

Though it was the last place she wanted to be, Sadie sighed and asked, "Can one of you give me a ride home?"

GRACIELA'S OLD TOYOTA pulled off the paved road onto the dirt driveway. Rocks crumbled under her bald tires as her headlights cut weakly through the midnight darkness. Sadie could see their house at the end of the driveway. Her mom always left the porch light on when Sadie was out late, but no lights greeted them tonight.

"Never understood why you guys live so far out here," Graciela said as the road bumped under them.

Sadie hadn't ever given it much thought, but now the answer seemed obvious. "I don't think Mom liked being in Red Valley much. I think she wanted room to breathe."

Her heart caught on the words, like skin on splintered wood. She was already switching to the past tense.

"And you never got a car?"

"Never seemed important, I guess."

Far from the lights of town, the sky overhead was overwhelmed with stars.

"You can stay with us," Graciela said when she put the car in park. "We'll have a slumber party, braid each other's hair, whatever. Like that time in the fifth grade when Julia fell asleep early so we drew all that shit on her face."

"You going to draw on my face?"

"I think you'd look good with a handlebar mustache, maybe a soul patch."

They laughed and Sadie didn't have the heart to say she didn't remember that slumber party, or who Julia was. She'd known Graciela forever, but as memories of a shared childhood faded, she often wondered what really held them together anymore.

"But seriously, chica," Graciela said. "You don't have to go in there. Not tonight."

Sadie stared at the black windows. There was nothing for her inside, except—hopefully—the Liar's ledgers. But she had come back for other things as well: a pile of dirty laundry, a coffee cup ringed with lipstick left on the table, a passive-aggressive note on the fridge about using the last of the milk. Echoes of her mother, fading.

"I'll be fine," Sadie said, her hand on the car door handle. "Thanks."

"Hey," Graciela said, grabbing her in an awkward hug over the center console. "You know I love you, right?

Maybe you're the Liar, maybe not, who cares? The world's gone to shit overnight, but I'm here for you."

Sadie touched away new tears and said her goodbyes. She stood on their sagging porch and watched Graciela's red taillights as they retreated up the long driveway and then turned and disappeared into the night. Sadie may not have much, but she had a friend who actually cared about her, and maybe that would be enough. At least for tonight.

The air inside the house was stale and stuffy. They didn't have A/C, just a rusty swamp cooler hanging precariously out one window. Sadie didn't bother to turn it on. The heat, at least, made it feel like the house wasn't so empty. She just stood in the living room for a while, soaking in old memories while sweat slid down her back.

Reading books on the floor.

Dancing barefoot on the ugly threadbare carpet.

Purposely annoying her mom while she tried to read the newspaper.

Yet even as she pictured these moments from her life, she felt strangely detached. Her memories felt far away, like a lost balloon floating into the summer sky. Whatever her life had been, it was something else entirely now.

Even though it was nearly 1AM, her appetite was finally back so she wandered into the tiny kitchen to find something to eat. The lunch meat in the fridge still smelled okay and she didn't see any mold on the loaf of white bread, so she slapped together a sandwich while the day's events cycled over and over in her mind. It felt like it had happened to someone else, not her. Some other unlucky girl whose hair still smelled like the deep fryer, who just had the worst day of her life and who was staring down more days like it. Some other girl who—

Sadie stopped. *What the fuck was that sound?* The knife she'd been about to use to cut her sandwich hovered in midair, shaking a little. She listened but the house was quiet now, so absolutely quiet that she could nearly convince herself she hadn't really heard anything.

But then she heard it again.

Laughter.

Despite the heat, Sadie's blood turned to ice. She gripped the knife's worn wooden handle until her knuckles turned white. A high-pitched tittering laughter floated down the hall from the bedrooms. It sounded like it was coming from her mom's room, but it was definitely not her mom's laugh.

"Who's there?" Sadie called. She held the knife out in front of her as she took a step toward the closed bedroom doors.

A pause, and then the laughter returned, even higher than before. The door to her mom's bedroom slowly started to open. A moment later, someone stepped out into the hall. It was too dark to see his face well, but he was only a little taller than Sadie, with skinny arms, lanky hair, and a loose-fitting shirt with a faded Nirvana logo across the chest. He took a step toward Sadie, but stopped when he saw the knife.

"I'm just here for the Liar's books," he said in a low voice that sounded nothing like the laughter she'd heard. "Tell me where they are and I'll go."

Closer to the light from the kitchen now, Sadie recognized him. His name was David, or Danny, or something like that. He'd been two years ahead of her at Red Valley High, a skater who rarely showed up for classes and barely made it to graduation. He had silver rings in his lip and eyebrow and a cold glaze in his eyes.

"Get the fuck," Sadie said, grief and fury and fatigue shredding her voice, "out of my house."

That maniac laughter returned, bouncing around the hallway and echoing in Sadie's head. Only, the overgrown skater boy's mouth hadn't moved.

Oh, God, Sadie thought. *He's a Laughing Boy.*

There were plenty of stupid kids in town who lost themselves to pot or heroin. Meth had become a problem too, especially in the rural parts of the county east of town. But for some, drugs would never give a good enough high, and in Red Valley, there were other options. Like inviting a demon into your head.

The first time someone explained it to Sadie, she was sure they were lying. Why would anyone want some monstrous thing crawling around inside of them? The answer: Because it feels so good. Nothing else could compare. It was like flying. No, it was like you'd spent your whole life blind and could now finally see. You understood the true measure of the world, the ancient mysteries, the forgotten tomorrows. That is, until the demon decided it wanted to stick around. Then you were fucked.

She could see the signs, now that she was looking for them. His fingers were a little too long, the nails a little too sharp. His irises were a little too blue, like some unholy icy light was pushing through cracks in the surface. When his pierced lips curled back, she could see his yellowed teeth tapered to sharp points.

And, of course, the laughter. Once the demon was riding you, its laughter would be ever-present, no matter how tightly you clamped your mouth shut. Its words whispered in your head and its will tugged at your hands and feet, begging, threatening, promising violence. But it was usually the laughter that drove people insane.

The only thing worse than a Laughing Boy was a Crying Boy, when the demon decided it wasn't having fun anymore.

"*Give us what we came for, bitch.*"

"How stupid do you have to be to break into the Liar's house?"

Danny said nothing, but the demon inside him couldn't remain silent for long. "*The Liar is dead, you stupid bitch. Now give us what we came for or we'll make you bleed.*"

How could they possibly know her mom had died already? She'd only left the hospital a few hours ago.

"So that means I'm the Liar now, idiot," Sadie said, putting as much spite as she could into her words to mask the tremor of fear. "I can make your life hell."

The demon cackled. "*Except, you're not the Liar yet, are you, girl?*"

"I don't want to hurt you," Danny said. "But *it* might make me. So please just give me the books."

Sadie pointed the tip of her knife at the front door. "If you don't want to hurt me, then leave," she said. "Walk out that door and don't look back. Or are you not in charge anymore?"

That sent the demon into a new laughing fit, while Danny just stared at her with his eyes leaking deathly blue light. Sadie's courage shriveled with every passing breath. She didn't want to mess with a Laughing Boy, but even if she wanted to give him the Liar's ledgers, she had no idea where they were. And as scary as he was, this punk was nothing compared to the King.

"I just need the books," Danny said, an edge creeping into his voice.

"They aren't here."

"I think they are."

"I don't give a fuck what you think." She held up the knife. "Liar or not, I think I can do something with this. You want to try me?"

Danny took another step and Sadie retreated, though there wasn't much room behind her.

"I'm only gonna ask one more time," Danny said.

"*Then we break your jaw and feed you your own hands*," said the demon.

"Get out," Sadie said. She held the knife as tightly as she could, but still it trembled. Her mouth was dry. A foul taste was rising in her throat. She tried to think, tried to decide, but the demon's bloodthirsty laughter filled her head and rattled her brain, like it was inside *her*, not Danny.

"*Kill her*," the demon whispered. "*Kill her.*"

"Go ahead and try," Sadie said. Her vision had gone dark around the edges. All she saw was the shaking tip of the knife and Danny's glowing eyes. She hoped her words sounded strong, because inside she was cowering, crumbling.

"I'm going to get those books," Danny said softly. "One way or another. I'm trying to be nice here. If I have to come back with my friends, you'll see they aren't so nice."

"Come a little closer," she said, raising the knife up a few inches, "and you'll see I'm not so nice either."

"*Oh, I like her*," said the demon. "*Let's find out what her liver tastes like.*"

Danny stared hard at her, but didn't approach. His too-long fingers agitated against the side of his legs, nervous energy desperate to get out. The unnatural light in his eyes flared brighter. The demon howled. But then Danny glanced away, toward the door, and Sadie realized he wasn't going to attack.

"I need the books," he said one last time.

"Get out," Sadie repeated.

The light in his eyes faded a little, then he shoved his twitchy hands into his pockets and made for the door. The demon just laughed and laughed. A moment later, they were gone, but the laughter hung in the air for a long time after like the smell of smoke.

CHAPTER FOUR

WHEN SHE WAS sure the Laughing Boy wasn't coming back, Sadie went back to the kitchen and threw the knife into the sink. The sound of metal on metal scraped her nerves and tore the threads of her resolve. Her hand, still cramping from her unyielding grip on the handle, shot to her mouth.

Oh, god, she thought when there were no other words left in her head. *Oh, god.*

She abandoned the sandwich and went to the front door and checked the locks. A distant part of her brain knew she was ravenously hungry, but there was too much acid in her gut and her head to even think about eating. She stumbled into the bathroom. She stripped off her sweat-damp clothes, turned the shower up as hot as it would go, and sat in the bathtub, letting the water scald her and hide the tears. She stayed there a long time, long enough to drain their temperamental water heater. Eventually she shut off the lukewarm water and dressed in the dark.

She went gingerly into her mom's room. The Laughing Boy had torn out drawers and scattered clothing and jewelry everywhere, but Sadie just stepped over the mess. She pulled back her mom's comforter and got into her bed. She remembered sleeping here with her mom when she'd had a bad dream or when the wind howled too loudly outside. She remembered the feel of her mom's arm over her, holding her, guarding her.

She pressed her face into her mom's pillow. Her scent filled her nostrils.

Sleep came easily.

SLEEP ENDED ABRUPTLY with a hard pounding on her front door. Sunlight slanted through the blinds. How long had she slept? Not long enough. Though her whole body hurt, Sadie crept from the bed to the window and peered through the blinds. A sheriff's car waited outside.

Panic jolted her the rest of the way awake. Why would the sheriffs be here? "Just a minute!" she yelled as she ran to her room and threw on some clothes.

She returned to the living room. The sheriff's deputy thudded on the door again and Sadie reminded herself to breathe.

She opened the door just wide enough for her face and nearly swallowed her tongue. The man on her porch was big, with a bright red mustache. He wore the usual khaki-colored uniform, though with fancier gold decorations shining on his shoulders. His badge gleamed on his chest. He had a brown broad-brimmed hat, polished black boots, and a hard, veined face. Sadie recognized him from his election posters glaring all over town. This wasn't a deputy standing in front of her; it was the goddamn undersheriff himself.

"Can... can I help you?" Sadie asked as she tried to regain her balance.

"Ma'am," he said, nodding his head toward her. He towered over her, blocking out the sun behind him. She thought he might have to stoop to come through the doorway. "My name is Undersheriff Hassler. Would you mind if I came inside so we could have a chat?"

Sadie's hands tightened involuntarily on the door. She forced her lips into the hint of a smile and asked, "What is this about?"

Hassler tried to match Sadie's smile and didn't do much better than she did. "It is already getting pretty warm out here, miss," he said, noticeably switching from *ma'am*. "I think we'd both be more comfortable in out of the sun."

"Sure," Sadie said, uncertain of what else she could say. "Come on in."

The big undersheriff blacked out the doorway as he stepped inside. Sadie retreated across the room to switch on the swamp cooler, which chugged and gurgled and screeched before belching out a bolus of fetid air.

The undersheriff's eyes traced slowly over the room in a manner trying too hard to look casual. "Lovely home you have here," he said as he removed his hat.

Sadie fought the urge to scoff. "What exactly can I do for you, Mr. Hassler?"

"There was an incident last night," he said. "An unfortunate incident that I hoped you could shed some light on."

Sadie swallowed. The Laughing Boy had stood exactly where the undersheriff was now. Did Hassler know he'd been there? How could he? Unless he knew *why* Danny had come. And who had sent him. "An incident?"

"Yes," Hassler said slowly as he completed his scan over her living room. "With one of my deputies in the hospital parking lot."

Sadie almost breathed a sigh of relief into the undersheriff's face. Of course that was why he was here. She'd nearly forgotten all about it. "Yeah, right," Sadie said. "That was... pretty bad."

"Pretty bad," Hassler repeated with a sour face, like he didn't care for the taste of the words. "A man lost three fingers and his livelihood. He'll never hold a gun or shake another man's hand again. He worked long and hard to wear that badge, and now he has to quit as a cripple." His mustache twitched. "So yes, pretty bad, and since you were involved, young lady, I'd expect you to show some more respect for his sacrifice."

It was no secret in town that Sadie's mom had a temper. It was the kind of thing you didn't really see coming. She could be all smiles and laughs one minute, but once you crossed the line, she'd hit you with both barrels. Sadie had been on the receiving end plenty of times, mostly deserved. And while she'd always told herself she wouldn't grow up to become her mother, she could feel that temper now, a blue-hot burst of color in front of her vision that blotted out the bulky man who had come to lecture her a few hours after she'd watched her mom die.

"Do you know why I was at the hospital, Mr. Hassler?"

Her mouth was tight, but the words found their way out anyway. "That wasn't rhetorical. Do you know?"

"Yes," he said after a heavy pause. "I heard about your mother."

"I was there to watch her die, Mr. Hassler," Sadie said. Bile churned in her gut and lent acid to her tone. "Yesterday I had a mom, now I just have a lot of shitty memories. And then to top it off, as soon as I walked outside, I ran into a pissing match between your cop and a King's Man. So yeah, I'm real sorry that guy lost his hand, but *with respect,* sir, I didn't do it, he brought it on himself, and we all got our own shit to deal with."

They stared each other down across the tiny living room. The whining swamp cooler filled the room with noise and reluctantly cool air. The undersheriff had an ugly little smile on his face, the kind of look a man gets when he's congratulating himself for not hitting someone who needs to be taught a lesson.

At last, Hassler shifted his feet and said, "I am sorry for your loss. I knew your mother by reputation."

"Yeah, well, everybody knew her by reputation."

"I suppose that's true," Hassler said. "Just like everyone knows the King."

Sadie felt a trap in there somewhere, and said nothing.

"Do you find yourself chatting with the King's Men often, miss?"

"Nope," she said. "That was a first."

"Alright," he said. "And have you spoken to him since?"

"No, but he did give me his card."

"Did he now?" Hassler said. "May I see it?"

"I don't think he meant me to share it."

The undersheriff exhaled out of fleshy nostrils. "Young lady, that *thing* you spoke to at the hospital brutally attacked a deputy in the line of duty. He is a public menace, like a rabid dog. Something to be destroyed. Yet I get the distinct impression that you are protecting him."

Sadie snorted a laugh. She knew better, but the anger was still inside her, burning her up. "I'm not protecting anybody. Not like the *King* needs me to protect him from you."

"Is that so?" the undersheriff asked coldly.

"The King protects Red Valley," she said. "I'd figure you'd be on the same side, not picking fights with him over parking spots."

The undersheriff turned his head away and stared out the window, back south toward Red Valley. Sadie knew she was making him angry too and was surprised at how little she cared.

"The law protects Red Valley," he said when he was done contemplating the horizon. "This isn't some godforsaken wasteland. This is the United States of America, state of California. Got a president, governor, all sorts of politicians. And we've got laws. And the most important thing about those laws is that nobody is above them."

"Not sure those laws were meant for things like the King," Sadie said.

"Or the Liar?"

The question sent Sadie back on her heels. She knew it was probably time to stop talking, yet words just kept coming out. "You drive all the way up here to accuse me of something, Undersheriff Hassler? Or my mother?"

He smiled at her discomfort, showing off teeth stained by coffee and age. "Like I said, I know—sorry, *knew*—your mother by reputation."

"So what?"

He came forward a few steps. Sadie was already up against the wall, so had no room to retreat. "When someone breaks the law, it is my job to prove it so justice can be served. That is the foundation of society. That's what keeps places like Red Valley from becoming... unseemly. But when that same someone can drive up here and ask your pretty mother to write in her little book and make all the proof disappear, well, the foundation becomes eroded."

"People asked her to make themselves look skinny without going to the gym," Sadie said. "Or bring back their dead yappy little dogs. Not cover up their crimes."

"Do you know every Lie your mother told?"

The question stung, but she pushed it aside. "No."

"But she wrote them down, isn't that right?"

Sadie's eyes narrowed. Now it all made sense. "You don't give a damn about your deputy and you're not here for me to give a statement." She shook her head. She was a little slow catching up to her new reality, but the rules were starting to make themselves clear. "You want my mom's ledger, just like everybody else."

Hassler tilted his head. "Everybody else?"

Shit. This was why you shouldn't let your mouth say whatever it wants. "That wasn't a denial."

Undersheriff Hassler sighed. It was a sound of disappointment, and of resignation. "You've inherited your mother's *unfortunate* disrespect for authority."

"I thought you said you only knew her by reputation."

He ignored that. "You are wrong, young lady, about a number of things. First, I care very deeply about my deputy and the loss he suffered. Second, I don't give a damn about your mom's ledger. I'm not interested in the kinds of scum who'd come up here and give their blood in exchange for covering up their sins. Those are symptoms. I'm after the cause."

"And what's that, Mr. Hassler?"

"The King," he said. "I want to take down the King."

Sadie wanted to laugh, but the way he said it gave her a chill instead. As far as she knew, the undersheriff wasn't anything special—anything *other*—so why did he sound so confident that he could take down something like the King? Arrogance? Stupidity? Or something else?

"You see, I know a little about the history of Red Valley," he went on. "And the *modifications* the King has made to the people here. The whole town is full of weird shit, but I don't think the King gives his power away from the kindness of his heart. Everything he does—his so called 'protection' of Red Valley—is carefully calculated."

Sadie doubted something as powerful as the King needed to bother with being careful around men like Hassler, but she kept that observation to herself.

Hassler lowered his head a little, like a bull about to charge. "So that leaves me with a very important question: Why'd he create the Liar?"

The books, Graciela had said last night. *He doesn't want anyone to read them. Must have something juicy in there, something real good.*

"I wouldn't know," Sadie replied.

The undersheriff smiled those stained teeth again. "Neither do I. But I think I would very much like to find out. You see, I strongly believe everybody's got a weakness, a way to make them hurt. Even things like the King. He's just better at hiding it than most. He acts like he owns this town, but he doesn't. He acts like he's a god, but he ain't. He's got a secret and I think it is written down in those Liar's books."

A new fear crawled up Sadie's back on spider's legs. *Had Hassler sent the Laughing Boy to get the ledgers?*

"Those books belong to my family," Sadie said.

"And you can keep them," he said. "I just want to know what they say."

"Did you ask my mom to see the ledgers? What did she tell you? Or were you too scared to get on her bad side?"

"I had hoped you might be more reasonable, but I'm starting to doubt that."

"Some things are secret for a reason, Mr. Hassler."

Hassler reached up and ran a meaty hand over his smooth chin. "I don't believe much in subtlety, young lady. It just complicates things that should be simple. I think a man should say what he means. So let me say what I mean: I will get what I aim to get."

An over-confident white man with a badge and a gun. How original, Sadie thought.

"Come November," he went on, "the sheriff is going to retire and I'll be elected as his replacement. Change is coming to Red Valley. Real change. We won't need things like the King or the Liar anymore. Everybody has a weakness, after all. So you need to take a good long moment to reflect and ask yourself which side of history you want to be on."

"Nice election speech," Sadie said. She suddenly remembered how hungry she was and decided it was time for breakfast. "If you want to pick a fight with the King, that seems insane, but I'm not going to stop you. I'm not going to help you either. I don't need him as an enemy. I've got enough to deal with on my own right now. Have a nice day, Mr. Hassler."

"I don't think you want me as an enemy either."

"Are we enemies now? Because I told you no?" Sadie sighed as condescendingly as she could. "Maybe you need a few moments of reflection yourself, Mr. Hassler, if that's all it takes. Hardly seems like the right attitude for the next sheriff of Red Valley."

He stared at her, measuring her. He must have expected something else when he drove up here, that a grief-stricken girl would be easy to push around. Well, he'd discovered otherwise. She may not be the Liar—not yet, anyway—but you didn't survive as the Liar's daughter by being an easy mark.

"Thank you for your time," Undersheriff Hassler said, replacing his hat on his head. "I look forward to our next meeting." He turned and went out the door and down the steps, his boots thumping heavy on the wood.

Sadie locked the door behind him. Her whole body was shaking with hunger, fatigue, and adrenaline. First the King's Man shows up, then a Laughing Boy, now the undersheriff. All of them very interested in her mom's books. None of them willing to go sniffing around until her mom was out of the way. Life had seemed so simple yesterday. She'd had problems, sure, but they were little things: getting to work on time, figuring out what to eat for dinner, accepting she'd never have much of a life outside of Red Valley. Now her problems weren't so little, not anymore.

First, she called Graciela. "I need your help."

"Say no more, chica," came the quick reply. "I'm on my way."

Second, she found the biggest bowl in the cupboard and emptied most of a box of cereal into it, and then drowned the little crispy oat squares in low-fat milk. She took her time eating it, chewing slowly, thinking. Planning.

Lastly, after washing her bowl and spoon—something her mom had always yelled at her for not doing—she methodically tore her house apart. Every drawer was opened, then emptied, then pulled out to check behind and beneath. Every shelf was cleared, every box dumped out. For the first time in her life, she was grateful that their house was small. She found broken pencils and ballpoint pens with chewed-on caps. She found old receipts and a couple cans of green beans that had started to bulge. She found little from her childhood; her mom had never been the type to hold onto crayon drawings or finger paintings. And her mom never liked how she looked in pictures, so they didn't even have any photos on the walls. Even up in the attic, she found only a few moldy boxes of Christmas lights and tinsel that they hadn't even bothered to hang last year.

And no ledgers.

I guess I shouldn't be surprised you were good at hiding stuff, Sadie thought as she surveyed the mess she'd made of their house. *That was kinda your thing.* What a lonely life that must have been, to have everyone confide in you but no one trust you. Was that the fate that awaited Sadie now?

Graciela found her sitting in a pile of crap on her living room floor. She took in the chaos and Sadie's grim face with wide, unblinking eyes.

"Um," Graciela said. "What the hell happened?"

Sadie stood up and wiped dust from her hands. "I'll explain on the way."

"The way where?"

"I need a ride to the far side of the River," she said. "I need to find my dad."

CHAPTER FIVE

"This is nuts," Graciela said as they neared the bridge. "You know that, right?"

"What I know is I've got to find those ledgers," Sadie said.

The town in all its expiring glory slid lazily by her car window. Honest Bob's Used Automotives had a sagging *Going Out of Business* sign across the half-empty car lot. In the park by the River, the grass was long dead and the trash cans spewed their contents onto the ground. No one played on the rusted playground. There were some signs of life by the Tastee-Freez, where kids hung around in sweaty clusters and licked melting soft-serve.

"You think your dad has them?"

Sadie shrugged. "My mom hid them somewhere. They aren't at our house or I would have found them. And he's the only other person I know she trusted. Sometimes."

They drove past a cluster of Hassler's election posters. His eyes seemed to follow them.

"You don't talk about him much."

"What's there to say? I've barely seen the dude more than a few times. I think he came to a piano recital once."

Graciela snorted. "You took piano lessons?"

"It didn't stick," Sadie said. "Neither did having a dad. I don't think he's much of the parenting sort. He sure liked Mom, though. And Mom liked him okay too, until she didn't."

The bridge stretched out ahead of them. They weren't alone on the road; it wasn't forbidden to cross over, after all, just stupid. Below them, the River churned. The never-ending drought had shrunk the River's reach, leaving newly exposed riverbanks to dry out like bleached bones, but still its black depths seemed limitless.

"And he lives over there?" Graciela asked, drumming her fingers on the steering wheel.

"The last I heard," Sadie said. "Don't know where exactly. But we need to find him."

"So your plan is...?"

"To ask nicely."

"Right," Graciela said.

"What?"

"You're not really the 'ask nicely' type."

"What the hell is that supposed to mean?" Sadie said, crossing her arms over her chest. "What exactly *is* my type?"

"'...she asked, nicely.'"

"Shut up."

"Real charming."

"I said, shut up."

They reached the end of the King's Peace halfway across the bridge. It was marked by a subtle shift in the light, like a cloud passing over the sun, only there hadn't been a cloud in the Red Valley sky in a long while. Inside the King's Peace, humans were safe from the other things. Outside, though, there were no rules.

As they left the bridge on the far side of the River, they passed a gas station with a couple decrepit pumps and dandelions growing between cracks in the pavement. Next door was a Chinese food place where Sadie remembered eating chicken chow mein with her dad once. A sign in the window announced: HELP WANTED, APPLY WITHIN. The sign's paper was yellowing from the sun, the tape curling away.

The light ahead turned red even though no cars were trying to cross. Graciela fidgeted in her seat and mumbled to herself. A sudden chill raced across Sadie's skin. She twisted and looked around. A man in a baseball cap sat slouching at a nearby bus stop. Dark eyes under the brim stared at Sadie. His mouth was pressed into a hard, thin line. As the light turned green and Graciela started forward, the man slid out of view and the chill faded.

"You sure about this?" Graciela asked.

"Hell, no," Sadie said. Something huge moved laboriously in the darkness between buildings up ahead, but she didn't get—and didn't want—a good look. There was a reason people like her stayed on the other side of the River. "And if I had a better choice, I'd be all over it. But I've got the King and now this undersheriff on me about the Liar's books. Plus that tweaking Laughing Boy who showed up at my house last night."

"Right," Graciela said, uneasy. "Those things give me the creeps. If I came home and one of them was giggling in my bedroom, I think I'd just burn down my house."

Sadie could picture the Laughing Boy's glowing blue eyes, his pointed teeth. She'd scared him off—for now, at least—but he'd be back. She shivered.

They pulled into a gravel parking lot just off the main road. This far from the rest of Red Valley, the peeling-paint apartment buildings and chain-link houses had thinned out, leaving plenty of room for *For Sale* signs in front of fields of dead crops. And for a dive bar.

"Roberto came here when he turned 21," Graciela said, eyeing the sheet metal structure with a broken neon sign that read TIPS BAR. It wasn't even lunch yet, but there were already plenty of cars in the lot. "Got in a fight with... something. Broke his nose and spent a night in jail."

"Looks like a classy joint," Sadie said. "No wonder Dad's supposed to be a regular." Sure enough, she recognized his dirty blue Thunderbird parked near the street.

"I don't think we're their normal clientele. They may not even let us inside," Graciela said. She usually didn't take crap from anybody, but ever since they left the King's Peace, her eyes hadn't stopped darting around and her hands hadn't stopped their nervous twitching.

Sadie unbuckled her seat belt. "We're young and female. We're every bar's clientele."

"I don't know, chica," Graciela said, glancing over her shoulder.

Sadie touched her arm; Graciela almost jumped out of her seat. "It's fine," Sadie said. "You can wait here. I got this."

"No," Graciela said. "You asked for my help. If I sent you in there alone, they'd kick me out of the sisterhood."

"You drove me out to a garbage bar on the wrong side of the River on your day off," Sadie said. "Your sisterhood card is safe."

"Oh, man," Graciela said. "I don't know..."

Sadie punched her in the shoulder. "Keep the getaway car warm. If I'm not back in five minutes, remember me fondly."

"I hate you sometimes."

"But you love me the rest of the time."

"Yeah," she said. "Vaya con Dios."

Summertime slapped Sadie in the face as she stepped out. She was sweating before she'd gone three steps toward the bar's front door. She didn't blame Graciela for wanting to wait this one out. This was a demonstrably stupid idea. The problem was, it was also her only idea.

She pushed the door open. It was so dark inside that she was blind for a moment while her eyes adjusted. Slowly the interior materialized. There was a long bar along one side and tables scattered elsewhere. A flickering jukebox warbled "Friends in Low Places" from just beside the entrance. A flat screen TV hung on the opposite wall; a soccer game was playing. The bar was about half full. She saw no sign of her dad. A few patrons watched the game. Some watched their drinks. Others watched her.

The bartender had a gray goatee, a snake tattoo on his neck, and bruised eyes that followed her closely as she stepped inside. "You lost, kiddo?" he asked.

Chairs creaked. Sadie ignored the stares.

"I'm looking for someone," she said. She rested her

hands on the smooth bar top, did her best to keep them from shaking. "Hoped you could help."

"You got ID?"

"Don't want a drink," she said. "Do you know Brian Holbrooke?"

"Who's asking?"

"His daughter."

A patron at the end of the bar chuckled at that and drained the rest of his beer. Sadie couldn't make out much of his face in the gloom. The more she squinted, the more his features swam and blurred.

The bartender, however, did not look amused. "You're in the wrong place, little girl."

She hadn't really expected them to be helpful, but still couldn't fight the anger simmering in her chest. "I *need* to find him."

"And I've never heard of him."

"His car is parked out front."

The bartender shrugged. "Don't know what to tell you."

"Fine," she said, turning away from the bar and looking out into the room. The jukebox chugged and switched to "Amarillo by Morning." A couple of the bar's patrons finished their drinks and wandered out into the bright noonday sun. Others slinked out the back entrance. Sadie tried to take a measure of those who remained. Most looked normal enough. Others, like the guy at the end of the bar still smirking into his beer, felt... off. Something about how their hands moved, or how the skin hung loose on their faces, or the unsettled shadows behind their eyes. A voice inside her head screamed for her to run, run, *run*.

"Maybe I'll just ask around."

But as she stepped away from the bar, the bartender's hand latched tightly onto her arm. "Girl," he said, his voice lower. "You're too stupid to see it, but I'm doing you a favor."

"You think I want to be in your shit bar right now?" she said, matching his volume. There was that natural charm that Graciela had mentioned. Maybe she wasn't the kind of person who smiled her way through life; too much like her mother. "I ain't got a choice. I need to find my dad."

"Whatever you think your problems are," he said, tightening his grip as his eyes darted around the room, "they can always get worse."

The bartender was a tough-looking man. His forearms were hard and veined. Scars stood out white on his hands. But Sadie saw something else too, when he glanced out at his patrons: fear. "I doubt it," she replied.

"I'm only gonna tell you this once more," he said. "Get the *fuck* out of my bar."

She looked down at his hand, his fingers digging deep into her bicep. "Unless you're telling me where Brian Holbrooke lives, I don't want your help."

He let go. He regarded her briefly, then shook his head. "Suit yourself," he said as he turned his back and occupied himself by straightening shot glasses on a shelf behind the bar.

Sadie rubbed her arm to get circulation going again. She felt the bartender's fingers—and his words—still weighing heavily. But like she'd told him, if she had any better ideas, she sure as hell wouldn't be here.

"I'm looking for Brian Holbrooke," she announced to the room. "Any of you know him?"

Silence.

"I ain't a cop," she said. "I ain't looking for nothing. I just need to talk to him. Any of you know where to find him?"

Someone near the TV raised the remote and increased the volume.

"I'm not trying to bother anybody," she said. "I just need—"

The patron at the end of the bar picked up his drink and slid down until he was right next to her. When she saw him out of the corner of her eye, he looked bigger. Less human-shaped. Though she still found it hard to make out specific details on his face, she could see he was smiling. It made her blood run cold.

"I know Brian," he said. His voice was quiet and a little raspy. His teeth were yellow and sour alcohol vapor hung around him like a cloud. "I know him real well. Old drinking buddies, he and I. Marvelous man, very generous."

"Great," Sadie said, fighting an urge to back away. "Do you know where I can find him?"

He leaned in a little. "Funny thing: he never mentioned having a daughter."

"We're not close," she said. "So, is he here?"

"You don't really look like him," he said. "You're much prettier."

"Thanks," she said, uneasy. "So about Brian..."

He reached out and patted her arm. His skin was rough, like sandpaper. The touch lingered a little and Sadie wanted to punch his blurry face. "This is a brave thing you're doing," he said. "Most people like you know to stay where you belong. Stay where it's safe. But not you. You come over here to our side of the River, stinking like the King, and start butting into our business. Asking questions. Making noise. Remarkably brave."

Sadie pulled her arm away and he chuckled and took another sip of beer.

"The thing is," he said as he wiped his yellow mouth with the back of his hand, "this isn't like the other side of the River. Over here, folks don't stick their noses in other people's affairs. Over here, we don't make noise when we should be quiet. Over here, we got whole fields full of gnawed-on bones from little girls who thought they were being brave."

She should be afraid—and she was, terrified even. The room was dark, rank, and unknown. She wanted to run for the welcome light and heat of the parking lot and tell Graciela to drive and not stop until the River ran underneath. But with the sound of the man's cloying feigned kindness still echoing in her head, she realized she wasn't just afraid; she was also pissed off.

"Spare me. I'm not some kid you can give nightmares to," she said. "I'm the fucking Liar of Red Valley." It wasn't true—not yet—but it was true enough.

The room got a little quieter. The man slurped the last of his beer and brought the glass down on the bar with a *crack*. "So," he said, his voice still quiet but suddenly far less sweet, "you *are* the King's special pet." He shook his head, his face smearing. "What a goddamn stupid thing to say in here."

He stood up and dusted off his jeans. Sadie took a step back, heart thundering. *When will you learn to keep your mouth shut?* That voice in her head sounded a bit like her mom, but then again, so had she, a moment ago.

"I think—" But the man never got to finish his thought before a nearly empty mug shattered over his head. He dropped to the floor in a haze of broken glass and beer.

Standing over him was a massive man with arms thick with muscle and dark with hair and ink. He nudged the fallen man with a boot. He didn't stir. Black blood crept along the floorboards.

"I tell you where Brian is, you stop interrupting the game?" the massive man asked, pointing a thumb over his broad shoulder at the TV.

Sadie nodded.

The bartender started to speak, but the big man waved him off. "She's made her bed, let her lie in it." To Sadie, he said, "He's in the back. Past the bathroom, on the left. You'll know which door." The big man returned to his place by the TV and the rest of the bar looked everywhere but at Sadie. The jukebox hummed and whirred and went quiet.

The bartender sighed and wiped some glass shards from the counter with a wet rag.

Sadie stepped around the pooling blood. If she just kept walking, maybe her legs wouldn't lock up and her hands would stop shaking. She moved quickly to the back of the bar. There was an unlit hallway there. She passed the foul smelling bathrooms and found an unmarked door, on the left. It had to be the one.

The door did not belong. It looked heavy, made of old wood stained a dark gray, with a heavy brass knob, like it had originally been made for a far nicer building and inexplicably moved to this dump. Where would a door like this in a place like this possibly lead?

It's not too late, she thought. *You can still run screaming.*

But she knew it wasn't true. It had been too late for a while now.

She put her hand on the cold brass, turned, and stepped inside.

CHAPTER SIX

THOUGH IT WAS hard to really see its edges in the gloom, it was clear the room beyond the door was far too large to fit inside Tips Bar. The air was frigid and smelled of old, old things. There was some weak light, though Sadie had no idea where it was coming from. The floor was hardwood covered in a lush rug. Low, leather-bound chairs lined one wall. Along the other wall stood a row of pedestals of differing heights. On each was a reconstructed skeleton of various animals, none of which she could identify, their forms twisted in pain, as though in the moment of their violent deaths. At the far end of the room, figures huddled around a small table, and as she entered, Sadie caught the end of a conversation.

"...you know I'm good for it," someone was saying. "I've always paid on time."

The figure closest to the door had his back to her. She could see a bald spot and the sun-reddened skin beneath. He was the one speaking, and she knew his voice. Brian.

"*Your debts compound,*" said one of the figures on the far side of the table. The voice sounded like a death rattle. She tried to get a closer look, but the figures were draped in almost complete darkness. She saw vague human-shaped outlines shifting in the shadows, but no clear details.

"I know, I know," Brian said, leaning toward the shadows. "But I've got a plan. A couple plans. I just need to buy some time, get some breathing room."

"*This is a story we've heard before, Brian.*"

"Yeah, I get it. But—"

Another of the shadowy figures held up a hand, or at least darkness congealed into the shape of a hand. "*It would seem that our conversation has an audience.*"

Brian twisted around in his chair.

"Hi, Dad," she said in a squeaky voice.

"Oh, shit," Brian muttered.

"Nice to see you too."

He got up quickly and crossed to her in a rush. He put his hands on her shoulders and pushed her toward the door. "You really, really shouldn't be here."

"I need to talk to you."

"You picked a real bad time, sweetheart."

"I didn't pick anything," she said. "But we need to talk."

"Fine," he said. "Fine. Sure. I was just finishing up my business. Wait for me outside. You don't want to be in here."

Sadie didn't argue. But as she turned to leave the strange dark room, a deathly voice stopped her.

"*You are the Liar's daughter,*" one of the figures said.

"Not anymore," Sadie said. "I'm the Liar now."

The shadows turned to each other. If they spoke, it wasn't in sounds Sadie's ear could recognize. Then they said, *"The Long Shadows offer our condolences. Both for what you have lost, and what you have gained."*

"Okay, that's enough," Brian said, pushing Sadie out the door. "I'll meet you outside."

Sadie shivered as the strange door slammed in her face.

WHEN SADIE RETURNED to the car, Graciela was waiting with saucer eyes.

"What happened to you in there?" she demanded. "You look like shit."

"I think you were right," Sadie said. "I don't think we're this bar's usual clientele."

Ten minutes later, Brian scurried out of the bar. Sadie met him by his car.

"So," he said nervously. He had on a sweat-dark shirt and cargo shorts. He looked worse than Sadie remembered, thinner in the arms and thicker in the gut. "Your mom's dead?"

"Classy way to start, asshole," Graciela said. Sadie shot an elbow into her ribs.

"Yeah," Sadie said.

"How?"

"Cancer."

"Shit."

"Yeah."

He ran both hands over his face, pulling at the skin. "She called me the other day. I knew it had to be bad if she was calling me. Hadn't spoken to her in years. It was nice to hear from her. Should have known something was wrong."

"What was going on in there?" Sadie asked, gesturing toward the bar with her chin. "With those... things."

"Don't worry about it," he said, the words coming out so quickly they got a little jumbled. "You don't want to be involved with the Long Shadows, trust me."

"You owe them money?"

"I owe them a debt." There was an edge to his voice now. "Like I said, don't worry about it."

"You could at least pretend to be happy to see your daughter," Graciela said. Sadie didn't stop her this time. She knew Brian wasn't going to greet her with a big hug, but she hadn't expected him to seem so annoyed.

"Sorry, sorry," he said. "I've just got a lot going on right now, I didn't mean..." He sighed, wiped some sweat that was about to drip into his eye. "That was a hell of thing you did, going in there like that."

"You've got a hell of a daughter," Graciela said.

"You said Mom called you," Sadie said. "What did she want?"

"Help," Brian said. "She thought someone might be after her, watching her. Didn't want to give me any details. She said she'd really screwed some shit up and was trying to make it right."

Sadie furrowed her brow. Who would have been following her mom around? Hassler? The King? And why? "Is that all she said?"

"It was weird, because she never really talked much about being the Liar, you know? But this time, it was like she needed to tell somebody, get it off her chest. She said she'd told a real bad Lie," he said. "And something got out of hand."

You could have told me, Mom.

"How were you supposed to help her?" Sadie asked.

"Wait for you, I think," he said. He fished his keys out of his pocket and popped the trunk of his car. He rummaged around and came out with a box. "She said she needed that kept safe for a little while, but I'm guessing she wanted me to hold onto it for you."

"And you kept it in your car?"

"Safer than my apartment, trust me."

Sadie pulled the box open. The cardboard was warm from the summer heat. Inside, she found a stack of old books held together with rubber bands. The ledgers.

"Did you look at these?" Sadie asked carefully.

Brian shook his head. "I don't need any more complications in my life. Frankly I'm happy to be rid of them."

So many pages, so many Lies. But they all looked aged, yellowed by time. None she recognized. "What about Mom's ledger?" Sadie asked. "Where is it?"

"Didn't see it in there," Brian said. "She never went anywhere without it. Guess she wasn't done with it yet."

He wasn't wrong; her mom rarely let her book out of her sight. Sadie had accused her multiple times of caring about it more than her own daughter, and her mom hadn't refuted her. But if it wasn't here and wasn't at their house, where was it?

"I need your help too," Sadie said after working up the courage. "I don't know anything about being the Liar, but ever since Mom died I've got half of Red Valley on my butt wanting me to keep these secrets or give up these secrets. The undersheriff was at my house this morning. And before that, the King's Man came to the hospital and—"

"Whoa, slow down," Brian said. He suddenly looked nervous. "You've got the sheriffs *and* the King after you?"

"I don't think the King is after me," Sadie said, though she still wondered what he truly wanted from her. "And the undersheriff wants these." She held up the ledgers. "So he can go to war with the King. Mom must have been in the middle of all of this and now that she's gone, I'm stuck with it. So I could use a hand. If you've got some time."

Brian glanced around the parking lot, as if he were looking for an escape route. "Look," he said. "Your mom asked me to hold onto those books for her, so I did. I'm not sure what else I can do."

"I don't know. You can give me a ride. Or some advice. Or twenty bucks. You know, your basic dad shit."

"I'm not really good at that."

"Yeah, I know. I've had plenty of years to notice," Sadie snapped back. *What is this guy's problem?* "Never too late to start now."

"What did your mom tell you... you know, about us? Me and her."

"She told me you were a dirt-bag, but a decent one."

"I'm not a decent anything," he said, his voice almost a whisper.

"Brian—"

"I'm not your dad," he said. The words came out in a gush, like they'd been trying to break free since the moment he saw Sadie inside.

"What?"

His face burned red and he couldn't look at her. "I liked your mom, always did. I knew her back in high school. She never had the time for me; didn't seem to like anyone, really. Later, we became friends. Maybe she got lonely, I don't know. But we never... you know. It never happened. When you came along, I didn't ask questions about who or whatever. It was fun sometimes, pretending. But that's all it was. Pretend."

Sadie felt her lips tighten and her lungs contract. The heat coming off the gravel was suddenly sweltering. And the man standing across from her suddenly looked very small.

"Pretend," Sadie repeated. The word tasted sour.

"I'm sorry," he said. "I don't want you to be mad or anything. I wouldn't have even told you, but with your mom gone now, it just seemed... I just felt like..." His words trailed off and he let them go, like they weren't worth chasing after.

"Now that she's gone and you know she won't ever sleep with you," Sadie said, "why keep pretending to care about her brat?"

"Hey, that's not fair," he said. "I cared a lot about your mom."

"Just not about me."

"It's not like—"

"No, no," Sadie said. "I get it. You don't have to explain." She needed to get out of there so she could breathe, so this bastard wouldn't see her cry. "Graciela, let's go. We've overstayed our welcome here."

"Aw, come on," Brian said, his voice stronger now that he could act aggrieved. "I gave you the books—"

Sadie stopped and held up the ledgers. "Did she ask you to give these to me? She didn't, did she? She asked you to keep them safe, but then I showed up and you saw an out, so you pawned them off on me. Well, thanks, *Dad*. I won't expect a Christmas card."

"And good luck with the Long Shadows, Brian," Graciela added before they got into her car and slammed the doors shut.

"So," GRACIELA SAID when they were back on the road.

"Shut up," Sadie said.

"Shutting up," Graciela said. "Want a hamburger?"

"Yes," Sadie said. "Yes, I do."

They drove back across the bridge and into the King's Peace. Sadie held the ledgers in her lap, but didn't undo the rubber bands. She was vaguely aware of their weight and knew they should command more of her attention, but she didn't care. Not after the morning she'd had. And the night before that.

They settled on the Treehouse Diner where Sadie worked. Sadie didn't really want to deal with Denise asking her to cover for one of the other waitresses, but they did have the best burgers in town and she got an employee discount. They got the booth in the back across from the coffee machine, where glass pots bubbled deep black liquid, despite the breakfast rush being long over. Sadie ignored the stares she got from the other patrons, their too-loud whispers.

The restaurant got its name from the tree growing right up the middle of it: an ancient oak with a trunk at least four feet wide. Most of the branches sprouted above the roof so they didn't have too many extra leaves to sweep up, and somehow the whole place didn't leak like a sieve. The story went that when they wanted to build the place, they cut down the tree, but by the next morning, it had regrown back to full size. They tried again, same thing happened. Eventually they gave up and built around it. Sadie wasn't sure if that was true, but she had seen bored jerks carve their initials into the wood while they waited for a burger, and by the next day, the marks were gone, the bark restored. Now the tree was a welcome steady presence in the diner, like a kindly regular who smiled and tipped well.

"I'm just going to say it," Graciela said when she couldn't take Sadie's silence anymore. "He was a total douchebag."

"Yeah," Sadie said. She didn't meet Graciela's eye. Instead she stared at the tabletop. At the Treehouse, the tables all had old newspaper clippings from the *Red Valley Daily News* embedded under a coat of clear varnish. From her seat, she could read about a record turnout for the rodeo back in 1957 or which families came to the Red Valley Baptist church potluck for Easter in 1907.

"I'm glad he's not your dad," she went on. "You don't need his douchebag genes messing you up. Your mom was right to stay away from him. What a tool."

"Yeah," Sadie said again, absently twirling a straw between her fingers.

"Seriously, chica. You don't need him."

"I know."

"But…?"

The straw flipped out of her hand and disappeared under the table. "Yesterday I had a mom and a dad. Today…" Sadie's voice trailed off into the bustle of the diner.

"Yeah," she said. They both sat in silence for a moment, but it became too much for Graciela and she said, "So, who do you think it is? Your dad, I mean."

Sadie laughed a little. She'd been too busy working over the events in the bar and Brian's revelation that she hadn't even thought about other options. "Mom wasn't really friendly with anybody else," she said, shrugging. "Maybe before my time."

"Maybe it was some dark, handsome stranger who came into town and swept her off her feet before his dangerous past caught up to him and he had to flee to keep you both safe."

Sadie snorted. "That sounds like one of those crappy telenovelas you love."

"*Una Pasión Peligrosa* is not crappy."

Sadie stared back with a raised eyebrow.

"Look, if you can't appreciate fine art, that's not my problem. That's just a failure of your upbringing."

"We certainly didn't watch a lot of *Una Pasión Peligrosa* growing up," Sadie said.

"What do boring white people watch instead? The local news? *Wheel of Fortune?*"

"*Murder, She Wrote.*"

"Is that a TV show?"

"Yeah," Sadie said, remembering. "An old lady solving crimes. Mom loved that stuff. Read a lot of books like it too. Murder mysteries at a bed and breakfast, solved by the local knitters' guild, that sort of thing."

Graciela blinked. "That is the whitest thing you've ever said to me."

Sadie laughed. The shows and books had been silly, but for some reason her mom had devoured them. She'd always toss the books after she was done, but Sadie had snagged a couple and read them herself. There was something to them, trying to work out the mystery before the big reveal. And while people usually did get murdered in the opening pages, death never really had the same weight in stories like these. You never got to know the victim; the stories weren't really about them. They were just a part of a harmless puzzle. As an ache grew in her chest and burned her eyes, Sadie longed for a world like that.

They ordered their food and Sadie set the ledgers on the table in front of her.

"So that's what everybody's after?" Graciela asked, nodding toward the books.

"I guess so," Sadie said. She unwound the rubber bands and spread the ledgers out. Any secrets inside these were old, the Lies forgotten by generations long gone from Red Valley. Sadie was more interested in her mom's ledger and the Lies she'd told. What else had she been keeping from her? And what had she meant when she told Brian about a bad Lie that had gotten out of hand?

"What are you going to do with them?"

Sadie ran a finger down the spine of one of the oldest ones. It was coarse under her thumb. Her mom had wanted the ledgers protected. The King had wanted them secret. The undersheriff had wanted them exposed.

What did *she* want?

"Maybe I should have just left them with Brian," she said. "I sure as hell don't need all this drama in my life right now. I never asked to be the keeper of this damn town's secrets." Yet even as she said this, she felt drawn to the books, to the words within, and to the mysterious women who had written them. Her family. Gone, but maybe not forgotten.

She opened one of the ledgers. There was a name inscribed inside: Alice Tully. Based on the dates aligned with each Lie, Alice was probably Sadie's grandmother, though she'd never met her. Her handwriting was terrible and the Lies fairly mundane, the same crap most people had come to see her mom for.

"Any great cosmic secrets of the universe?" Graciela asked.

"People are vain and stupid," Sadie said, turning a page. "I can't believe what people are willing to give up for such petty shit. Oh, but here's a good one: 'Nobody will ever find Alexander Harbaugh's body.'"

"Nice. And just to be clear, that is exactly the kind of thing that would happen in *Una Pasión Peligrosa*."

Their food arrived and Sadie set the ledger aside. They ate in silence, food being one of the few things that could keep Graciela quiet for long. Sadie chewed slowly, absently, barely tasting the greasy fries. Her mom had told her that the King gave the Liars their power. He'd done similar things all over Red Valley through the years, as his magic infused the town. But the Liar's power was unique, and particular. What Lies did the King want told?

She brushed salt from her fingers and found what looked like the oldest ledger. The corners were fraying and the ink on the cover had faded from black to brown. The spine cracked slightly as she gently opened it. It too was inscribed on the inside of the cover: PROPERTY OF MARY BELL. Sadie turned the first thick page and found its Lies.

The ledger was separated into columns. The first column was a date, followed by a long block where the Lies were written out. The last column held a space for the blood. The stains had long turned the color of rust, but Sadie still felt a chill at the sight of them. She fanned through the pages briefly. There were hundreds and hundreds of entries, each marked with blood. How much life had been burned up with these Lies?

Mary Bell's handwriting was small and neat, though the cursive lettering was a bit strange for Sadie. She returned to the first entry.

August 1, 1862   *In this book, I will write only truth.*

An interesting way to start. Sadie kept reading.

October 2, 1862   *Sarah Jane Macalister is a tall woman with beautiful blonde hair.*

October 19, 1862   *Jacob Baker came back from the foothills with 10 gold nuggets.*

November 4, 1862   *The Rev. Robert Joseph White still believes in the power of the Almighty.*

She read the last one aloud to Graciela.

"But he'd still know, right?" Graciela said. "He'd know it was a Lie."

Sadie remembered Mrs. Bradford and her yappy dog. So much of what people told themselves were already lies, long before the Liar got involved. Maybe some people just needed a little help. "I think these Lies might be true enough for..." Her words died in her mouth.

"What is it?"

"Oh, God," Sadie said. *No, no. That can't be right.* She read the line again, careful to understand each looping letter. She hadn't misread it.

"Tell me."

The hamburger started to crawl its way back up Sadie's throat. "Trust me," she said. "You don't want to know."

December 20, 1862 The King of Red Valley is not dying.

CHAPTER SEVEN

SADIE'S HEART BEGAN jumping in her chest. Her hands went cold and tingly. The noise of the diner was muted in her ears, like she was listening from underwater.

The King of Red Valley is not dying.

Which was a Lie. Which meant the King was dying. And had been for a long time. And the first Liar had covered it up.

Sadie wasn't exactly clear on what the King actually was. There were guesses and rumors, old stories shared in hushed tones around town, but no one claimed to have any real information. The King hadn't been seen by anyone, as far as Sadie knew. But what the King *did* was more apparent. She'd just witnessed it, when they'd dared to venture outside of the King's Peace. The world was full of monsters, but the King kept the people of Red Valley safe. Whatever the King was, the things outside were terrified of him and so stayed away.

Things started to make sense now: why the King's Man

had been so concerned about the ledgers, and why the undersheriff wanted them. And why the King created the Liar in the first place. If the great dark things outside Red Valley knew that the King was dying—that he was vulnerable— maybe they wouldn't be so afraid of him. Maybe they wouldn't stay away.

"So," Graciela said. "You wanna talk about it?"

"Nope," Sadie said. "Not really."

"That bad, huh?"

Most secrets were just embarrassing. Others were maybe shameful. But a secret like this was dangerous. Deadly. "Yeah, that bad. Sorry, I think it's better if I keep this one to myself."

"I guess that's part of this whole Liar gig. Keeping the secrets, like the King asked."

Sadie closed the ledger. "And here I thought being the Liar would be fun."

Graciela shrugged. "Whatever it is, your mom handled it, right? So you can too."

She had a point. Her mom had known this secret too, but no one had bothered her about it. No one had started snooping around until her mom was gone. And her grandmother must have known, and her mother, all the way back to Mary Bell. And they'd kept the secret. Because they were the Liar, and no one screwed with the Liar.

"I need to learn how to do what my mom could do," Sadie said. "And fast."

"So, how do you do that? Learn how to Lie and all that."

"I have no idea," Sadie said. "I think my mom was supposed to teach me." So why hadn't she? Especially once she knew about the cancer?

"Huh," Graciela said thoughtfully.

Sadie let a French fry drop. "What?"

"Nothing."

"No, that was something. You have an idea." Sadie narrowed her eyes. "And judging by the look on your face, it's a bad one."

"Oh, yeah," Graciela said. "Real bad."

"Spill it."

Graciela finished off her Cherry Coke and wiped salt from her hands. "What if you could talk to your mom again?"

Sadie's skin tingled and her lunch flopped in her gut. "What do you mean?"

"Beto," Graciela said. Graciela's eldest brother was a brujo, but Sadie didn't know much more about him. He was older than them, intense even when they were all kids, and never much interested in his little sister or her friends.

"He can talk to the dead?"

Graciela nodded. "I heard him talking about it once with some of his brujería friends. It sounded like it wasn't easy or safe, but they could do it."

Mom, Sadie thought. *Are you out there somewhere?* Sadie had never given much thought to what happened after death. Just being alive was enough work on its own. But if there was a chance? *You didn't help me when you were here. Can you help me now?*

"Let's go."

"You'd better let me do the talking," Graciela said when they parked in front of her house. "Beto doesn't know you very well, and since he got out on parole, he's… well, even more of his usual charming self."

"Yeah, that seems smart," Sadie said, a little relieved. "And, thanks for everything today."

"Don't thank me yet."

They found him in the garage. The air inside was stale and smelled of gasoline. A 1973 Mustang stripped to gray primer and sitting on cinderblocks took up most of the middle of the room. Every corner was full of crumbling cardboard boxes laced with spiderwebs. Beto sat cross-legged on the stained concrete next to the car. His eyes were closed and sweat ran freely down his face.

"Roberto," Graciela called as they entered. "Need to talk to you."

Sadie saw him wince at the interruption. His eyes opened slowly and stared at them both with dark, unimpressed eyes. He was shaved bald, save for a thin black mustache and a wispy soul patch. Tattoos crawled up his forearms; she didn't remember those from before he went to jail. Sadie didn't know what he'd done—no one really talked about it.

"We need a favor," Graciela said.

He closed his eyes and sighed.

"Hey, I'm talking to you," Graciela said, snapping her fingers in front of his face. Sadie was starting to question the wisdom of letting her do the talking. "Don't make me go get Mamá."

His eyes opened again. His irises were nearly black, like wells too deep to see the bottom. Sadie saw something in there, more than just the natural antipathy an older brother has for his annoying little sister. There was anger, sure: coiled tight and ready to strike. But also power. Sadie couldn't nail it down any more than that, and wasn't sure she would have even noticed it a week ago, before her world went a little crazy, but it was there.

"What do you want?" he asked.

"A favor, like I said."

"And why should I do anything for you?"

"It's not for me, dumbass. For my friend."

His gaze turned fully to Sadie. She met it and held it. Maybe there was power moving behind her eyes too.

"I know you?" Beto asked.

Graciela groaned in exasperation. "She's been my friend since kindergarten."

"We've met," Sadie said. "A few times."

"Don't look familiar," he said. "So what do *you* want?"

"We need you to do your brujo thing," Graciela said.

Muscles tensed along his jaw and neck.

"My mom just died," Sadie said quickly before Graciela could irritate him more. "And she's left me in a lot of trouble. I need to talk to her. I don't need long, just a few—"

"And you think I can talk to the dead?" he asked, his voice sharp. "Who told you a fool thing like that?"

"I heard you," Graciela said. "You were talking with Esteban and Paco."

"You listened in on my private conversation?"

Graciela laughed. "Nothing's private here. You want privacy, move out of your parents' house, tough guy."

Storm clouds crackled in those deep eyes. He pointed at the door. "Get out."

"Don't be like that," Graciela said. "We're just—"

"Get out." His words hit like falling on concrete. Sadie was sure she imagined it, but she could have sworn she heard some of the bottles on the shelf next to her rattle.

"Fine," Graciela said. "Come on, let's go."

"Just you," Beto said. He jerked his chin at Sadie. "She can stay."

"Oh, no," Graciela said.

"I don't like your tone," her brother replied. "And if your little white friend wants a favor, then she and I need to talk business."

Graciela looked at Sadie. Sadie felt her blood racing. The heat in the garage bore down on her like a heavy wool blanket, smothering her in sweat and fumes. She had remembered Beto being intense, but this was something else entirely. She didn't like what she saw in his eyes. But the only way out of this mess was forward, and she was starting to discover that things that used to scare her didn't seem all that frightening anymore.

"Go ahead," Sadie said softly. "I'll be fine."

"If you touch her…" Graciela said, before launching into a litany of rapid-fire profane Spanish that Sadie could barely follow. "I'll be inside. Kick him in the balls if you have to."

The door to the garage clicked shut.

"Nice car," Sadie said into the hot silence.

"It was, once," Beto said. "Maybe will be again someday. So Javi tells me you're the new Liar of Red Valley."

"Javi told you that?" Sadie was surprised; she'd never heard Graciela's youngest brother talk much.

As if he could read her thoughts, Beto tapped his temple.

"Javi talks all the time. You just have to know how to listen. Now, is it true? You're the Liar?"

"I guess so," she said. "But that's what I need to talk to my mom about."

Beto nodded, considering. "Even if I could do the thing you think I can do," he said, "I can't. Condition of my parole. Sheriffs in this shit town don't like brown men using magic."

Sadie's shoulders slumped. All that for nothing. There had to be others in Red Valley who could help her, but she didn't know how much time she had. But she couldn't expect Beto to risk getting sent back to jail for someone he barely knew.

"Alright," Sadie said. "Sorry to bother you."

As she turned to go, Beto said, "Hold up, gringa. Not so fast. I didn't say no." He stood up and stretched out his legs. "I'm just providing you with the necessary details for this negotiation."

"Is that what we're doing? Negotiating?"

He smiled a little, though his storming eyes didn't settle. "I've got something you want, you've got something I want. So yeah. A simple business transaction." He pulled out his wallet and retrieved a crinkled picture of a pretty girl with a round face and long black hair. "This is my girl, Teresa. Been together since high school. Waited eighteen months for me to get out of that fucking prison. Met me at the front gate."

Sadie didn't know what to say to that, but handed the picture back.

"We found out last week that she's pregnant," he said.

"Congratulations."

Now the smile broadened and the clouds thinned a little. "Gracias. Still can't believe it. It's one of those things, happens all the time. Nothing more normal in the world, people having kids. But when it's *you*, when it's *your* kid, there aren't any words for it. It's magic, just as much as anything a brujo or a Liar can do."

Did you feel that way, Mom, when I came along? And what about her dad, whoever that was? Had he beamed like this when he talked about Sadie? And if so, how long had that lasted, before he disappeared from her life?

"I'm sure you'll make a great dad," Sadie said.

"I hope so," he replied. The gloom darkened his face again. "But that's where you come in, Liar girl. I don't know how this whole Liar shit works, but I know you can change things. I need you to write in your little book. You write that I never went to prison. I don't care if I know it isn't true. I need my kid to think it's true. I don't want them thinking about that every time they look at me. You can do that?"

Sadie thought about all the stupid Lies her mom told for people, and wondered if she told Lies like this, too. Maybe some things were worth the Liar's Price.

"Yeah," she said. "I can do that."

"Good," he said. He sounded a little relieved. "Then we can do business."

"So you can let me talk to my mom?"

He held up his hands. "I can commune with the spirits. That's not the same thing. But it can be done."

"You've done it before?"

"I've heard of it being done," he corrected. "By my elders."

She was about to get angry before she remembered she'd never told a Lie before, but had promised to do so for him. So maybe it was an even trade after all. "Okay," she said. "What do we need to do?"

"This is the tricky part," he said. "We need some things, if we're going to do this. Things you maybe don't have."

"You didn't tell me that before we negotiated."

He shrugged. "It's not my first negotiation."

"Just tell me what we need."

He held up a finger to count. "We need a conduit," he said. "Lucky for you, that's me." Another finger. "We need a crossroads."

"Is that like, Washington and Main Street?"

"That," Beto said, "is an intersection. I'm talking about a true crossroads."

Sadie's eyes flicked around the garage as she thought. What made a 'true crossroads'? What the hell did that even mean? Where two roads came together, right? How was that different than just any old street corner? But there was more to it than just roads running into each other. People had to make a choice at a crossroads. Take a diverging path.

"I know where to go," she said at last.

"Good," he said. "Because those were the easy ones. We need a piece of something alive that can never die."

"What does that mean?"

"I'm not finished," Beto said. "Magic makes sense, but this is more than just magic. We're talking about breaking the laws of the universe, not to mention the laws of the County of Red Valley. This shit isn't easy, otherwise people would do it all the time."

"Fine," Sadie said. "What else?"

"You need an icon of the dead."

"What, like a picture?"

"That'd work. But you also need the blood of the dead."

Sadie felt light-headed and not just from the heat of the garage. She thought she might throw up. "Why would I... I don't have my mom's blood." They'd cremated her, on her mom's wishes. She was gone, really, totally, completely gone. Sadie didn't even have a picture of her.

Beto shrugged. "Nothing I can do, then."

No, no, no. Not when I'm this close. Just when she thought she might see her again, her mom's face slipped away a little further in her mind. *Did you have to leave me with nothing I could use to help myself?*

Sadie let the anger in, felt it burn hot inside, consuming all the air in her chest. She swallowed a scream and screwed her eyes shut, for a breath, two. Then opened them again. She did have something: the ledgers. They were full of blood, but only the blood of those telling Lies. But she remembered what she'd read in Mary Bell's book, her first Lie: *In this book I will write only truth.* That had been Mary's Lie. Mary's blood. That had been the first Lie in every ledger, so if she could find her mom's ledger, she'd have her mom's blood too.

But she had no ideas left on how to find her mom's ledger. And little time before the undersheriff or the Laughing Boys came calling again.

"So all you need is blood and an icon?" she asked Beto.

"And a piece of—"

"Yeah, yeah, something that can't die." Sadie needed to get out of the airless garage, but her mind was already turning, moving. Plotting. "I'll be back," she said, wiping a bead of sweat from her forehead. "Then we can do business."

Beto sat back down on the concrete, hands resting lightly on his knees. "I'll be waiting."

CHAPTER EIGHT

"TODAY'S BEEN STRANGE, no doubt," Graciela said as they parked. "But I never expected to end up here." She shuddered a little. "I mean, you're great and all that, but our friendship has its limits."

Sadie smiled briefly before she opened her door and heat outside pummeled her. "Stay close," she said as they hurried inside. "I'll make sure no books jump out and bite you."

The Red Valley County Library didn't look much like a library from the outside; in fact, it had once been a grocery store. When the original building burned in a mysterious fire back before Sadie was born, they'd reclaimed the abandoned structure, replacing aisles of pre-packaged dinners with the works of Tolstoy and Dickens. Sadie knew the place well; she could still picture the spinning racks of children's books, the colorful covers staring hopefully back at her. When they stepped in through the glass doors, the musty smell of old paper suddenly made her six years old again.

"So you used to come here, willingly?"

"Books are your friends," Sadie said, soaking it in. "Think of them like telenovelas for your mind."

"*Telenovelas* are telenovelas for my mind, you elitist—"

Sadie shushed her and jerked her head meaningfully toward the busy kids' section only a few feet away. A few of the moms eyed them with that judgmental glare you only earn after bringing your special bundle of joy into the world.

They found the local records room in the back, next to the sections on WWII and the Gold Rush. A librarian sat behind a nearby desk. She was older, with long graying hair that hung loose past her shoulders. She wore a mismatched collection of jewelry around her neck, beads, crystals, and chains all tangled up.

"Can I help you young ladies?" she asked with a welcoming smile. Graciela flinched at the question, but Sadie smiled back.

"I'm doing some family research," she said, nodding to the local records room. "My family has been in Red Valley a long time, so I was hoping to find something about them here. Specifically any pictures that might have been in the local newspaper or something."

The librarian looked a little more closely at Sadie, but if she saw something of note, she kept it to herself. "We've got records that go back before the founding of the town," she said. "Though few photographs back that far."

"Can we take a look?"

"Certainly," she said. "Let me show you."

The records room was cramped. Shelves filled the walls and books and binders filled the shelves. There was a single computer with a tiny screen that took its sweet time to boot. Once it came to life, the librarian showed them how to search.

"Who are we looking for?" she asked.

"Try 'Mary Bell,'" Sadie offered.

"Ah," the librarian said with a little nod. "Your family *has* been in Red Valley a long time."

"You know who Mary is?"

"I've spent my life studying our town's history," she said. Her fingers played idly with the beads around her neck. "And whatever the era, the Liars always play a part. Don't know what pictures we might have of her, but we can look."

They ran the search. Only a few records were returned. One was a title for a 10-acre plot of land on the edge of town in Mary's name.

"It would be unusual for a woman to own land at that time," the librarian noted. "But Mary would have been an unusual woman."

Sadie smiled at that. She knew nothing about her family—just another thing her mom hadn't bothered to share with her—but she liked the idea that they'd all screwed with the status quo.

"But no pictures?"

"I'm sorry, no."

They searched for some of Mary's descendants, all the way up to Sadie's mom. The Liars appeared in records here and there, including a few times in the newspaper, but no pictures. Maybe her mom hadn't been the only one in her family to disconnect herself from the rest of Red Valley.

"Dead end," Graciela said.

"I'm sorry, girls," the librarian said. "I'll let you poke around a bit, if you'd like. Let me know if you need anything else."

She left them alone. Graciela eyed the books surrounding them suspiciously. Sadie stared at the cursor on the screen, mocking her: blink, blink, blink.

Sadie searched for Mary's name again. One of the records had caught her eye. She opened it up. It was an article from the newspaper from 1871 and there was a photograph included, just not of Mary. It was a grainy black-and-white picture of an old Victorian-style building with a gabled roof and pointed tower. Two men in old-fashioned suits and even older-fashioned mustaches stood in front, scowling at the camera. The caption at the bottom read, "Pictured, Thomas Gray, owner of the Gray House, and friend Charles Hooper, before the mysterious disappearance of the house and occupants last Thursday."

Graciela looked over Sadie's shoulder. "The Gray House. I remember going on a field trip there in elementary school. It was... creepy."

"Everything in Red Valley is creepy."

"Fair enough."

"And look here," Sadie said, pointing to the section highlighted by the search. "'When asked about the strange disappearance, Red Valley resident and long-time associate of the missing gentlemen Mary Bell said, "I'm glad they left. This town didn't deserve them. They were too pure for Red Valley. Too good. I wish them well, wherever they are now."'"

"So the caretakers knew your great-great-whatever-grandmother."

"Maybe they have something we can use," Sadie said. "A picture or something. It seems like a longshot, but those are the only shots I've got right now."

"Is the Gray House even, you know, *there* right now?"

"One way to find out."

It wasn't.

The lot on Washington Street was empty. There were houses on both sides, but in between was just a dirt lot, devoid even of weeds. Caution tape sagged between wooden stakes along the border. A sign posted right in front was blazoned with: ABSOLUTELY NO TRESPASSING. The ink had started to fade under the relentless sun.

"Real welcoming," Graciela said.

Sadie said nothing. Of course the Gray House was gone. That was just the kind of week she was having. She squinted at the fine print on the trespassing sign and read it aloud. "'Private property of Thomas Gray. If you are trespassing when the Gray House returns, you will be wiped from existence. You have been warned.'"

"I don't remember the casual death threats from when we toured here as kids," Graciela said.

Sadie had few memories of the trip, but that was unsurprising. Kids rarely appreciated the things they were forced to experience. And the Gray House wasn't just a well-preserved relic from an older era. No one was quite sure how they managed it—or frankly, why—but the caretakers of the Gray House had tapped into some of the King's latent magic and found a way to step outside of time. One minute, the stately Victorian building would be looming over Washington Street, then the next, it would be gone. Months or years would pass, then then poof—it would be back, exactly like it had been when it left, roses still in bloom. Had there ever been a time when the caretakers had been revered for their unique power? Sadie doubted it. Just another weird, dangerous consequence of their proximity to the King.

"So, what now?" Graciela asked. "Back to the library?"

Though she was looking at just dirt, Sadie felt something else there, like an unexpected pressure. She felt it in her chest and inside her skull. It reminded her of what she'd felt in Tips, trying to look at the patrons, and what she'd seen in Beto's endless eyes. "No," she said absently. "There's nothing at the library."

Sadie stepped up to the caution tape. There was nothing here, either. She could see all the way to the houses on the far street. A few cars drove by. But when she turned her head and snuck a look out of the corner of her eye, it was almost like...

"I don't think we're supposed to go in there," Graciela said as Sadie ducked under the tape.

"You always do what you're told?"

"Usually breaking the rules doesn't involve getting wiped from existence."

"You buy that nonsense?" Sadie asked. She took a few more steps into the lot. Her footprints were the only things disturbing the dirt. "Sounds like what a cranky Victorian-era magician would write if he wanted to keep kids off his lawn."

The strange feeling was stronger now, but even as she reached for it, it slipped away. This was starting to piss her off. *A little help would have been nice, Mom. Just a few notes on how all this shit was supposed to work, would that have been too much to ask?* She waved her hands in front of her and swept only air. But then for a moment, she caught a whiff of roses.

This was the King's magic, just like the Liar was. Just like *she* was.

"Hey!" Sadie yelled.

Graciela jumped. "What?"

"Not you," Sadie said. She focused hard on the strangeness, on the unnamable otherness she could somehow sense. "Thomas Gray! I need to talk to you!"

Movement in her peripheral vision. Sadie spun, but there was nothing. "I'm a descendent of Mary Bell and I need your help!"

"I don't think they can hear you," Graciela said.

"Sure they can," Sadie said, mostly to herself. The Gray House might exist outside of time—whatever that meant—but it was anchored here, and she could feel it. Maybe they could feel her too. Louder, she called, "Mary said you were good and pure. That Red Valley didn't deserve you. Well then, get out here and *prove* it!"

People were watching them now, from the far sidewalks or behind pulled window blinds. She was making a scene. *Let them look*, Sadie thought. *What they think won't matter if I can't figure this Liar thing out.*

"I think maybe we should…" Graciela was saying, but Sadie stopped listening. She smelled roses again. The air was filling with the heavy scent. And if she looked closely, she could just make out—

"Oh, shit." All around her, the Gray House was returning. Ghostly brick and stone and wood appeared like fog, creating garden, house, and wall. Some of it right in front of her face. Some of it inside of her body.

Sadie ran. Maybe the warning on the sign was just to frighten people off. And maybe it wasn't.

"Come on!" Graciela yelled.

Sadie's feet slapped the dirt. Then the gravel garden path. She crashed through a hedge that was almost nearly real. Echoes of leaves brushed her face. Memories of branches pulled at her clothes. Then she burst out onto the sidewalk, nearly knocking Graciela over, just as a stone wall and gate settled into place.

They stood on the sidewalk for a minute, breathing heavily, staring at the house that hadn't been there a moment ago.

"Holy shit," Graciela said, and Sadie couldn't have said it better.

The building stood tall and sharp, just as it had been in the picture. Now, however, instead of being surrounded by fields and a dirt road, it was bordered by plain tract houses and a busy paved street. The blue and white paint looked fresh, without a crack or smudge. A tall brick chimney crowned the roof along the west side of the house. The building looked to be at least three stories high, but the haphazard windows made it hard to identify floors. The main tower stood well above every other building in sight on Washington Street. From its upper window, Sadie imagined you could probably see all of Red Valley. The wall surrounded the entire property, blocking some of the rose gardens from view and funneling visitors through a single iron gate, where a sign hung from a chain: THE GRAY HOUSE. ALL WELCOME. ADMISSION $10. GROUP RATES AVAILABLE. INQUIRE WITHIN.

When no one appeared from inside, Sadie approached the gate. "You coming?" she asked.

"Do I have a choice?"

"You aren't curious to meet the impossibly old friends of my long-dead ancestor?"

"Well, when you put it like that…"

They walked cautiously along the stately garden path just inside the gate. Sadie marveled at it. Stuff like this didn't grow in Red Valley, not anymore. The plants themselves must be well over a hundred years old, if ages could still be measured when the passage of time no longer universally applied.

They climbed the oddly steep steps to the front door and knocked using the bulbous brass knocker. A moment later, the door opened. On the other side was a man dressed in a fine black waistcoat and purple silk tie. His hair was dark and slick with pomade. He had a mustache that refused to end, disappearing into bushy chops that cascaded down his cheeks. He wore round wire-rimmed glasses and a pained expression.

"So," he said sourly. "Brazen self-centeredness runs in your family as much as does magic."

"Um, hi," Sadie said. "I'm a descendant of—"

"Yes I *heard* you," the man replied. "You made your point quite clearly. And with volume. Otherwise, we would not be conversing."

"Oh," Sadie said. "Okay. So, can you help me?"

"Help you?" the man asked. "No. Dear me, no. I responded to your summons to admonish you for trespassing and to demand your silence. I have not come to be where I am today by offering my help to any waif barging in off the street, even if she can reach out to us when we are away. Though it might appear otherwise, my time on this earth is precious and limited. Good day. And do keep your voice down in the future."

As he made to close the door, Sadie stopped it with her foot. "Please," she said. "I need your help. I'm in trouble and I have nowhere else to go."

The man's face hardened as he stared down at Sadie's foot and then back up at her. His arching expanse of beard made Sadie want to laugh, but she saw nothing amusing in his calculating eyes.

"Of course you are in trouble," he said. "You're the Liar, aren't you? Liars track trouble everywhere they go, like dung stuck to your shoes."

"Um, ew?" Graciela said.

"Great metaphor," Sadie said. "Really nails the whole, 'I hate you even though we just met' vibe you're going for here. But if what you want is to be left alone in peace and quiet, then your best move right now is to invite me in, serve me tea or whatever, and help me do what I need to do. Because if you think I won't camp out on that sidewalk with a bullhorn and scream the lyrics to Backstreet Boys songs at your invisible windows all night long, until you learn how miserable eternity can actually be, then don't pretend you know me just because you've met my ancestors, okay?"

They locked eyes and stared each other down across the threshold, across generations, until finally a voice called from inside the house. "Thomas, stop grandstanding. Just let them in."

The man—Thomas, apparently—paused for another long moment, then exhaled a weary, resigned sigh. "I knew how this was going to go the moment I opened this door," he said. "Congratulations on being just as stubborn as your mother. And her mother. And frankly, every accursed woman in your mendacious family. Come inside."

Sadie and Graciela exchanged a look as Thomas disappeared into the dim house. "What's 'mendacious' mean?" Graciela asked.

"I think it means he likes us," Sadie said.

"Backstreet Boys?"

"Shut up," Sadie said. "It worked, right? Come on."

The wood floor inside the Gray House creaked under their feet as they stepped inside. Just ahead, a tall staircase with narrow steps disappeared up into gloom. Hazy yellow sunlight filtered in from windows in two side rooms. When Sadie's eyes adjusted, she discovered that their reluctant host was not waiting for them and they had to hurry to catch up.

They reached him in a small library off the central hallway. Expensive-looking plush chairs flanked a red-brick fireplace and bookshelves covered all the remaining wall space from floor to ceiling. Sadie stole a glance at the books on display: Dickens, Brontë, and Keats, but also Hemingway and Faulkner, and then Grisham and King and Gaiman.

"See anything you like?" The question came from a man sitting in one of the chairs. Unlike Thomas, this man was clean-shaven, with pale skin and light blond hair. And also unlike Thomas, he was smiling.

"Quite a collection," Sadie said. "Though some doesn't seem... period appropriate."

"Guilty," the blond man said. "I didn't magically flee the Victorian era only to be stuck reading Victorian books. We don't usually let the school tours come back here. Might ruin the mystique if the caretakers appeared too human."

"Charles," Thomas said, chiding.

"What?" Charles replied. "You're the one who invited these ladies inside."

"At your insistence."

"Oh, you were going to get there eventually, however you'd like to pretend otherwise," Charles said with a dismissive wave of his hand. "I just hurried us along."

Thomas didn't argue that point. "They may be our guests, but that does not mean we have to be so... informal."

Sadie noticed that Charles hadn't gotten up from his chair. He had a woolen blanket over his legs, despite the heat outside. Thomas stood by the empty fireplace and scowled.

"So you guys are really from the past?" Graciela asked as she looked between both men. "That isn't just some marketing gimmick to trick kids?"

Thomas scoffed at the question, but Charles just laughed. "We prefer to think of it as the ever-changing present."

"That's not really an answer," Sadie said.

"Why are you here?" Thomas asked. "You've come for our help, but I do not see how we could possibly assist you, whatever your troubles."

"My mom died," Sadie said. "Yesterday, actually." So much had happened since that still moment in the hospital room that the memory of it was already receding, though the pain was still vivid, a bright burn in her chest.

"Oh, I am so sorry," Charles said.

"That," Thomas said, "is not really an answer, is it?"

"Man, I remember you being a lot nicer when we came on the tour," Graciela said. "Now you're kind of a dick."

Thomas sighed. Charles looked at him carefully, as if he recognized the sound and wanted to calm him, but Thomas did not return the glance. "The tours are a performance," Thomas said. His voice was hard-edged. "It is part of our agreement with the lovely people of Red Valley. We give their insufferable children a glimpse into a glorious, nearly forgotten past, and they don't build a gas station in the lot where my house stands when we are… away."

Sadie nodded toward the front of the house. "The sign out there, the warning. It is… real? Wiped out of existence?"

"Very real," Thomas said. "Anything standing here when we return from outside of time is instantly and forever eradicated, a process that I am tempted to initiate immediately if no one in this particular year will be bothered to answer any of my bloody questions."

"Thomas, please," Charles said. "Don't be such a boor. We so rarely have guests. And perhaps now I remember why that is," he added with a wink to Sadie and Graciela.

Before Thomas could offer another rebuke, Sadie stepped forward. "My mom died, which I guess means I'm the Liar now. Since then I've had the King and the undersheriff and a number of other weirdos making demands of me. Making threats. I need to be able to protect myself."

"No one can make demands on the Liar," Thomas said. "Not unless they want to face her wrath, terrible as it is wont to be. The Lies she could tell, not to mention if she got ahold some of their blood. Once that goes in the ledger, the Liar's Price is due, whether the blood's owner agrees or not."

"See," Sadie said, "that's just it. I don't know anything about being the Liar. I don't know the rules. I don't know how to make the magic work."

Thomas and Charles shared a weighty look now. There was a great deal of history there, but little Sadie could read.

"We've known our share of Liars," Charles said. "In fact, as you seem to have deduced, Mary Bell was a dear friend of ours."

"Yours," Thomas corrected under his breath. "Dreadful woman."

"But," Charles went on, choosing to ignore him, "I must confess that we're no experts on the Liar's gift."

"No," Sadie said, "but I'm hoping you can help me talk to someone who is." She explained her plan in brief. She had a moment of pause before describing it, but then realized talking to the dead might not seem so bizarre to two men who could step out of the current of time.

When she was done, Thomas nodded slowly to himself. "I'll admit it sounds a bit mad, but not impossible. Red Valley is a very peculiar place; and while I believe there are others like it, there are not many. The rules of the universe bend here. And sometimes they break."

"Because of the King," Graciela said.

"There is power here, that much I know for certain," Thomas said. "I could not be definitive about its source."

"Thomas is an expert at uncovering Red Valley's reluctant secrets," Charles explained with a slight grin. "That's how he saved our lives."

"Is that why you took the Gray House out of time?" Sadie asked. "Your lives were in danger?"

Thomas's scowl deepened, but he seemed more annoyed at Charles than Sadie. "We left our time in search of a more enlightened future," he said gruffly. "In more ways than one."

"What have you found so far?"

"Progress," Thomas said. "Slow and disappointing progress."

Sadie considered Charles's immobility and the pallor of his skin, and what life might have been like in Red Valley in the 1800s. She had barely remembered her tour at the Gray House, and certainly nothing of its inhabitants. But now she saw them not as relics, but as human, faced with their own insurmountable problems. But they hadn't given up; they'd broken the rules.

"So you think talking to the dead might be possible here?"

Charles held out a hand, and Thomas stepped over and took it and held it gently. "The dead are on a journey of their own," Thomas said. With his fingers laced with Charles's, the edge was gone from his voice. "We see them, sometimes, when we are between the past and the present. Distant shadows on a long, winding road."

"Can you speak to them?"

"It is not our place," Thomas said. "And I do not want to draw unwanted attention."

"I have Mary's blood," Sadie said. "But I need an icon, an image of her. Something for the brujo to focus on."

"Indeed," Charles said. With some great effort, he allowed Thomas to help him up from his chair. He moved steadily, if a bit slowly, out of the library and into the hallway. A few minutes later he returned holding a white handkerchief bordered in pink lace, and handed it to Sadie. She unfolded it. Inside was a very old photograph— or perhaps a very new one, to Thomas and Charles. It was a portrait of a woman in a wide white dress. Her hair was dark and piled on top of her head. She had a ribbon around her neck and a sternness fixed on her lips.

"That's Mary. She gave this to me," Charles said wistfully, "when I told her that we were leaving. Something to remember her by, she said. Though, I think she was more upset about losing Thomas than me," he said, winking again.

"Dreadful woman," Thomas repeated, but this time with a hint of fondness.

"This is perfect," Sadie said. She almost wanted to cry. After hitting so many brick walls, it was unreal to be holding what she needed in the palm of her hand. "May I borrow this?"

Charles nodded. "Keep it. You never knew her, so

it's right that you have it. I won't need a photograph to remember her."

"She was a memorable lady?" Sadie asked.

"Oh, God," Thomas muttered.

"Maybe with a little luck, and the right magic," said Charles, "you'll see for yourself."

"Thank you. And, sorry I made you, you know, exist again."

Before Thomas could reply, Charles said, "Think nothing of it. We've been gone a good while now, so it will do us well to stretch our legs."

"Are you going to pop out of time as soon as we leave?"

"No," Thomas said. "It takes time to prepare the process. And Charles is right. We should pause a moment to take stock of Red Valley in its current form. Maybe there is at last something of value here."

Sadie held up the picture. "Then I'll come back and let you know if I can speak to Mary. But now, if you'll excuse me, I've got some rules to break."

CHAPTER NINE

THAT EVENING, THEY all piled into Graciela's Toyota: Sadie, Graciela, Beto, and Ashleigh, who came over as soon as Graciela told her what they were planning to do. "I've seen some shit in this town," she'd said, "but nothing like this." Sadie was a bit irritated Graciela had called her— did they really need spectators?—but silently she agreed with Ashleigh's sentiment. The creepy King's Men, the things lurking just outside of town, the Liar's gift, all that seemed normal. Or if not exactly *normal,* then at least expected. But now they were painting outside the lines, making up new rules.

But maybe that was more common in Red Valley than she ever knew.

They had to make a quick stop at the Treehouse Diner for one last item.

"Denise," Sadie called when she came in, "I'm going to borrow one of the tree's branches, okay?"

Denise was counting money at the bar. She didn't even

look up. "Sure," she said. "It'll grow back by the morning anyway."

Sadie selected a small enough branch and broke it off where it reached the trunk. She felt a little guilty doing it, even if the tree would recover, but she needed a piece of something that couldn't die. She patted the rough bark and whispered, "Thanks, old buddy."

Armed with the blood, the icon, a piece of immortality, and a conduit, all they needed now was a crossroads. Sadie told Graciela to drive south. They passed the last houses in town, then the farm supply store flanked by green tractors, and then the shady-looking Texaco station that was always at least forty cents a gallon more expensive than anywhere else. They passed the town's welcome sign: WELCOME TO RED VALLEY, it said. A NICE PLACE TO LIVE. And they passed the reach of the King's Peace once Main Street became Highway 147.

"You sure about this?" Graciela asked as they left the protection of the King's oversight. Outside the car, a sweltering night had fallen hard, dropping the temperature under 100 but just barely. "Things got a little nasty when we went outside the Peace last time."

"Not sure I want the King spying on us when we do this," Sadie said. "I don't think he minds breaking the rules himself, but I think he expects everyone else to follow them."

And still, the farther out of town they got, the worse Sadie felt. She wasn't sure if she was nervous about what they were trying to do, or worried it wouldn't work, or worried that it would. Whatever it was, it tied her stomach up in painful knots and made her head ache like somebody was inside her skull and trying to claw their way out.

"You look like shit," Graciela said as she stole glances over at Sadie. "You gonna puke? Don't puke in my car."

"I'm fine," Sadie said, though she didn't feel fine. She looked out the window and saw the road sign for Paso Verde, 37 miles. "Stop here."

They pulled over into the dirt on the side of the road and got out. There were no street lights this far out of town, so Graciela left her headlights on. The beams shot out over the highway, illuminating the crossroads.

Highway 147 and State Road 18. If you took the way south, you'd reach Paso Verde in a little more than a half hour. Sadie had never actually been there, even though it was close by, but she'd heard it was a lot nicer than Red Valley. They had a state university with a better reputation for parties than academics, but for some of her old classmates, it had been a way out, a way to a different future. Not for Sadie.

If you took the road east for about 10 miles, you'd reach the new Walmart Distribution Center, which everyone had been talking about when it opened last year. Starting wages were $3 above minimum, if you didn't mind the backbreaking work or the unpredictable hours. If you stayed on at least 5 years, you could start to earn a pension. Another kind of escape.

The road west went into the hills, disappearing behind tight curves and sheer drops that usually claimed a few lives every year. If you survived the drive, eventually you'd arrive at the barbed-wire and concrete guard towers of the California Men's Penal Colony, where the state sent the criminals it wanted to forget.

And the road north went back to Red Valley.

Four roads converging: the prison, the college, the DC, and Red Valley. If this wasn't a true crossroads, Sadie didn't know what one was.

"What now?" Graciela asked.

Ashleigh looked back down the dark highway. "What happens if a car comes?"

"Get out of the way," Beto said.

Sadie walked to the center of the crossroads and held out the ledger, the branch, and the photo to Beto. A blade-thin moon hung over the distant foothills where miners had once prayed for gold. "So what do we do now?" she asked the brujo.

"I have no idea," he said. "I've never summoned a dead white woman before." Before Sadie could say anything, he held out his hand for the talismans. "Would you look at your face? Relax, I know what I'm doing. Mostly." He spread his feet on the asphalt and closed his eyes. Graciela started to say something snide, but Sadie cut her off. Eventually Beto said, "But there is something here. Power coming through. I can feel it."

Ashleigh put an arm around Graciela's waist. "How come you can't do any magic, like he can?"

"Tell your chica I'm already taken, Gras," Beto said. "But I'm flattered."

"Ugh," Graciela said. "Magic is nothing but trouble. I don't want any part of it."

"Then why did you come?" Beto asked. "I didn't invite you."

"Will you just shut up and open a portal to Hell or

whatever? It's creepy being out here. Anybody could be watching us."

Sadie scanned their surroundings. There were empty fields on all sides. The remains of an almond orchard stood to her left, skeletal trees lined up in withered rows. Something flew above them almost without a sound; she hoped it was just a big owl.

A humming filled the air. Beto had squatted down in the center of the crossroads, the talismans spread around him in a triangle. His fingers were wide and pressed against the road. His eyes were closed and the low rumble of his voice danced across Sadie's skin like electricity. The night seemed to grow darker, deeper, colder.

"This is sweet," Ashleigh whispered. "So much better than watching TV."

"You're crazy. TV is safe. I never died watching TV," Graciela said. "Never had my soul sucked out, or my brains eaten, or…"

Sadie stopped listening and just focused on Beto. She stepped a little closer and saw that he was trembling, little tremors running up the muscles and tattoos on his arms. His jaw was set hard, his teeth grinding. Whatever he was doing, she could feel it, like a sudden drop in air pressure, like a storm coming. It made her forget the twist in her guts and the pounding in her head and focus just on him, and the highway beyond.

I wish you could have been here for this, Mom.

I wish I could see you one last time. To tell you to go to Hell. And that I love you.

She didn't know how long it took; that moment seemed to both last for hours and be over in an instant. But suddenly Beto's humming stopped and his eyes snapped open and he said, "Oh, fuck."

The road ahead began to shimmer. And then move.

Highway 147 was gone. In its place was a winding dirt road that stretched to a distant gray horizon lit by ghostly silver stars. Along the road were trees, or something like trees, with tortured black branches laden with rotten fruit that swayed in a silent wind. There was a sign, where the highway sign had been, but it was written in a language Sadie had never seen. The letters wriggled like worms digging through rot when she tried to focus on them. There were other things moving in the distance, heavy and dark, things Sadie could give no name to, but they did not seem to notice her and came no closer.

And then she saw someone on the road, coming toward them.

"You did it," Sadie said quietly.

"I guess I did," Beto said. "Not sure if that's a good thing."

The traveler approached. Her gait was steady and sure, as if she knew the path she walked well, and she did not seem surprised to find Sadie waiting for her at the end.

"Greetings, girl," the traveler said with a voice like an echo. She was a tall, sturdy woman in a cotton gingham dress with a pack on her back. Her hair was pulled up in a tight bun and her eyes were empty and bright, like staring into a candle flame. "I wondered how long it would take before one of my seed stirred up enough hellfire to seek me out. Come on now. You'll catch flies with your mouth open like that, so let's hear it. What stupid thing did you do?"

CHAPTER TEN

SADIE GAPED AT the traveler and the colorless world behind her. Dreadful questions chased all other thoughts away. Is that what it meant to be dead, to walk endlessly and alone on old roads under a hostile sky? It certainly wasn't the Heaven or the Hell she'd heard about in church. What would the congregation of the First Church of the Risen Christ make of the cold wind coming through this sundered crossroads? What would they make of Mary Bell, eyes afire, hands on hips?

"Out with it, child," the traveler said. Her form blurred as she moved, an imperfect image on a bleak canvas. "I can stay here but a moment. The road goes on and I'm going with it. Standing still eventually draws unwanted attention."

An unwanted tear raced down Sadie's cheek. "Mary. My name is Sadie."

"Sadie," Mary said. The name sounded strange when spoken by a woman dead for over a hundred years, but also somehow reassuring. "I can see it in you. You're one of mine?"

Sadie nodded as she wiped away the tear with a fingertip. "Great-great-great-granddaughter, or something like that."

"Something like that," Mary said.

Sadie heard Ashleigh and Graciela whispering behind her: "Is this really happening?" "Shut up!" "Am I high right now? Tell me I'm high." "Shut up shut up."

"Mary," Sadie said, "I need your help. My mom died."

"I thought so," Mary said. She turned back over her shoulder and stared off at something Sadie couldn't see. "I felt it. I always do when another one arrives, even if I don't know her name. Her journey's just starting. Could be that we'll cross paths someday, she and I. I've walked stranger roads."

"She died and never taught me how to be the Liar," Sadie said. "And without that, I'm—"

"—going to get killed?" Mary finished for her. "Trust me, girl. I know. Been a long time since I was in your place, but the world don't change much." Her searing eyes narrowed. "You have my ledger? You've read it?"

"Enough of it."

"Good. Then you know what being the Liar's really about."

Sadie nodded. You don't speak secrets out loud in Red Valley, and Mary seemed to be of the same mind.

"People will kill for the truth, Sadie," Mary said. "They've done it before and they'll do it again, just give them cause. The Lies hold things together. You don't have to like them, nobody asked you to like them. You just have to tell them."

Sadie held up one of the ledgers. "How do I do it?"

"Find yourself a book. Doesn't matter what book, so long as it's yours. In there you're going to write your first Lie, the Liar's words."

Sadie remembered what she'd seen in the ledgers. "*In this book, I will write only truth.*"

"There's a smart girl. Maybe you are my seed. Write those words and seal the Lie with your blood."

Sadie considered this then asked, "But what is the Liar's Price for that Lie?"

Mary's ashen face creased with shadows. "A smart question. I can't rightly say, but it won't truly matter. The Liar never lives long. We burn hot and then we burn out. And then we walk the old roads, and wait for a meeting like this."

Sadie could feel a gathering tension in the air. The crossroads was growing weary. "And is that it? Then I can write new Lies?"

"You make it sound easy, but it ain't. And it ain't fun. But yes, the power will come. You'll know it when it does."

Sadie didn't like the sound of that, but she kept that to herself. "And then what?"

"Lying's an art form, girl. Some of us are better at it than others, I expect, just like lies of the worldly kind. When you write a Lie, you have to hold it in your mind. Picture a world where such a thing could be true. The Devil is in those details, child. The words on the page are just a marker. Some of it comes from the one wanting the Lie, but the real Lie is born inside your head. Focus on it, breathe life into it. But most importantly, you have to *believe* it."

"But how can I believe something I know isn't true?"

Mary frowned. On her void-scarred face, it was an unpleasant sight. "Come now, I thought you were smart. People believe things they know ain't true every day of the week and twice on Sunday. And like I said, it's an art. You'll get better. It'll break something in your soul, getting good at lying, but you'll get better. You'll start lying to yourself. And believing it."

Did that happen to you, Mom? What lies did you believe?

"Pay attention, girl," Mary said sharply. "Telling a Lie will become easy, with time. Too easy. Never forget that once it is told, there's no taking it back. Once it escapes from your head into the world, it has a life all its own." She looked back down the road, something of a longing in that stare. "But there are limitations, of course."

"Limitations?"

Mary's thunderbolt eyes shifted, like she was staring off at something Sadie couldn't see. She held a bony finger to her lips and looked like she might be ready to flee at any moment. From somewhere far off and across that strange divide, Sadie heard an awful, mournful wail growing in intensity. The sound burrowed into her head and filled her mind with visions of sloughing flesh, of matted hair being ripped out in meaty chunks, of bulbous flies drinking all moisture from bloodshot lidless eyes. Sadie thought she was going to be sick, thought she was going to go insane, but then the wail began to recede and the visions faded.

"Apologies for that," Mary said. When her eyes returned to Sadie, they looked pitying. "Before you ask, trust me that you don't want to know. Let's just say it's important to remember we're never alone out here, and that people spend too much time fearing death when they should fear what comes after."

Sadie tried to blink away the afterimages and focus on the task at hand before all her resolve bled out on the road. "You were speaking of the limits of the Liar's power."

"Right, there's always a catch in life," Mary said. "Take the Liar's Price for example. A hellish thing, but you can't make something out of nothing. The Price is higher for bigger Lies, or for Lies about somebody else. If I wanted to tell Lies about myself, well, that's my prerogative. But Lies about another are costly, sometimes too costly. And," she added casually, "of course the Lies don't mean nothing outside of Red Valley."

"Wait, what?"

Mary clucked her tongue. "Your mother didn't tell you much of anything, did she? I guess not, or you wouldn't have violated the laws of men and nature to bring me here." She laughed and the sound rattled the marrow in Sadie's bones. "The Lies are tied to Red Valley. Men came to me, begging for gold nuggets the size of their testicles. All well and good, but if they rode out of town, their sacks would be empty by the time they reached San Francisco. That kind of coin has to be spent locally. Hear me true: Being the Liar is powerful magic, but it don't mean a thing in the big world, Sadie. Not much does."

So that's why you never wanted to leave this town, Mom. Here, you were a queen. Out there, you ain't shit. Neither am I, I guess.

"Sadie," Mary said. "The road's bending."

More tears. Sadie ignored them. "Why did the King choose you, choose us?"

"No good asking why. I gave up guessing at the King's mind a long time ago, girl."

"Have you ever seen him?"

"Yes, once," Mary said. "I wouldn't recommend it."

The fiery stars over Mary's head were fading. The dirt road under her feet was turning back to asphalt. The cold air was turning into summer heat again. *Not yet, not yet!* Sadie moved closer, but as she did, Mary's form moved away, like chasing a mirage.

"It's nearly time, girl. Got to move on while there's still road to walk."

Sadie pushed tears away with both hands and let her anger rise to burn away the rest. She had no family, no connection to those who came before her, except for a ghost who couldn't stay still. "I'm all alone," Sadie said, her voice quiet so only Mary could hear. "I don't think I can do this."

"Girl," Mary said as she situated her pack on her back. "None of us do. And yet we keep doing it. Don't forget that." Mary looked beyond Sadie, back along the highway toward town. "Trouble's coming for you. You didn't ask for it, but it's coming. Red Valley don't have much, but it ain't lacking in trouble. You have what you need to see it through. Trust me on that, girl."

"Thank you," Sadie said softly.

"It's been my pleasure," Mary said. "I'd say we should chat again soon, but I don't expect I'll be walking this way again. This road always goes on, never back."

The world was almost right again. Sadie hated how

normal it looked. She wasn't ready for normal yet, maybe never again.

"Mary!" Sadie called as the traveler turned to go. "I almost forgot! Charles Hooper sends his greetings."

"Does he now?" Mary said, her voice a long way off. "So they made it work. Good for them, the crazy fools. Tell them..." But whatever she said was lost across the barrier between this life and the next as it closed with a final gust of frigid air.

A new grief washed over Sadie, for things lost she never knew, for those she might have loved, if time and death had allowed it. And for an image of her mom, walking a gray road shadowed by something like trees, alone. *I wish you could have stayed here a while longer*, Sadie thought, thinking of both Mary and her mom.

"Not gonna lie," Graciela said, her voice breaking the thick silence that had fallen over the deserted highway, "that was some crazy shit."

Beto said nothing. He stared down the road where Mary had been, his face grim. What had he seen when he stared out at that wasteland or heard that foul wailing?

"You get what you need?" Ashleigh asked.

"I think so," Sadie said. Her mind was still reeling from the horrible visions she'd endured, but it hadn't been for nothing. She needed a ledger. And some blood. Her own blood.

Spotlights burst over them like unexpected sunlight. Red and blue lights pulsed behind the blinding glare and voices began shouting, shattering the evening calm. The sheriff patrol cars had come up on them without headlights, slipping silently across the asphalt. The deputies appeared a moment later, dark shadows backlit by a blaze of white.

Beto tried to run, but they were ready for him. Three burly men with black batons were on him in an instant, pinning him to the ground. They clubbed at his arms and legs until he stopped fighting then clubbed some more. His face was shoved into the highway until the skin split and blood oozed down his forehead and into his eyes.

Graciela and Ashleigh were forced to their knees, black pistol barrels and barked threats shoved into their faces. Sadie alone was untouched. She stood frozen in a sea of violence, her heart cracking vainly against her ribs.

"I did warn you, young lady," said a voice from behind the line of cars. A big shape moved in front of the lights, broad shoulders and broad-brimmed hat cutting a sharp silhouette. "I told you that you didn't want me as an enemy."

Sadie stared the undersheriff down as his face came into view. "I thought you were interested in stopping people breaking the law, Mr. Hassler. We're just having a bit of car trouble."

"I'm interested in stopping the biggest law-breaker of them all," Undersheriff Hassler said, his voice booming over the road and the dead fields. "And I *will* stop him. And if I catch a few others along the way, well, then even better."

Sadie stuck out her chin back up the road. "The King's back that way. If you want that fight, go have it, and leave us alone."

The undersheriff stopped in front of her. He blotted out the spotlights, setting the edges of his frame ablaze like a man-shaped solar eclipse. He lowered his voice and smiled a little under his red mustache. "You know it isn't that simple. I asked you for your assistance in this matter. I thought you might be motivated by civic pride. But now I see I must be more persuasive."

"You going to arrest us? What for?"

"Illegally impeding a thoroughfare," he said. "Reckless mischief." His eyes moved away from Sadie and lingered on Beto, still trapped under 400 pounds of deputy. "Violation of parole."

"He did nothing illegal."

Hassler coughed a laugh. "Oh, we saw your little performance. Even in Red Valley, use of magic is a privilege, not a right, and your little friend there gave up his rights to the State of California." He shook his head. "Always sad to see such wanton recidivism. Never surprising, but always sad."

"Go to Hell," Graciela yelled before she was shoved to the ground and handcuffed.

When Beto saw this, he pushed against his captors and shouted in Spanish. The deputies were caught off balance and one even fell over on his butt, but that just made the others bear down harder. Sadie winced as the batons came down again and again.

"You need to understand," Hassler said. "I'll send that vato back to prison until he's an old man, and my men will break his legs before he gets there. Your girlfriends here won't be in jail long, but long enough to lose their jobs and good name. I will *ruin* them. And you need to know that this is just the start. It gets much worse from here. I'll impound this car and sell it for scrap. I'll take your house as a civil forfeiture. Listen here, girl: I will burn down your life."

Sadie stopped looking at Hassler. Instead she forced herself to look at Beto's blood on the road and at Graciela and Ashleigh, handcuffed in the dirt, faces smeared and terrified.

"I don't know anything," Sadie said, her lips shaking.

"I don't believe that," Hassler said. "After our last little chat, I think you couldn't help yourself. I think you read through your momma's books and found what I was looking for. It's only human nature, can't blame you. But that means that you can end this right now. You tell me what I need, and I'll forget about what we saw here tonight. You get on the right side of this war, and there will be mercy."

She felt no true loyalty to the King, whatever he was protecting them from. But she had no interest in helping the undersheriff take him down. What would that even mean? She didn't know what the King was, but doubted they had a cell big or strong enough in the county jail to hold him.

But she did know a secret. A weakness. Something the King wanted to stay well hidden. He may have even given Mary Bell the Liar's power just to hide this very thing away. And they'd kept it hidden all that time. Until this moment.

"You can't beat the King," Sadie said.

"You let me worry about that," Hassler said. "Tonight, you should be focusing on the fact that I can beat *you*. And everyone you care about." His eyes—flashing red and blue, red and blue—stayed on Sadie but he turned his head toward his men. "I think that suspect is resisting arrest, boys."

Beto shouted in pain. He tried to cuss out his assailants but got a boot in his face instead. Blows rained down on him: fists, batons, boots. Beto didn't even bother fighting back, but that didn't stop them. Nothing would. Nothing could.

Except Sadie.

"Fine!" More tears, more grief. "Fine. I'll tell you. Just leave them be."

The deputies stopped, hands hovering, ready to continue if necessary. Undersheriff Hassler waved them off. "I'm glad you decided to see reason. Like I said before, everyone has their weakness. So tell me. What does he not want us to know?"

"I shouldn't..." Sadie said. Anger and sorrow boiled up inside her, stealing her words. "I shouldn't say it out loud. The whispers—"

"Don't give me that horseshit," Hassler said. "Tell me, or that boy will never walk again."

Sadie looked at Beto. His head was down, his face hidden. She thought about how he'd looked when he told her that he was going to be a father. She thought about the Lie he wanted her to tell, the new future he hoped for.

"The King is dying," Sadie said.

There was a tickle across the back of her neck. Words swished around her, like leaves caught in a breeze, but the air was still. *The King... the King*, the words said, soft and low. *The King is dying. Dying.*

You don't tell your secrets out loud in Red Valley. The whispers are always listening, and when they hear something secret, they take it and spread it to the last place in the world you would want it told. It was easy to believe that parents made this up to teach kids to be careful and not to gossip; it would be a good lesson in a town like this, even if it were just a fable. But what is easy to believe is rarely true, especially in Red Valley, and the whispers were very real.

If Undersheriff Hassler heard the whispers, he didn't show it. Instead he tipped the brim of his hat to Sadie and said, "Dying, huh. Well, that is something. Thank you. Sorry we had to do this the hard way, but glad we could come to a reasonable resolution."

"Fuck you," Sadie said, her voice distant.

Hassler ignored her. "This will be good for Red Valley. Very good. The King's been pretending to be almighty for too long. Now I know he's full of shit. Thanks again. Have a safe drive back to town." He motioned for his men to return to their cars. They unlocked the handcuffs and gave Beto one last half-hearted kick before disappearing behind the blinding lights.

Oh, God, Sadie thought. *What have I done?*

CHAPTER ELEVEN

NO ONE COULD say why the whispers did it, what they gained, what they truly wanted. No one was even sure what they were: ghosts, echoes, spirits, or something else. But two things were certain, deadly certain: They were always listening. And they hated the King.

The King is dying.

The King is dying.

The King is dying.

They had put many a petty secret in many an interested ear, over the years. Sometimes they lingered to watch the ensuing chaos for reasons all their own. And sometimes the telling was enough. But this secret was not like the others. This was the secret they had been waiting for. Yearning for. And they knew exactly where to take it. Which ears would be most interested.

Some of the King's enemies were close. They crouched in darkness outside the King's Peace, bitter, baleful eyes watching the River's far shore. Some pondered how to fight the King in his own lair; others simply waited—patience was a virtue among their kind. The whispers reached them first and breathed into them seductive truths.

The King is dying. His strength is a Lie and his Liar is gone. The time for vengeance grows near.

Fanged smiles grew. Talons tore the earth. And dark faces turned to the Red Valley bridge.

The King had amassed many foes across the ages, and these were of the lesser sort. Dangerous to the weak and unprotected, but the King was neither. They might hate the King, but they were no match for him, and they knew it. But the whispers also knew the old hatreds, remembered stories of blood and battle long forgotten by the mortal world.

Dying or not, the King was not going to be defeated by a lesser foe.

But there were others.

POLICE TAPE FLAPPED in the wind as exhausted officers held back the surge of neighbors and reporters. Behind them, the flames reached high in the night sky, devouring the building and casting the world in red.

"Let them do their jobs," the police told the crowd, speaking of the firefighters slowly losing the fight.

A family of five had been in the house. No one had come out.

One face in the crowd watched with a different gaze than the others. For him, the fire was not tragic; it was art. It was perfection. He only wished he could get closer, to feel the heat on his skin. He never felt more alive than watching the little hairs on his arms singe and wither under the force of the flame. He craved it, loved it, needed it.

He hadn't known the people in the house, but that wasn't the point. It wasn't personal, never personal. He would watch anything burn, but a fire that consumed a life, well, that burned all the brighter for it. In such a fire, he sometimes thought he could see flickering faces cheering him on, calling him home.

The firefighters' hoses could do nothing. The crowd let out a gasp when the roof collapsed. They were afraid, all of them. This was the third arson fire in San Bernardino in the last two months, and with the state so dry, who knew how big it could get, how far it could spread?

One face in the crowd smiled. He shouldn't have but he couldn't help it. Not when watching something so beautiful, dancing just for him.

The whispers moved among the people, searching.

They were not searching for the arsonist. He was a monster, but a frail one. A human one. They were searching for something much older, something in the fire. Flickering faces, smiles in flame.

The King of Red Valley is dying, the whispers said to those who waited behind the flames. *All he took from you can be retaken. All he owes can be paid.*

Those who waited behind the flames could speak no words, but they could hear. And they could act.

The newspapers the following morning would go with the headline: *Deadly Fire Extinguished in Unexplained Manner.* Below the picture of the ruined house, they would quote the fire chief: *We don't know why the fire went out like that. Sometimes these fires have a mind of their own. We're just glad we were able to contain it to the single structure and no more homes were damaged.*

The whispers moved on. And the ashes, flying high in hot summer air, moved north.

THE HUNTER IN the darkness stalked the great open spaces between the cities of man. It was not afraid of men or their cities; it was afraid of nothing. But it was never truly dark in a city, and it preferred to hunt in the dark. It crouched on the old dead tree overlooking the freeway far below. Cars sped along at eighty miles an hour, tiny smudges of ugly light in an otherwise unblemished night. It wished it could kill them all, drive them away, but it had given up that dream long ago. They bred too quickly, these men, and were too easily replaced.

It flexed its wings. Their leathery expanse blotted out the sky. Oh, it felt good to hunt again.

There were others out here, hiding in the cracks of civilization, but it ignored them. They were nothing and they knew it. When its shadow crossed over the moonlit hills and arroyos, they cowered, and this was right and good. It had haunted the dark skies since before man crawled upon this earth and deserved to be feared. To be honored by their fear. *Harut*, the hunter had been called. *Baphomet. Chemosh. Azazyel.* And Death.

Claws tensed and mouth open, it was about to take to the air when it heard the voices. They sang to it—only to it—a song it had longed to hear for many an age.

The King of Red Valley is dying, the whispered song said. *He is weak. He is unprotected. He will fall.*

It considered these words. There *was* one thing that it honored with its fear: the King. It felt no shame in this; all wise things feared the King. Even if the King were dying, it would not wish to face the King in battle. Not again.

And yet.

It could continue to hunt among the cactus and juniper. It could snuff out one light at a time, knowing it could never stop them all. It could be the most feared shadow in the dark and face no challenge, no risk. But it would always know there was something worse out there. Something hiding in Red Valley.

Something that it could hunt, if the whispers could be trusted.

And what was a hunt without a challenge? Unworthy.

It pumped its wings and rose into the night. The old tree shuddered as it went.

FEW ALIVE KNEW of this place, and those who did, knew to avoid it. There are things better left undisturbed. There are bones that are meant to stay buried.

The whispers knew of this place. How they learned of it was a secret they never told. This, and only one other: why they truly hated the King. And it was that hatred that made them go where nothing—no creature or spirit—ought to go.

They found in this shadowed place a skeleton of a creature unlike any other who walked the earth. These were old bones, ancient when the world was new.

Weathered by sand and the passing of ages. Forgotten. But the whispers did not come for the dead. They came for the presence that lingered there, the one for whom there is no name that can be spoken, not by men or gods. The old enemy. The speaker of lies and truths unknowable. The gathering darkness. The one who—in another time, a lost age—nearly killed the King.

The King is dying.

Nothing moved. The ground was as still as a grave.

Louder then, the whispers repeated their secret. *The King is dying.*

There was a rustle among the bones.

He is weak. He is—

Something moved and the whispers were gone, fear outstripping boldness.

There was a sound then, in that ancient place. A rushing. A breath of wind. A sigh.

Not far away, a woman walked a dusty trail with her dog, as they did every day. The dog—a brown-black German shepherd—trotted alongside his master with a casual, graceful stride. The woman moved carefully on the uneven terrain, though her thoughts were elsewhere, consumed by a tyranny of small worries.

Something moved around them, like a breeze in a night without wind.

The dog stopped. Its fur stood on end. Its teeth shone. A low rumble grew in its chest.

The woman stopped, too, the insignificant concerns in her mind suddenly gone.

The dog lunged. There was no hesitation. Ten years he had lived with his master and never once considered doing her harm. Now he went for her throat.

But this was not his master, not anymore. She had been wholly burned away, replaced by something else, something for which there was no name, not among beasts or men. And the dog, driven to violence by baser instincts than he had ever known, knew in his soul it had to be destroyed.

But he was not fast enough.

The woman walked on. She did not hurry; there would be time. Others would come, certainly, but she did not concern herself with them. They were nothing. They would fade away, as had the ages of the Earth as she waited, and then there would only be her. And the King.

One last time.

CHAPTER TWELVE

THE DRIVE BACK to Red Valley happened in silence. Beto had barely been able to get into the car due to his injuries. They wiped up the blood as best they could. Sadie wanted to say something, to thank him, to apologize to him, anything, but when she looked into the cold expanse of his eyes, her words fled. Graciela was angry—furious— but had no outlet for that fury. Ashleigh was in shock and looked at no one, said nothing. Sadie gripped Mary's ledger and stared out the window at the town passing them by.

They took Beto back to their house. His girlfriend Teresa met them at the door. Graciela's mom appeared as well, then her dad. Spanish flowed over shouting and tears but found no purchase in Sadie's mind. All she could think about was Beto's face, spotlights shining on black blood as the blows fell. She thought she should explain to all of them why she'd needed Beto's help, why it had been so important, but she said nothing. It wouldn't matter.

She could have never reached Mary Bell without him, but that didn't seem to matter much anymore. Not to his family, anyway. She knew how to become the Liar, but that wasn't going to stitch Beto's scalp back together, or take the limp out of his step.

After a low, heated exchange, Ashleigh left on her own without a word to Sadie.

"Come on," Graciela said. "I'll drive you home."

They said nothing until Graciela put her car in park outside Sadie's dark house.

"I'm really, really sorry," Sadie said. Now that she'd finally gotten it out there, it wasn't as freeing as she'd hoped. She still felt the weight of what happened pressing down on her shoulders. "I didn't know that was going to happen."

"Yeah," Graciela said.

"You believe me, right? I told you the undersheriff came over to harass me, but I had no idea he was following us."

"Yeah, I know," she said.

"Do you think Beto is going to be okay?"

"No idea. They beat him pretty bad."

"Yeah," Sadie said and hated how weak it sounded. She didn't know what else to say, but was going to try something when Graciela spoke first.

"Hey, so I wasn't going to say anything," she said. She wasn't looking at her, just staring at the dashboard. "After your mom, well, I figured you didn't want to hear it. And then today, we were having fun, driving around town, playing detective. But then that thing with your dad, I don't know. Just seemed like there wasn't ever a good time."

Sadie's mouth went dry. "What? Tell me."

"When the summer's over," Graciela said, "Ashleigh's moving to Paso Verde. And I'm going with her."

"*What?*" Sadie said, her voice too loud. "You're leaving?"

"After tonight, can you blame me? I don't know why anyone would want to live in this shit town, with the King's Men and the sheriffs and everything else."

"Of course it's a shit town," Sadie said. "It's always been a shit town. But we've been stuck here together."

Graciela let out a long-held breath. "I don't want to be *stuck* somewhere anymore."

Sadie knew the right words to say: *I'm so happy for you. You're going to love it there. I can't wait to come visit you.* But they just wouldn't come out. They just curdled in her mouth, sour and hot. Instead, she said, "I can't believe you're leaving me."

"I knew you wouldn't understand," Graciela muttered.

Her mom was gone. Her real dad was gone and Brian couldn't even be bothered to pretend. Her whole world was upside down, and now her best friend—her *only* friend—was moving away, chasing some dream of a slightly better life in a slightly better town. No. No, she didn't *fucking* understand.

"Have a nice life, I guess," Sadie said as she shouldered the door open.

"Seriously? You're going to be like that?"

"Like what?" Sadie snapped. "You want me to pretend like we're going to still see each other? 'It's only forty miles, we'll meet for brunch on Sundays!' Bullshit. You're leaving. I get it. I mean, I really do. I hate everything about this place. Well, everything but you. So I guess everything now."

"You could leave too."

The thought hit her low and hard. She wasn't sure why. It wasn't like she'd never considered it. Every kid in Red Valley had. But now, with the idea just out there, it seemed completely ridiculous.

"I'm the Liar."

"So?" Graciela finally turned to face her. "What does that even mean? You've been running around all day, picking fights, stirring shit up. All so you can become the Liar. What if you just... don't? Will it really matter?"

Sadie's ears were ringing. The sound made it hard to think, hard to focus. She wanted to scream. Then the ringing shifted and sounded instead like the machines at the hospital, the ones keeping her mom alive, until they stopped.

Sadie's mom never really had many friends. There had been Brian once, but that hadn't lasted. There were people who needed something from her, people who owed her favors, and people who were afraid of her, but that was it. No family, no friends, just her ledger and her crappy little house and her ungrateful daughter. That's why they lived way out here, far from town. Sadie had always thought it was a lonely way to live, but maybe now she understood it a little better.

"That's all she left me," Sadie said. There was no fire in her words, no force. She had wanted to scream, but now she was about to cry. "Being the Liar's all I've got. Maybe it seems stupid, but it's all I've got."

"Chica..."

"I hope you and Ashleigh are happy together," she said. "See you around."

Sadie watched Graciela go. Overhead, the night was speckled with stars far more benign than those in Mary Bell's sky.

Graciela's revelation almost made her forget about what had happened at the crossroads. Almost. She'd had no choice. She'd had to tell the undersheriff the King's secret. Even now, alone in the almost cool darkness, she didn't regret it. But she did not believe for a moment that the King would understand. He'd sent his Man to make it clear he wanted the ledgers—and their secrets— protected, and she hadn't even lasted a day.

And worse, she knew the whispers had heard it. It wasn't every day that the new Liar gave away one of the oldest Lies in Red Valley. It would spread, and she had no idea what that meant, for her, for the King, or for Red Valley.

On her doorstep, she found a bag and a note. She took them inside. The note was hand-written, the paper taken from a pad with the St. Elizabeth's Hospital logo in the header. *Here are your mother's belongings,* the note said. *I'm sorry I missed you, and so sorry again for your loss.* It was signed by Nurse Abagail.

Sadie dumped the bag out onto the kitchen table. Her mom's clothes were there: a loose, faded purple shirt she often wore around the house, jeans that were frayed from use and not fashion, cheap sandals thin at the heel. A smaller bag contained her earrings and a necklace, simple yellow gold jewelry in need of a cleaning. Her pocket knife was there too. Sade touched it gently, the white handle shining in the kitchen light. She lifted it up for inspection.

It was heavier than it looked. Solid. She placed it against the front left pocket of the flat jeans, right in the worn spot where her mom had always kept it.

She also found her mom's car keys. In all the craziness of the last few days, she hadn't thought for a moment about her mom's car. She guessed it was still sitting in the hospital parking lot.

Of her mom's ledger, however, there was no sign. Maybe it was in her car? Sadie doubted she would have left it somewhere so insecure, but there weren't many other options. She remembered what Brian had said, that her mom had told a real bad Lie. Her mom had been the Liar for a long time without much trouble, but this felt different. Not because she was dead, but because she had asked Brian for help. Her mom never asked *anyone* for help. Whatever that Lie had been, it was lost until Sadie could find that ledger. And that might be precisely why it was missing.

Leaving the remnants of her mom's final day on the table, Sadie went to her bedroom and pulled a box out from under the bed. She used to keep little pieces of her childhood under here: the old toys, the waxy crayons and chewed pencils, the artwork that had never been hung on the fridge. It had all been tossed away over the years, a steady ritualistic purge, but not *everything*. After a few moments, she found what she was looking for: her diary.

She'd always aspired to be the kind of person who kept notes on their life in witty, breezy prose, but she'd only ever written one entry and that hadn't taken up even a single page. The cover was midnight blue with a bright orange spine, where she'd written in black marker: *Sadie's*.

She took the diary back to the kitchen and found a pen in the junk drawer. She sat at the table, pen in hand, and once again wondered at what her life had become in just a few days. Monotony had given her existence a misleading sense of permanence, but that rug had been pulled out from under her, true enough. And there was no use looking back.

Sadie tore out the first page of the diary and crumpled it up without reading it. Time for a new page. She wrote the date. And then the words.

In this book, I will write only truth.

She stared at what she'd written while the ink dried. *What were you thinking when you wrote these words in your ledger, Mom? Were you alone too? Who told you what to write? What Lies to tell, which to refuse; when to run, when to fight. And why didn't you tell me any of this? What did you hope to save me from? Or were you saving yourself?*

Sadie set down the pen and picked up her mom's pocket knife. She slid the blade out. It came easily and locked firmly in place. She tested the edge with her finger: still very sharp.

"Fuck," Sadie said when she cut the pad of her thumb on the blade. She hadn't expected it to hurt this much. She sucked on the wound before she reminded herself that blood was the point. Maybe the pain was the point, too. She let the blood well up, then swiped it across the page next to her words.

Something lit up inside of her. A fire, a light, a surge of power; something. She was glad she was sitting down, because her world began to swim. She thought she might be sick, then she thought she might be blind. Then the visions came.

A weathered man with a crippled leg.

A young woman with a burn scar across her face.

Blighted crops.

Empty pockets.

Vanity. Want. Need. A thousand Lies, ten thousand. Rushing over her, through her. After a moment of panic, her mind sharpened and she tried to focus, tried to see the secrets her mom had hidden away, but there were too many of them. A flood of truth, now known only to her.

And then a final image: something huge and black, waiting in darkness, with eyes like fire.

When the kitchen came back into view, sweat beaded on her upper lip though her skin was like ice. Her diary—her ledger—lay open in front of her. Her blood had seeped into the paper and was starting to dry. The clock over the sink ticked away. She absently ran her index finger over the cut on her thumb. It didn't hurt quite so much anymore.

And that was that. She was now the Liar of Red Valley. Would the townsfolk start driving up the dirt road to see her now? What secrets would they lay bare in the hope she could hide them away? What trust would they begrudgingly place in her, because they had no other choice? And would she help them?

Sadie had barely ever left Red Valley. She could remember a vacation or two when she was a kid—a trip to Yosemite, a few days at Disneyland—but that was it. She'd imagined a wider world out there, with its own beauty and magic and monsters, but that's all it was: imagination. This place was all she knew.

But she'd never felt at home here. She'd lived in this house her whole life—her childhood had seeped into every creaking floorboard, every carpet stain—but never felt like she belonged. Even weeds put down deep roots if they grow long enough. So why hadn't Sadie?

They'd need her now. They'd hate her for it, but they'd come.

If she survived long enough.

She closed her ledger. In the bathroom, she salvaged an old *My Little Pony* bandage for her thumb. In her bedroom, she found pajamas and an all-too-inviting bed. Her problems would still be waiting for her when she woke up, but now maybe she had something to fight back with, if she could figure out how to use it. She climbed into bed and listened to the house settle and the crickets outside her window until she fell asleep. It didn't take long.

She woke a few hours later, her heart thudding, terror sharp on her tongue. Though the dream was fading, the afterimage was still bright and vivid, like staring too long into the sun: burning red eyes towering over her in the darkness.

"Oh, fuck it," she said and swung out of bed.

She found the card the King's Man had given her. She hesitated a moment, then dialed the number. A click. Silence.

"I want to meet with the King," Sadie said into the phone.

Static on the line. Then a voice. "He will see you tomorrow." Then the line went dead.

CHAPTER THIRTEEN

AFTER THAT, SADIE slept just fine.

She woke late morning. Her body ached with the blissful weight of long, deep sleep. Everything looked as she remembered it from countless other mornings. Light filtering in through the dusty aluminum blinds on a room mostly devoid of decoration.

Nothing had changed, and everything had.

She showered, dressed, ate, and waited. They'd been light on the details on the phone, but she knew they'd come for her. Everyone in town knew where the King lived, but you didn't just show up at his front door and ring the bell. Sometimes kids tried. Sometimes they even came back.

Sure enough, just as the day was getting unbearably hot and just as Sadie was starting to get impatient, a sleek black car with a tan roof came rumbling down the driveway. Not a Cadillac, this time; a 1949 Buick Roadmaster with a shiny grille that made the car look angry. The King's

Man who stepped out was not the same one from the hospital; this one was older, bald, and jowly. He wore a double-breasted navy suit with gold buttons and a yellow necktie. But he had the same mirrored sunglasses and the same dead facial expression.

Sadie met him on the porch. She had on an old backpack with the ledgers—including her own—inside. Her mom's pocket knife was tucked into her jeans.

"You must be my ride," she said as the King's Man approached.

He cocked his head to the side. The sun glinted off his polished scalp. "The King wishes for you to come to his home."

Don't talk to the mirroreyes, went the conventional wisdom in Red Valley. *Don't get in their way. And don't get in their car*. But Sadie had left wisdom—conventional or otherwise—behind a few days ago. The King was going to find out she had revealed his secret sooner or later, and when he did, she had no doubt she'd find a King's Man waiting for her. Better to just rip the *My Little Pony* Band-Aid right off.

"Good," Sadie said. "I was worried today might be a normal day."

The car's interior was pristine, like she was the first person to ever sit inside. The seats and steering wheel were stitched in red leather. The seatbelt clunked into place with real heft. There was nothing cheap or plastic in this car. It smelled like money, and like dust. The King's Man slid mechanically into the driver's seat. The car started, though Sadie didn't see him turn a key. His hands gripped the wheel firmly at 10 and 2. Sadie briefly considered small talk, then remembered her previous experience with these... men, and thought better of it.

To get to the King's home, they had to drive through the heart of Red Valley. People were out on the streets, riding bikes or skateboards or pushing strollers. They all stopped as the King's Man drove by. Stopped, and stared. Sadie stared back, wondering at the expressions on their faces. What emotions were betrayed were subtle: a quick downcast glance, a tightening grip on the wrist of a child. A hardness around the mouth. There was no love in Red Valley for the driver of this car, and no love for its passenger either.

They kept driving. Cars pulled over, as if they were an ambulance with blazing lights and sirens. Pedestrians didn't even approach the crosswalk until they had gone. Stop signs did not slow them down. Red lights meant nothing. The King's Man drove slowly, deliberately, the speed limit the only traffic law he didn't ignore. He drove safely, all things considered, just not legally.

As they left the town behind, the King's Man turned off on an unmarked one-lane road that slowly rose into the foothills. Twisted oak trees overgrew the road on both sides, crowning it like a tunnel. Leaves filled the runoff on both sides. Through the tortured branches, Sadie caught a glimpse of their destination.

There was a high hill just outside of town, and on top of that hill, a white house that overlooked everything: the valley, the highway, the town. The hill itself was surrounded by an iron fence topped with spikes. The lands beyond were wild with dead and dying weeds. There was no lawn, no gardens, no real sign of life at all. The car stopped at the gate and the King's Man got out to swing it open, and did so again to close it behind them. Sadie jumped a little when it clanged shut, the sound rattling around in her head.

The driveway snaked up the hill for half a mile or more, climbing higher with every foot. Sadie looked back the way they had come, but saw only yellow grasses and gray-brown trees. She got her first real close look at the house as the car neared. It was bigger than it appeared from a distance, built in a plantation style, with tall white columns flanking the red double doors. A heavy wrought iron lamp hung suspended by chains over the porch. The porch itself, which wrapped around the front of the building and disappeared into the back, was bigger than Sadie's whole house. It reminded Sadie of the Haunted Mansion ride at Disneyland: stately and formal and sinister.

The car pulled into a detached garage. There must have been a dozen other cars parked inside, all covered up with canvas tarps. Sadie wondered how many people in Red Valley could even park one car in their garage, let alone a fleet.

The King's Man led her out of the garage and up to the main house. As she got closer, she was surprised to see cracking paint and cobwebs marring the façade. The steps up to the porch sagged, the wood old and failing. One of the windows on the bottom floor was broken.

The front doors were unlocked; they walked inside. The floors were made of wood that groaned with every step. She immediately thought of the Gray House, but while its interior had felt cramped, this was massive.

Dual staircases with ornate railings wound up on either side to a second story. A broad hallway between them disappeared into the depths of the house. Empty rooms waited on either side of the front doors. Every room Sadie could see, in fact, was empty. There were no rugs or furniture, no paintings or photos on the walls. She felt like her breaths were echoing back at her. There was nothing here, just a thin coating of dust everywhere except down the middle of the main walkway, where a myriad of feet had cleared a path.

The King's Man matched those footprints without a word, and so Sadie followed. The emptiness of this house high on the hill pressed down on her as she went deeper. She saw rooms with closed doors and silently prayed they stayed closed. Discolored wallpaper hung peeling away from the wall. They passed a kitchen that looked as though no meals had ever been cooked there. The house—grand beyond anything in her experience—was a husk.

They stopped in front of a staircase leading down into what appeared to be a basement.

"The King doesn't greet his guests upstairs?" she asked, wary of the dark stairs.

"The King waits below," said the King's Man.

"Is he trying to be creepy, or is that just a fun side-effect?" When she glanced up at the King's Man's blank expression, she quickly retracted the question. "Of course it's creepy, sorry. That's your thing. Lead the way."

The basement too was empty, though the walls here were lined not with plaster and drywall, but stone. It was cooler underground and she was grateful. The basement seemed to span the entire house. At the darkest end, a wide doorway had been carved into the stones.

"Is that his throne room or whatever?" Sadie asked.

"The King waits below," was the only reply.

Further in, she noticed a string of small alcoves set back into the wall at regular intervals. The first were empty, with no lights or decoration or any other discernable purpose.

"What are these—?" Her question was stolen away when she passed the next one. A man stood in the alcove, hands at his sides, mirrored eyes staring straight ahead. He was young, maybe twenty-five, with shoulder-length black hair and thick sideburns. She gave out a quick gasp when she saw him, but the man did not react. In fact, he didn't even appear to be breathing.

Her guide did not wait for her. She moved away from the alcove and kept walking. The next was empty, but she recognized the man in the one after that: the King's Man who met her at the hospital and had come with the shovel to her home. She carefully stepped closer to him and waved a hand in his face. Nothing.

"And here I was worried about the creepy staircase," Sadie muttered.

There were more dormant King's Men as she kept going: tall, short, young, old. Their clothing was a mix of styles and value, but nothing Sadie had ever seen someone else wear outside of old pictures. All had the same sunglasses and empty faces.

Her guide had stopped at the doorway. She caught up to him. The air pouring from the door wasn't just cooler, it was frigid. She had a million questions, but guessed the King's Man wouldn't be offering any answers on this tour.

"The way below is long," the King's Man said. "Take care."

He stepped through into the dark and she followed. A moment later she heard a click and soft white LED lights came on. This chamber was smaller and round. In the center of the floor was the start of another set of stairs, spiraling down into an abyss so deep and black that Sadie saw no bottom.

The King's Man stood at the top of the stairs, waiting. It seemed that she was meant to go the rest of the way alone.

"The King waits below," she said under her breath as she started down.

The stairs were made of stone, and were narrow and smooth. Every step she took felt like her foot could go flying out from under her. There was no railing, just the rock face on one side and the abyss on the other.

Just as the lights from the upper room were too far away to illuminate the path down, more LEDs began to glow, fixed into the rock. Sadie was momentarily grateful, before discarding that wholesale. If the King wanted to make it easy to get down to see him, he should have installed an elevator. But she doubted ease was anywhere on the King's mind.

The next set of lights that came on as she passed were older: flickering yellow bulbs that cast a golden glow on the way below. Deeper in, more lights snapped to life. These appeared, impossibly, to be gaslamps. She could hear a soft hiss and the tick of heating glass as the flames danced. They threw jagged shadows out over the abyss that made Sadie want to hug the wall even closer.

Mary Bell had said that she'd been to see the King. Had she walked down these very steps? And what about Sadie's mom? Had she been granted an audience like this?

When the gaslight faded, pitch torches roared to life, but even their red light showed no end to the winding stair. *How long have I been descending?* The hill leading up to the King's house had been tall, but not this tall. How deep into the earth was she? She looked up and saw only darkness. It was only for a moment, but was dizzying; before she could catch herself, her foot slipped on the next step and she tumbled forward.

Her hands slapped the dark rock and found only pain, no purchase. She rolled, scrambling, slipping, and the abyss opened up in front of her, a hungry expanse of nothing. Her fingers dug into whatever she could find until she finally jerked to a halt.

Her body dangled over the edge, her feet kicking only shadows. The torches had gone out and she couldn't tell which way was up, or even see what she was holding onto. She could taste blood in her mouth.

She exhaled a long-clenched breath. "It's okay," she said, panting into the black. "You just have to—"

Then her grip failed and she fell.

CHAPTER FOURTEEN

SADIE'S SCREAMS FLEW out into the darkness ahead of her, and she followed closely behind. Her arms and legs thrashed in the void, finding nothing. Terror clamped down hard on her heart and images of Mary Bell walking her lonely road flashed in her mind.

But then her fall inexplicably began to slow. Something held her up in the emptiness, and it set her down on her feet, at the bottom of the abyss at last.

I'm... not dead? Her breathing rasped in her ears. *Holy shit.*

For a moment, Sadie's entire world was impenetrable darkness. Somewhere far off there was the drip, drip, drip of water. Then she saw a soft green glow ahead of her. The walls were far away now, opening up to a massive chamber that she could not see the end of. She moved toward the closest wall—careful on unsteady legs—and found the end of the winding stair, and the source of the light: the cavern rock was covered in a glowing green algae. She brushed it with her fingertips and they came away flecked with bioluminescent light.

"**Few enter this place,**" boomed a voice as loud as thunder. Sadie had to clamp her hands over her ears to fend off the sudden, shattering noise. "**And even fewer enter in such dramatic fashion.**"

She turned away from the glowing walls, toward the vast dark that filled the cavern. There was something familiar about this; she could feel it in her bones. Yes—in her vision, after signing her ledger. And in her nightmares last night.

But she'd asked for this. Her great-great-great-grandmother had stood here, and so could she. "You're the King of Red Valley," she called out into the dark.

A deep rumble spread throughout the chamber like an earthquake. A laugh, perhaps. "**I am King of many things,**" the thunderous voice replied. "**I am King of the air and sky, of the rock and stone. I am King of ages that have been forgotten and those that will never be seen. I am King of fire and shadow.**" Two great red eyes opened above her. The eyes were as tall as she was, and contained endless depths of power, malice, and flame. "**And yes, little Liar, I am King of Red Valley.**"

Something moved in the dark. What she thought had been the far wall of the cavern shifted just enough to tell her she'd been wrong. That it was alive. There was no discernable shape, no limb or face. Only the eyes. And the darkness.

"**Do I frighten you, little Liar?**"

Such a stupid question. Sadie had never been more terrified in all her life. Her imagination was fevered with thoughts of claws or fangs or even tentacles, but those would be preferable to the unknowable shadows that filled this deep well. But what really made her want to scream was his sheer impossible size. Whatever he was, whatever true horror was hidden just beyond the reach of her eyes, it was on a scale that made her feel—not like a child, but like a raindrop falling into the ocean.

With something as massive as the King, it seemed less a matter of if he could kill you, than if he'd even notice he'd done it.

But she wasn't going to tell him that.

"Yes, I am afraid," Sadie said, twisting a finger in her ear. "Afraid that I'm going to be deaf before this conversation is half over."

The cavern trembled with the King's laughter. Somewhere out of sight, rocks probably bigger than her fell and shattered on the stone.

"Is this preferable?" the King asked in a new voice, something more human.

"Yes, thank you," Sadie said. "And thanks for catching me when I... fell."

"Of course," said the King. "I did warn you to take care before you started down."

Sadie's brow crinkled. "That was you? You speak through the King's Men?"

"They are my eyes, ears, and voice. They go where I cannot."

"What are they, exactly?"

"What do they look like?"

"They look human," Sadie said.

"And so they are," the King said. "Or nearly so. They

served me in their lives, and they serve me still. My blood runs in their veins."

Sadie wondered if the King believed such a transformation to be a punishment or a reward. The distinction probably did not matter, nor the victim's willingness. "You know the people in town hate the King's Men. Everybody's afraid of them."

"As they should be," said the King. "I protect my subjects. I honor them with my forbearance and mercy and demand little in return. But one thing I do require is fear. It is instructive. It is... a reminder. Man is always seeking to control his world. Without proper fear, he forgets his proper place in the true order."

Like Undersheriff Hassler, Sadie thought. He had a very different idea about the true order.

"I mourn the loss of your mother," said the King. "She was a bright star in a dim night. This world was better for her presence."

"Thank you."

"But the world turns," said the King. "Old fades, replaced by new. I sense the power in you. Raw, untamed, new, but there. You will take up your family's heritage? You will safekeep the secrets of Red Valley, little Liar?"

Sadie swallowed. "Actually," she said, "that's why I asked to see you. I... failed."

The fiery red eyes regarded her without blinking. "Yes," said the King. "I know."

"You... you do?"

The darkness moved again, grinding like an avalanche. Heat radiated all around her, making Sadie's skin sweat. Whatever the King was, it felt like he had come closer.

"The ambitions of foolish men in Red Valley are not unknown to me."

"So you know that the undersheriff thinks he can stop you?"

The King snorted. "Greater beings than he have tried and failed. He is of no consequence. Or he was, at least, until he forced my long-kept secret to be revealed."

"So it's true," Sadie said. "That you're dying?"

"Let me tell you a story, little Liar," said the King. "In a time before the reach of mankind's memory, I walked this world like a god. The sun burned far hotter then, and the nights were bitter cold. Such a world was hardly fit for life. So I told the sun to calm its fires and demanded that the night draw back its cold. They resisted my command at first, as many have. But they relented, in the end, as all things do.

"But I was not alone in the world. There were not many, but there were others, and they did not want the world to be full of life. They wanted it for themselves. They thought I was a fool, and they thought me weak. They were wrong, and I showed them that. Our battles broke the world, shattered continents, created seas, ripped canyons and toppled mountains. But I showed them their folly and the world was better off without them."

Pride had crept into the King's booming voice. Sadie wondered how much of his story was true, but she did not doubt he had defeated many of his enemies. The thought of other creatures like him in the world was hard to hold onto. She'd always known about the strange things who lingered on the far side of the River, but they were nothing like this.

"There was one," said the King, "who proved a challenge to me. I will not speak its name. It ought never be spoken by gods or men. Its power is in annihilation and the void. Life is abhorrent to it, and withers at its touch. And so we fought. For an age, we fought. Until at last I struck the final blow.

"But," said the King, "I did not escape this battle unscathed. Before its defeat, my unspeakable enemy delivered to me a great wound. The pain of it was like the sundering of the world. Though I was victorious, I was weakened by the ordeal. I required rest. Therefore I searched the world over, and at last came to this place. Beneath the earth, I slumbered long to recover my strength. In time, humans settled the land above me.

"I came to love this place and its people. They became my people. I lent them my strength and my protection. I gave them power."

Like the Liar's gift. Like Beto's brujo magic.

"But your wound hasn't healed?" Sadie asked.

The King sighed; the sound was like a hurricane. "No. No matter how long I slumbered, the wound does not heal. I no longer believe it can. But I still have enemies in this world, some small and some great. If they knew I was still so weak, they would strike—not just at me, but also my people. If they came to Red Valley, the town would not survive."

Sadie considered this. "So is that why you created the Liar? To hide away your wound?"

"You are clever, little Liar," said the King. "I have great power. I can shape and I can mold. And I can destroy. But I cannot change. I am as I have always been. But humans, you are forever changing, forever evolving. Over the ages, I learned that my power could be used to guide that evolution. So I found a suitable servant and gave her the power I needed to protect us all."

"Mary Bell."

"Yes," said the King with a shuddering laugh. "Whom you recently met, if I am not mistaken."

"What do you know of the road Mary walks now?"

"Nothing," said the King. "The dark roads are closed to me, their purpose and path unknowable. If I could have saved her from death, I would have, but I have no dominion over life and death. I cannot grant immortality. And perhaps this is for the best. It is exactly that frailty that allows you humans to change, to grow."

Sadie was not interested in hearing from an immortal being about the usefulness of human mortality, not when she'd watched her mother die a few days before. But she did not challenge him; something like him would never understand such a loss.

"So Mary's Lie kept your enemies from learning that you are still wounded," Sadie said. "So they stay away, because they are still afraid of you."

"Precisely," said the King.

Now it was Sadie's turn to sigh. "But then I spoke your secret."

"Yes," said the King. The great red eyes turned, looking off at something Sadie couldn't see. "And now they are coming. I can feel it. Old, terrible things. The hunter in the darkness. Those who wait behind the flames. And my greatest foe, the unspeakable one."

"I thought you defeated it."

"Defeated, yes," said the King. "Destroyed, no. Some evils cannot be destroyed."

Sadie dropped her eyes. She'd been the Liar for less than a day but had already revealed a nearly two hundred-year-old secret and brought certain destruction to her home town. But should she have just let Beto be beaten and thrown back into prison? That couldn't be the right answer either. There had to be another way.

"But can't you fight them?" Sadie asked. "I know you're hurt, but it's your fault they're coming here at all."

"My fault? This is how you speak to your King?"

Sadie hadn't meant to offend, but bristled at his tone. "We didn't invite a bunch of monsters to our town. They're coming for you."

The King growled and Sadie felt it in her gut. "You forget your place."

"My *place?*" Sadie's jaw tightened. "My place is trying to figure out how to live with a worthless job in a dead-end town. My place is realizing I'll be living paycheck to paycheck for the rest of my life. My place is figuring out how to pay for burial expenses for my mom, who didn't even tell me she was dying."

The towering black bulk of the King shifted closer, close enough that the air around her stirred with his warm breath. It smelled of wet soil and of iron. Of blood. "You know nothing of the horrors I have spared you and your people."

"Well I don't feel particularly *spared* right now, your majesty," Sadie snapped. Part of her brain knew how stupid it was to pick a fight with a being who could crush her without breaking a sweat. But most of her brain was just sick of his shit. "You didn't save my mom from cancer.

I went outside the King's Peace for five minutes and weird things with fake faces threaten me because they can smell you on me. And the undersheriff—"

"**Silence!**" His voice rose, filling the cavern, filling Sadie's skull. From somewhere in the cavern came a leathery scrape across the stone and Sadie imagined a massive fist coming to crush her where she stood. "**I will not be insulted in my home, not by you or any other. This world is a dark, inhospitable place and you are weak. If I left you on your own, you would be prey. You would be carrion. You would be *nothing*.**"

His eyes raged with molten fury. The heat of it washed over her and prickled her skin. But Sadie had her own anger and she wasn't ready to calm down and grovel at the King's feet—if he even had feet. She was ashamed at giving away the King's secret, but she'd done what she had to. No one told her how to be the Liar. If the King was so powerful, why had he trusted his weak subjects to keep his secrets safe? Because he had to.

"I didn't give you your wound," Sadie said. "I didn't make enemies with the Hunter in the Dark and all those others. I didn't ask to be a soldier in your war, and neither did Mary. But you recruited us anyway, because you needed us."

They stared at each other across the distance between then, the Liar and the King, the speck and the storm. Sadie felt the weight of those awful eyes bearing down on her and wanted to look away. Hell, she wanted to *run* away. But her problems weren't going to solve themselves, and in the end, she really had nowhere to run. So she stood. And she stared back.

"It has been too long since I had an audience like this. I had forgotten the stubbornness of your family," said the King. "When mortal creatures come before me, I am accustomed to their fear and hatred. But defiance, that is a rare trait. The first Liar was similarly defiant. It was partly why she was chosen."

Internally, Sadie let out a huge sigh. *Okay,* she thought. *Guess I'm not going to die quite yet.*

"I meant no offense," Sadie said. "But I stand by what I said."

"As you should," said the King. "I have rested here for a long time. I am fond of this place. I do not wish to see it come to harm. And it was brave of you to come here and tell me what you had done, on your own. That is admirable. So to answer your impertinent question: yes, I will fight, if it comes to that. And I might call on you, as I did your forebear, for aid."

Sadie didn't know what to make of this creature lurking under the hill. Other than his size and power, was he any different from the things inside of Tips Bar? Why should she trust him? Why should she want to help him? But, strangely enough, she did.

"Alright," she said. "I'll help, if I can. But I still have a lot to figure out with this whole Liar thing."

"See that you do," said the King. "You have enemies of your own."

Don't I know it, Sadie thought. Sensing their time coming to an end, Sadie braved one last question. "My mom," she said. "Did you know her?"

The King paused a moment. The cavern was perfectly still as he considered his answer. "We met," he said. "She came before me, as you have done. She stood near where you stand now. I was fond of her as well. She proved an able servant."

What did you think of him, Mom? Were you scared? Did you trust him?

"Thank you," Sadie said.

"Take better care on your ascent. The way above remains treacherous."

CHAPTER FIFTEEN

CLIMBING OUT OF the King's well sucked. The path just kept winding and winding. Sadie did her best to keep her feet under her and away from the edge. She walked for what must have been hours, though in the dark it was hard to know for certain. When she finally stepped back into the basement, her legs felt like hardening concrete and sweat was running down her back. The King's Man was waiting for her, as if he hadn't moved a muscle since. He probably hadn't.

"The King thanks you for your time," the King's Man said. "And wishes you a safe journey home."

She'd always found the King's Men strange: their emotionless faces, their weird clothes, their delayed way of talking. The strangeness had gone way up when she'd seen the others waiting in the basement, unmoving. But after talking to the King himself and knowing that he spoke through these peculiar puppets—that his blood flowed inside them—Sadie was about ready to slap this bald man in a suit in his pale face and run screaming.

"Actually," Sadie said as she fought to keep hold of herself, "I was hoping you could give me a ride. I need to pick up a car."

As the King's Man drove away, Sadie twisted in her seat to stare back up at the King's house. People in town were always guessing at what it was like inside, what the King was like. Now she knew, and wished she didn't. She'd imagined him being much like her, like a human, living alone in his big white house on a hill. A sad, noble, mysterious benefactor. Maybe that was the whole point of the empty manor: the illusion of normalcy. Would the citizens of Red Valley feel differently about their benevolent protector if they knew the truth? Would they storm the hill with pitchforks and torches? Who was she kidding: they wouldn't care. People had to find a way get food on the table; they didn't have time to worry about the dark things lurking on the edge of town, as long as they stayed there.

Once the trees hid the manor from view, Sadie spared a thought for the King's warnings about his enemies coming to Red Valley. He didn't seem afraid, though how would she know? And he said he'd fight, but he'd been wounded fighting these things before, and he'd been stronger then. He'd claimed that their previous battles had destroyed everything around them, which made Sadie wonder how Red Valley would fare. The King said that he cared about the people in the town, but she doubted that would be enough to spare them from becoming collateral damage.

They turned off the side road and started back toward town. What would Graciela think when she told her that she'd been to see the King? Or when she tried to describe him?

But even as she thought this, she remembered Beto's battered body and Graciela's averted eyes when she dropped her off. She probably needed to give her friend some time, and hope that would be enough. They'd been friends since grade school, and Sadie couldn't imagine—

The front tires in the heavy car exploded in a loud bang. The car began to swerve all over the road as the King's Man tried to control it, steel rims gouging the asphalt. Sadie sloshed around in the backseat, the loose seatbelt barely holding her in place. The car turned sideways and finally came to a stop blocking both lanes of traffic.

Sadie spilled out of the car just as the sheriff's deputies arrived. There were three patrol cars waiting for them. Sadie glanced back and saw the spike strip they had laid out on the road.

Oh, you stupid, stupid men.

"Get your hands in the air and get out of the way," one of the deputies demanded. His gun was pointed right at Sadie. She raised her hands, but did not move.

"You don't want to do this," Sadie said, her voice fluttering with adrenaline.

"Stand aside!"

"Listen to me. One of your deputies just went to the hospital," Sadie said in a rush. "You all heard about it, you must have. He went up against one of the King's Men, and got his hand bitten off." She locked eyes with the closest deputy, a young man with a bead of sweat on his nose and a leveled shotgun. "I was there. I saw it. I heard him scream. He thought he could beat the King's Man, but he never had a chance."

"Get out of the way or be treated like the enemy," one of them said. He was an older man with a black mustache and jowls that hung over the collar of his uniform.

"Enemy?" Sadie said. "This isn't a war."

"Yes, it is. And you're about to be on the losing side, little girl."

There was a groan of metal as the driver's door opened. All five deputies trained their pistols and shotguns on the King's Man. Sadie's gut filled with sour dread. This was not going to end well. She inched off the road into the dirt and knelt down, her hands on her head. The deputies barely even looked at her.

"Put your hands where we can see them and step away from the car, sir."

The King's Man did not move.

They're all about to die, Sadie thought.

The King's Man did not raise his hands. They hung limp at his sides, as usual, as he walked around the car and stood in front of the firing squad. His mirrored eyes surveyed each of the deputies in a slow arc.

"The King finds this unexpected interruption," the King's Man said, "displeasing."

"You are under arrest," the deputy with the black mustache said.

"On what charge, Deputy Lester Jones?" said the King's Man.

"Put your hands up!"

The King's Man cocked his head. "No."

"Put your hands up," Deputy Jones said, "or we'll be forced to open fire."

Oh, hell. They weren't here to arrest the King's Man; they'd come to kill him. They were even stupider than she thought.

"The King wishes—"

But they didn't let him finish. "Time's up."

The King's Man started to move, but was too late. The deputies fired as one and the world suddenly roared with noise. The bullets and shot tore into the King's Man. He staggered back against the car, and the windows shattered under the barrage. Dark blood—the King's blood—burst out on his blue suit and spattered his pale skin. He stayed on his feet longer than any human could, his face registering nothing as his body was cut apart.

The cacophony stopped when their guns ran empty. The King's Man slumped to the road and did not move. The deputies didn't move either, just stared at the bloodied man and ruined car over their smoking guns.

"He was unarmed," Sadie heard herself say. Her voice was muffled in her ringing ears. "He did nothing wrong. And you shot him!"

The deputies belatedly remembered Sadie was there. "Shut up," the older one said. "He was resisting arrest."

"So you murdered him?"

"You said it yourself. Those things are dangerous to everyone in Red Valley."

"No, just to morons who pick fights with them."

The deputies were looking uneasy and a bit surprised. They were in uncharted territory now. And there was a witness.

"You're under arrest," the deputy said as he started toward Sadie. He tucked his pistol away and retrieved handcuffs instead. "Things have changed around here. If you're working with the King, then you've got no place in this town."

"The King's been here longer than any of us," Sadie said. "There wouldn't be a town without him."

"He's got to follow our laws, like everybody else," the deputy said. He didn't have the ironclad confidence in his voice that she'd heard from Undersheriff Hassler. He sounded like he was repeating something he'd been told but wasn't sure if he believed. "Now get up."

But before Sadie could stand, the King's Man spoke. No, that wasn't right. The King's Man's mouth was open, but his lips didn't move. This voice came from the King's Man, but it was a different voice altogether, one that boomed across the road and echoed off the nearby hills, one that Sadie recognized.

"**You miserable ingrates,**" said the King of Red Valley. His words were like a cataclysm. "**I have held back the outer darkness. I have given you life and bounty. I have stayed my own wrath when you make a mockery of my power. And this is how my endless patience is welcomed. With violence.**"

"What is this?" the young deputy asked Jones. "What do we do, sir?" But he didn't have any answers; none of them did. They just stared around at the empty hills as the terrible voice surrounded them and spoke of doom.

Sadie felt the ground under her start to shake.

"**You assault my anointed with your petty weapons of war. You confuse my infirmity for your strength. You are** nothing. **You are not worthy of my violence. But blood demands blood.**"

The road split open. Deputy Jones tried to jump out of the way of the widening expanse, but it swallowed him like a hungry mouth and he vanished beneath the earth. His screams lasted only a moment before they went silent. The other deputies scrambled back to their patrol cars as more cracks appeared.

"**I will not be mocked.**"

One of the patrol cars tipped front-first into a new chasm. Metal bent and snapped; glass shattered. The other cars backed away at frantic speeds, even crashing into each other. But they did not seem to notice, and they did not slow until they disappeared around a turn in the road, their sirens fading to nothing.

The King's voice fell silent and the road began to knit itself back together. After a few moments of unnatural twisting and grinding, it almost looked as if nothing had happened. There was no sign of Deputy Jones or the swallowed patrol car.

Sadie just knelt there, hands still on her head. She knew the King was powerful, even before meeting him in person, but she hadn't expected this. The very earth of Red Valley responded to his commands. What the hell did Undersheriff Hassler expect to do against that? The King's Man they'd shot still hadn't moved. His dark blood spread across the road. Some of it had been smeared on the lenses of his mirrored sunglasses.

War, the deputy had called it.

She heard a car coming down from the manor before she saw it. It was the Cadillac she'd seen before. But he was not alone. Two more old cars followed, one painted green, the other yellow. Unreadable faces stared out from the windshields of each.

The first car crept around the ruined one and stopped near where Sadie knelt. The King's Man stepped out and opened a door for her.

"The King requests that you complete your journey in alternate transport," he said.

Sadie looked at the fallen King's Man. "What's going to happen to him?"

"The King wishes you to remain focused on the tasks before you," the King's Man said. "He apologizes for the unfortunate delay."

"Right," Sadie said as she got to her feet.

The King's Man paused, head turned. Then he said, "The King promises that the source of these disturbances will be addressed. And soon."

Sadie didn't know if that should make her feel relieved or terrified. Or both.

CHAPTER SIXTEEN

THE SECOND KING'S Man dropped Sadie off at the hospital. Thankfully, they saw no more sheriff's deputies on the way. The parking lot was mostly empty, and Sadie found her mom's red Nissan without much trouble. She allowed herself to forget what she'd seen beneath the King's house and on the road afterward and just focus on the freedom a car would provide.

But any excitement at the thought faded as she approached the driver's side door and looked inside. Her mom's car was a mess, as always: food wrappers littered the floorboards, gum wrappers filled the ashtray, a paper coffee cup with a ring of lipstick around the mouth sat cold in the cup holder. And the weight of her mom's absence clamped down on Sadie's chest like a vise.

She sat on the curb next to the car. Tears spilled out and dripped onto the concrete. She tried to catch her breath, but the sobs stole it away. Her mom was gone and was never coming back. She was gone and Sadie was left, like an old paper coffee cup, half empty and alone.

You should have told me, Mom. About everything. I would have listened. But you got too good at keeping secrets. Too good at believing the Lies, just like Mary said. Too good at keeping people away.

Or maybe Sadie would just have to learn to do the same. Couldn't get hurt that way. Couldn't get left behind.

When the tears stopped and Sadie could breathe again, she fished the car keys out of her backpack and unlocked the car. The inside was blistering hot, but Sadie welcomed the heat as she thumbed away the last of the tears from her cheeks.

Unsurprisingly, there was no sign of her mom's ledger anywhere. It couldn't be that easy.

"Alright, you piece of junk," Sadie said as she tried the key in the ignition. "I need something to go right for once." The engine groaned, shuddered, and gave up. Sadie swore and wished her mom had done more Lies for Honest Bob. "C'mon…" she said through gritted teeth, but the engine still wouldn't turn over.

Sadie rested her forehead on the steering wheel. She could feel the tears threatening to return. *Mom, you died and left me with just secrets and crap. All I need right now is for your stupid car to start. Is that too much to ask?*

She turned the key one last time and pumped the gas. The car coughed and belched black smoke, but then the engine turned and the car came to life. Sadie exhaled and allowed her shoulder muscles to unclench. The A/C kicked in and blew frigid air into her face. She closed her eyes and just let the warmth of the car seat and the coolness of the air conditioner seep into her body.

Alright, she thought after a wonderfully long self-indulgent moment, *you have a car, twenty bucks in your wallet, and a quarter tank of gas. What are you going to do with it?* After talking with Mary Bell, she knew the basic rules of being the Liar, but what she needed was experience. She needed people to know she was a threat.

And she had an idea.

She drove to the only drug store in town and bought a jumbo pack of Band-Aids, some rubbing alcohol, and a bag of cotton balls. The cashier gave her a look that she pointedly ignored. Then she drove back to the Treehouse Diner. Denise met her at the door, grease-stains on her apron and a ballpoint pen behind her ear.

"How you doing, hon?" she asked when Sadie came inside. "You ready for me to put you back on the schedule?"

Sadie smiled weakly. "Not yet. I still need a little time to process… everything. But I think I can help out another way." When she explained her idea, Denise raised a penciled eyebrow, but she didn't object. It was an unconventional way to drum up business, but business was business.

There were probably a dozen people in the restaurant enjoying their late lunch. A few older couples, some kids near the back who'd mostly just ordered water, a family with towheaded toddlers who were throwing food on the black-and-white tile floor. Sadie grabbed a glass from the counter and got up on one of the barstools and clanged on the glass with a butter knife.

"Excuse me, can I have everyone's attention, please?" And then she had every eye in the room on her. None of them looked particularly pleased. "Thanks. I promise I won't take much of your time. Some of you probably know who I am—or, at least, who my mother was. Well, she died. And now I'm the Liar of Red Valley, I guess."

Wrinkled scowls hardened on some of the older couples. The toddlers' mother mostly ignored her while she tried to keep one kid from shoving a French fry in the other one's nose. Dishes getting washed clinked in the kitchen.

"I need some practice," Sadie went on before her resolve could completely wilt. "So today we're having a one-time special offer. Everyone pays the Liar's Price, but the Lie itself is..." She paused a second, remembering how light her wallet was, and the cost of gas. "The Lie is ten dollars only." Denise made a clucking sound with her tongue and Sadie added, "Right. That's ten dollars only *with* a purchase from this fine eating establishment."

Murmurs began. Some faces still glared at her, but others had softened and become thoughtful. How many people in Red Valley had been interested in coming to see the Liar, but couldn't afford what her mom charged? How many people had Lies worth the price?

"Okay," Sadie said, suddenly feeling strange standing on a barstool. "I'm setting up shop in the booth back there. Tell your friends." She got down, smiled awkwardly at Denise, then took her ledger and supplies and retreated to the back booth. And waited. Denise brought her a glass of ice water. She took a sip, and then waited. A puddle of condensation gathered around the base. And still she waited. Nearby, the ancient oak tree creaked slightly. Whatever Lies people in town had, maybe they didn't want them told in front of God and everybody by a window at the Treehouse. Maybe that's why her mom had moved them so far out of town.

A woman came and slid into the booth across from her. Sadie hadn't noticed her when she'd been giving her announcement. She was in her early fifties, with graying black hair and a forced smile. Foundation caked around her eyes and mouth and some of her lipstick had rubbed off on her teeth. Gaudy gold earrings dangled from each ear.

"So," the woman said. "How does this work, exactly?"

"I'm figuring that out myself," Sadie replied. She picked up her pen and opened her ledger to the first page. "I think you tell me what you'd like to have change, and then I write it down, and then we go from there."

The woman's smile slipped a little. "Just like that?"

Sadie nodded. "Just like that."

"And only ten dollars?"

"Special price. Today only."

"Right," she said. She was clutching the strap to her purse with two tight fists. Veins stood out on the backs of her hands. "I met your mother once. Never got the nerve to ask her how much it would cost. I never have had much money, and my husband would never agree to..." She trailed off and looked out the window. There was a bus stop near the corner. A few cars drove lazily past. A kid rattled by on an old skateboard.

"Maybe now's not the best—" Sadie began.

"No," the woman said, blinking away unacknowledgeable tears. "Special price, right? Today only." She sighed and pressed her lips together. "I've not been handling it. My therapist tells me I'm doing *great* and my husband just won't talk about it, but I'm not doing great. I'm not going to ever do great. I just... but then you hopped up there and said you're the Liar now, and I've got ten dollars right here." She dove into her purse and came up with two fives. "My husband never has to know."

Sadie's mouth was dry. She'd wanted to be the Liar so she'd be protected, so maybe she could make a better life for herself. She'd thought that the magic would be the hard part. Maybe she was wrong.

"What would you like me to write?" Sadie asked softly.

"If I want to change something," the woman said, "will it just change for me? Or everybody?"

"I think that depends on what I write," Sadie said. "If you wanted to change something for everybody, that Lie would be much more costly. If you wanted to change it for yourself, I think the Liar's Price would be lower."

"Good," the woman said. "That's good. I don't need it changed for everybody. Everyone else seems to be doing just fine. I'm the only one who can't move on."

"Alright," Sadie said. She was in no hurry, since she'd just been waiting before the woman came to take her up on her offer, and the woman was clearly not ready to be pushed.

The woman let out a little grunt as she tried to will the tears from forming. The muscles around her mouth and chin were straining from the effort. "It was twelve years ago," she said, maybe hoping speaking would distract her. "That should be long enough, right? Time is supposed to heal all wounds, they say. Well that's *bullshit*."

Her hand shot up to her lips, surprised at her own vulgarity. Sadie just smiled and waited.

"I'm sorry, I'm not usually like this," the woman said. "Oh, who am I kidding? I'm always like this. That's why I was eating alone today. Friends are there for you at first. They bring you casseroles and tell you they're praying for you. But there's a limit. They don't tell you that, of course. They let you grieve for a while, but eventually they get bored. When you refuse to get better, they stop coming over. Nobody wants to be reminded about death."

Sadie had hoped her first Lies would be changing someone's hair color, or making someone a bit thinner or taller. But she doubted that's what this woman had in mind.

"I lost my son," the woman finally blurted out, louder than she meant to. "Twelve years ago. He knew the rules, we taught all our kids the rules for living in this awful town. But Nick always liked to take risks, always pushed the boundaries. Drove me crazy with worry."

A rogue tear escaped and ran down her face. Sadie handed her a paper napkin and she dabbed it away.

"He went in the River," the woman said. "I can't tell you how many times we told him not to. He was a great swimmer. He was a strong boy, a good boy. But you don't go in the River. Everybody knows that. Nick knew that. But he just had to see for himself."

Sadie pictured the black churning depths of the River and shuddered. She'd been curious about what lay beneath, but never enough to dip even a toe into that dark water.

The woman went on. "We had the funeral, even though

they never found a body. My husband even got him a plot and a headstone. I think he thought it might help me, if I had somewhere I could go to say goodbye. It didn't. Nothing did. Nothing fills a hole like that. It just grows and grows and eats you up inside."

Sadie felt a pang deep in her heart, in that broken place that couldn't heal since her mom had died. She could only imagine what the reverse might feel like. She didn't want to imagine it.

"How can I help?" Sadie asked.

The woman pointed at the ledger. "I want you to write down that I never had a son. I have three lovely daughters who miss their mom. I have a husband who doesn't even look at me. I've tried to push through, to come out stronger on the other side, and that isn't going to happen. I just want to forget."

"You know about the Liar's Price?"

"I do. What… what do you think that would cost me?"

Sadie shook her head. "I really don't know, I'm sorry." Nick was gone, had been gone a long time. Writing him out of her life wouldn't be a small Lie, but it wouldn't be the biggest either. Maybe the cost wouldn't be that high.

"That's fine," the woman said. "Whatever it is, I'll pay it. Whatever time I have left can't be like this. I won't let it be like this."

"Okay," Sadie said. "What's your name?"

"Marilyn," she said. "Marilyn Stevens."

"Okay, Marilyn," Sadie said. She looked down at the ledger and gripped the pen. Her first Lie. A horrible, ugly Lie that just might let this woman live again. Sadie wrote the date, and then she wrote:

Marilyn Stevens never had a son named Nick.

"I'm going to need some blood, Marilyn."

"Oh, right," Marilyn said, a bit flustered. "I forgot about that part."

Sadie took out her mom's pocketknife. "Don't worry," she said, "it's very sharp." She cleaned the blade with some rubbing alcohol then motioned for Marilyn to hold out her hand, which she reluctantly did. Sadie pressed the tip as gently as possible into the meat of her thumb until blood welled up.

"Just mark here," Sadie said, and Marilyn smeared her blood into the Liar's ledger. As she did, Sadie felt something stirring inside of her. She recognized it from when she had put her own blood in the book. The Lie was taking shape. She focused, concentrated. She imagined a life for Marilyn without the burden of loss, full of joy at the lives of her three remaining children. She imagined a world without Nick and without the agony of his absence.

And then it was done.

Sadie handed Marilyn a Band-Aid for her thumb.

"How long before...?" Marilyn started to ask, but then trailed off almost sleepily. Her eyes fluttered a bit. Then her whole countenance changed. Her back became a little straighter, her shoulders less bunched. Her face relaxed and her eyes brightened. She smiled at Sadie, a little confused, then abruptly stood and walked out of the Treehouse.

I'm so sorry, Nick, Sadie thought. *Wherever you are.*

Sadie collected the ten dollars that Marilyn left and tucked it into her pocket and resigned herself to more waiting, but then a moment later another person was sitting across from her. She leaned out of the booth and looked down toward the front of the diner. A line of people snaked between the tables and out the doors. Denise was walking down the line, taking orders.

"Alright," Sadie said to her next client. "What can I do for you today?"

SADIE LIED THROUGH the dinner rush. Denise had to call in extra help in the kitchen. Sadie caught a glimpse of Javier bussing a load of dirty dishes to the back, but he didn't look up at her. Most of the people who sat across from her were strangers, though she recognized a few. Some were very reluctant to tell their secrets; others were thrilled they were getting such a great deal. Most weren't happy about getting cut though, no matter how cheap the price.

To Sadie's relief, they were mostly petty little Lies, nothing like the first one. She regrew hair and removed cellulite, changed eye color and fixed broken family heirlooms. One grateful woman asked if Sadie could make her husband less fat and lazy, but Sadie had to demur. These were harmless things, simple things, but with each one Sadie felt her power—and her confidence—grow a little. Maybe she could be the Liar after all.

When the line finally ran out, Denise came over and slapped a pile of bills on the table.

"What's this?" Sadie asked.

"Your split of the tips," Denise said. "Never had so many happy customers."

Between the tips and her Liar's fees, Sadie now had more cash than she'd ever had in her life. And she'd been giving away her talents at a reduced rate. As her abilities grew, so could her fees. Maybe she wouldn't have to spend the rest of her life praying for enough to pay for gas.

She gathered up her things and her money and shoved them into her backpack. As she did, something caught her attention about the tree at the center of the restaurant. She walked over and ran a finger over the spot where she'd broken a branch off to assist in the summoning of Mary Bell. The branch hadn't regrown. A few of the other branches didn't look right either, and a few dried leaves crunched under her feet.

"Denise," she said. "Is something wrong with the tree?"

The owner didn't look up from where she sat counting the day's take. "That tree has a mind all its own. If there's something wrong, it doesn't bother to share those details with us mere mortals."

All of Red Valley had been looking dried-out and withered for a while now, as far back as Sadie could recall. But until today, she'd never seen the old tree affected by the drought—or anything, for that matter. She wondered how much more the town could take.

She took a slice of apple pie to go, and stepped outside. The sun was long gone and the night almost felt like it was cooling down. Mosquitos buzzed angrily in her face but she brushed them away with her free hand. She was headed for her mom's car when she glanced over at the bus stop. A single person stood there, and Sadie thought she recognized her.

"Courtney, right?" Sadie asked.

The girl waiting under the yellow street light looked up sharply, surprised to hear her own name. It had been a while since Sadie had seen her, but she hadn't changed much: still perfect and blonde, dressed for Sunday morning in a floral sundress and white pearls.

"Hi," Courtney said, a bit cautiously.

"I'm Sadie. We went to high school together."

"Right," Courtney said. "Sorry, it took me a minute."

"That's fine," Sadie said. "It's been a while since then."

"Yeah."

Sadie wasn't sure what had drawn her to speak to Courtney, so wasn't sure what to say next. During high school, you spend every day with these people. They're a part of your life, whether you like it or not. But after graduation, they're just gone, like a death. She remembered Ashleigh's story about seeing Courtney at Planned Parenthood, but figured that wouldn't be a good ice-breaker.

"So you still live in Red Valley? I thought you'd go off to college somewhere."

"I did," Courtney said with a weak, sad smile. "Wasn't for me. So I came back home. Been back a year or so."

Sadie had been staring at people for hours. All sorts of people: rich, poor, young, old, friendly, grumpy. She'd listened to their stories and written their Lies and watched their faces. She'd noticed which ones fidgeted with the silverware on the table, which ones didn't make eye contact, which ones kept watching the door. Now she turned her honed evaluations on Courtney. Arms crossed tight over her body. Mouth pressed firmly closed. A little too much makeup around the eyes, barely hiding the puffiness. Courtney was a brittle porcelain doll ready to crack.

"Find any good work in town?"

"A few odd jobs," Courtney said, shrugging. "Mostly volunteering at my church."

"That probably doesn't pay too well," Sadie observed.

Courtney laughed a little. "No, not really. What about you?"

"I've been stuck here ever since graduation," Sadie said. She pointed over her shoulder at the Treehouse with a thumb. "Waiting tables, getting discounts on apple pie."

"I've had worse jobs."

"Me too."

"I heard about your mom," Courtney said. "I'm so sorry. She was real nice to me."

Sadie had to blink a few times as she processed this. She hadn't expected Courtney to remember her, let alone her mom.

"When... when did you see my mom?" Sadie asked.

Courtney looked down, her cheeks reddening. Behind her, the crosstown #2 bus lumbered up to the stop and its doors hissed open. "That's my bus," she said. "I should go."

"Yeah, sure," Sadie said. "Nice seeing you again."

"You too," Courtney said. She stepped up into the bus, paused for a second as if she might say something else, but then just hurried on inside.

Sadie watched the bus as it drove by. They'd never been friends in school, barely said a word to each other as far as Sadie could remember, but now Sadie couldn't help but feel a little sad for her. She'd had a chance to escape Red Valley, but here she was again, trying to find a life in a town with little to spare. Whatever her secrets, Sadie hoped she'd find some peace.

*   *   *

SHE ATE THE apple pie as soon as she got home. She was originally only going to eat half and save the rest for later, but that plan—and the pie—didn't survive very long. As she ate, she idly flipped through the ledgers of her ancestors and wondered at the lives they'd lived and the Lies they'd told, long before Sadie came along. She saw a glimpse of them in these words, a thin outline of people she'd never know. And she wished—not for the first or last time—that she had her mother's ledger, too.

Sadie left the old ledgers on the table, but took her own down the hall and flopped onto her bed. Her book was now filled with many of her own Lies, and her mind was full of many new faces. For the first time in her life, people in Red Valley needed something from her; and she was able to give it. Some people at the diner hadn't been happy when she'd set up shop, but most of them were eager for her help. Maybe the Liar didn't have to be hated. Maybe she could do some good.

Though she tried not to, she couldn't help but think of Marilyn, and of Nick. She'd taken something from that woman, something irreplaceable. Was she really better off without her memories, as painful as they were? Sadie couldn't even guess, but she had seemed a changed person after the Lie took effect. Her finger traced over the words. How many Lies would it take before she stopped second-guessing them? The previous Liars had hundreds and hundreds in their ledgers. Had that been enough?

I miss you, Mom, Sadie thought. *I wish you could have seen me today. I kicked serious ass.*

Bone-tired, Sadie was about to let herself drift to sleep when she remembered she hadn't turned off the kitchen light. She used to think an 8-hour shift at the diner was exhausting, but that turned out to be nothing compared with confronting cosmic horrors and rewriting reality. Luckily, they also seemed to pay better. She went back out into the living room and turned off the lights. She was about to head back to her bedroom when something out the window caught her eye. She lifted the blinds and peered out.

There were blazing headlights at the end of her driveway. Not just one pair; she counted four. She couldn't see the cars themselves, but it was clear they were blocking the road. Her blood ran cold. Who would...?

But then, through the open window, she heard the sound of high-pitched laughter echoing down the driveway.

CHAPTER SEVENTEEN

OH SHIT OH *shit oh shit*. The Laughing Boys.

Sadie wanted to run but her legs wouldn't move. *No, no.* With everything else she'd been doing, she'd forgotten about the Laughing Boy. Though the headlights were nearly blinding, she thought she could see wisps of demonic blue light floating out there in the night. Coming closer. There were a *lot* of them. And they weren't coming to ask nicely.

You have to go. Now.

Finally moving, she ran back to the kitchen and gathered up the old ledgers and shoved them deep into her backpack. She thought about running for her mom's car, but that would mean going toward the Laughing Boys, and they'd blocked the driveway anyway.

She'd have to run.

The laughter was coming through the walls now. And the voices.

"Come on out!"

"We won't hurt you! Just give us what we want!"

"*Yes we will! Make her hurt. Make her scream!*"

"*We want to taste her agony!*"

She burst out the back door into the night. The Laughing Boys were still all out front and didn't see her break for the trees. There was no moon and she could barely see the uneven ground, but that didn't slow her.

She hadn't made it far before her foot caught on something hidden in the darkness and she fell hard. Pain shot up her leg from a turned ankle, but she bit it down until her eyes watered.

"We know you're in there!" came a voice from near the house.

"*We're going to make you hurt, stupid little girl!*"

Sadie lay motionless in the dry leaves. The Laughing Boys had the house surrounded now. There were at least a dozen of them, maybe more. Some had baseball bats, some knives, others just closed fists. Their strange laughter filled the night. What would happen when they didn't find her or the ledgers? Would they leave?

She heard broken glass. They were inside.

She needed to move, to get away while they were distracted. But when she slowly got to her feet, her ankle screamed at her and her vision swam. She had to rest against one of the trees to keep from losing her balance.

"Where is she?"

"*Find her! Find her! We want to play!*"

Something crashed inside the house. More glass shattered.

Sadie limped around to the trees on the side of the house. She knew these well; she'd played among them her whole life. She couldn't get away fast enough, but she could hide. As everything she owned was smashed up inside her house, she found the tree she was looking for. She started to climb. It hurt—it hurt like *hell*—but even with her twisted ankle, she was able to find her footing.

The tree's rough bark felt good as it bit into her hands. She tried not to think about the pain or the fear and just focus on that bark and on climbing just a little higher.

When there was nowhere left to go, she settled into the crook of two large branches, where she'd sat many times as a girl. It used to be smooth here, worn down by her frequent visits. But no more. She wiped away a few tears and pressed into the tree, wishing herself invisible.

"She's gone!"

"I told you we should sneak up on her."

"Find her! Kill her!"

Sadie could see some of the Laughing Boys through the living room windows. They tore pictures off the walls. They shattered the plates in the cupboards with their bats. They kicked holes in the drywall.

Others were still outside. They'd already smashed the windshield on her mom's car and slashed the tires. One was carving his name on the hood with a knife.

A tall Laughing Boy with long blond hair and a denim vest studded with silver spikes came out the front door and stood on the porch. His black combat boots thumped heavily on the wood. The others seemed to give him a wide berth as his otherworldly eyes scanned the night. For a moment, Sadie felt the blue cold gaze on her hiding place, but thankfully it didn't linger.

Danny, who'd come to her house that night, came out just behind the blond boy. He'd been terrifying when she found him hiding in the dark, but now he looked small and meek.

"Are you out there?" the blond Laughing Boy called. "I know you are."

"*We can smell you!*" said his demon.

"It's fine, Kyle," Danny said. "She's gone."

"You asked for our help, Danny," said Kyle. "We're helping."

"I just wanted the book. We don't have to break everything."

"*Break everything! Break it all!*" added his demon.

A particularly giddy Laughing Boy came out, holding something high over his head. Sadie squinted. *Oh, fuck.*

It was her ledger. She'd been reading it on her bed and forgotten about it when the Laughing Boys showed up. She'd grabbed the old books, but left hers behind.

Kyle grabbed the book and flipped through it, then tossed it to Danny. "That what you're looking for, Danny my man?"

Sadie squeezed her eyes closed. The pain was hot in her leg and anger hot in her chest. That was her ledger. So little of what she had in life was truly hers. She lived in her mom's house, drove her mom's car, even wore some of her mom's old clothes. But that ledger was *hers*, dammit. It was her blood on its first Lie.

Danny shook his head. "This ain't it."

"Danny, Danny, Danny," Kyle said, sounding disappointed.

"It's the wrong one. The Lie was in her mom's book. It

looked different, had a different cover. And these Lies are all new ones."

Danny knew what her mom's ledger looked like?

Kyle came down a step and shouted into the night. "I know you can hear me, little girl. Our brother here just wants your mom's book. He just wants to keep a secret safe, that's all. You can appreciate that, I'm sure. Come on out so we can discuss this like the proper civilized people we are."

Sadie doubted they'd be understanding if she explained she had no fucking clue where her mom's ledger went, or why everybody was so interested in it. These things had come up here looking for blood.

"Very well," Kyle called. He grabbed the ledger from Danny's hands and tossed it back into the house. To the others, he said, "Light it."

The demons' laughter polluted the night with wicked, vile glee. A few of the Laughing Boys ran back to their cars, returning a few moments later with oily gas cans.

No, Sadie thought. *No, no, no.*

They first doused the car, but then began pouring the gasoline all around her house. They poured on the carpet inside, on the walls, in the sink. On her entire life.

When the gas cans were empty, Kyle gathered up his companions. "She might be running for it. You, take one of the trucks back down the hill, make sure she isn't following the road. The rest of you, fan out in these trees. She won't get far."

"We'll find her. Oh, yes. We'll find her."

"We'll eat her face!"

"We'll eat her soul!"

Kyle turned back toward the house. He pulled a cheap lighter from his vest. With a click, he produced a small orange flame.

"No one fucks with us," he said as he held the lighter up. "No one."

Then he threw it into the gasoline vapors.

The fire caught fast and quick. Flames lapped hungrily at the plastic siding on her house and spread all along the front. The porch resisted for a moment, then began to burn. Smoke rose into the sky and wild red light lit up the night.

Sadie nearly suffocated on the scream stuck in her throat. Her fingers bit into the tree's bark. Her whole life had been spent in that house. Every memory she had of her childhood was in there. Everything she had of her mom's was in there too. It was like watching her die all over again.

The Laughing Boys began to spread out into the oak trees. Sadie hugged the tree tighter and tried to be invisible even as the growing fire illuminated everything. Two of the blue-eyed junkies walked right under her. One held an aluminum baseball bat, the other a machete. Their demons cackled and tittered like this was the best night of their lives, all the while whispering what they were going to do to her if they found her. Sadie couldn't even breathe. And all she could think about was her ledger. For a moment, she considered just leaving it. Could she just make another? Or would her power burn up with it? But her resolve didn't waver long. She had to get it back. She had to save something from that house or she might just lose her mind.

From her vantage point, she saw no more Laughing Boys. They'd all disappeared into the forest. There were acres to cover between the house and the nearest neighbor; there was no way to quickly search it all.

Just stay here. They can't find you here. Wait until morning.

But that would be too late. Everything would be ash by then.

She made her way down the tree as quickly as silence and her ankle would allow. The fire was only growing hotter; she didn't have long. She tried to land mostly on her good foot but the impact still shot spikes of pain from her ankle to her eyes.

Forget it, she told herself. Waiting wasn't an option. Pain wasn't an option. She had to move.

She limped across the driveway, not even looking at the smoldering ruin of her mom's car. She could feel the fire hot on her face now. The meager azaleas they planted last month next to the porch had already been consumed. Through the windows, she could see the walls she'd drawn on with crayon as a kid starting to blacken and crack. The open front door was a wall of angry fire. But beyond, just at the end of the hallway leading to the bedrooms, she saw where her ledger had fallen. It was still safe, but she couldn't get to it from here.

She hurried around the side of the house to her bedroom window. She could smell gasoline, but it hadn't caught yet. She could see a yellow flicker inside. She pushed up on the glass, but it didn't budge. Her mom had always harped on her to close and latch her window when she left. Don't make it so easy for intruders, she'd said.

Nearby, Sadie saw the stack of firewood they kept for the stove during the winter. She pulled off the tarp and brushed away the spider-webs. Somewhere in the dark night, she heard someone shouting, but it was too far away to hear clearly. She grabbed a decent sized hunk of split wood and struggled back over to her window. She hefted the log with both hands and smashed it into the window.

The log bounced off and out of her hands. She tried to catch it, put too much weight on her ankle, and fell, screaming. She clamped her lips down and when that didn't work, buried her face in the dead grass and roared pain, grief, and fury into the ground.

Then she forced herself to her feet, picked up the log, and hammered at the window until the glass exploded inward. She dragged the wood along the frame to clear away the jagged edges, then grabbed the inside sill and pulled herself inside.

Her room was full of choking smoke. The fire was just outside the door and creeping closer with every passing moment. The whole house shuddered like a dying animal. Sadie knocked broken glass from her palms on her jeans and nearly fell onto her bed. She rolled off the side and onto the carpet. She stayed low, under the smoke, and peeked out into the hallway. The fire was coming, but there was her ledger, near the doorway. She scrambled for it on all fours and smacked away a few embers that had started to smolder on the cover.

Got it. Almost there. Almost out.

Sadie hurried back to the bedroom away from the approaching flames. She let herself down out of the window gingerly and avoided making her ankle any angrier. *Just keep moving.* She had her ledger, so she just had to get away from the house before the Laughing Boys returned. She was miles from town, but she'd figure that part out later. Now she just had to move.

When she turned away from the fire back toward the trees, the blond Laughing Boy—Kyle—was there, watching.

"So rude," Kyle said with a leering grin. "We knocked on your door, but you didn't invite us in."

"*Just a rude little girl,*" said his demon, laughing. "*A rude little girl who needs to be taught some manners.*"

"I don't know you," Sadie said. "I never did anything to you."

The Laughing Boy chuckled and shook his head. "I would have thought the Liar would be better at lying." He took a step toward her. She wanted to move away, but could feel the flames hot on the back of her neck and knew there was no retreat that way. "Danny asked you nicely. He just wanted to keep a little secret, but you had to be a bitch about it."

"I'm the Liar," she said. "Being a bitch about secrets is my job."

"Ooh, such a serious face," Kyle said. "It isn't very pretty. Give us a smile."

"Go to hell."

The Laughing Boy's smile melted. "I should have known you couldn't be reasonable. What a shame."

"*Cut out her tongue. Let her choke on her own blood!*"
The fire danced in the Laughing Boy's glowing blue eyes. His fingers twitched.

Sadie lunged for the split log she'd used to break the window just as the Laughing Boy lunged for her. She got the wood up to swing like a club, but then he was on her. He grabbed at the log with abnormally long fingers, tipped in hooked claws. She pulled back, but felt it slipping through her grasp. The fire was hot on her back and the Laughing Boy's breath hot on her face. He smirked at her and pulled her closer.

"I'm going to make you—"

She didn't let him finish. Now that she was inside his reach, she planted her good foot and drove her other knee up and hard into his balls. His horrible demonic eyes went wide in surprise and gut-wrenching agony and his hand dropped away from the log to cradle his groin.

Sadie brought the log down on his head with every ounce of fury in her body. The impact jarred the log out of her hands, but Kyle went down. It was enough.

Her ankle burned hotter than her crumbling house, but still she ran. Smoke and terror stung her eyes and blurred her vision but still she ran. She had nowhere left to go, but still she ran.

Until those hooked claws caught her.

They sunk into her backpack and nearly pulled her off her feet. The blond Laughing Boy, his face half covered in blood, shouted something unintelligible in both his and his demon's voice together, and went to yank her to the ground.

But just as he did, Sadie slipped the straps off her shoulders. Suddenly finding no resistance, he stumbled and tripped backward onto the front porch.

And into the flames.

He screamed. Sadie ran.

CHAPTER EIGHTEEN

SADIE STOPPED RUNNING when her legs gave out. She slid into broken branches and brittle leaves. Behind her, the orange glow that had once been her childhood home was as distant as dawn. Her heart threatened to break her ribs. Sweat and tears dripped off her chin.

Her ledger, her ancestors' ledgers—and all the money she had in the world—had been in that bag. Everything she had that mattered.

What am I going to do now? How can I even—No, she interrupted her own thoughts and tightened her hands to fists. She'd lost everything, but she was alive. For now. She needed to focus on staying that way.

The night was dark but it was not quiet. Laughter echoed all around her, some far off, some far too close.

A booming voice full of pain exploded into the smoke and star-filled sky. "Find her! Find that bitch and bring her to me!"

Howls of predator joy and hunger burst out in response.

The laughter of madmen rang out and sank under Sadie's skin, into her brain, into her soul. She forced her eyes away from the fire's light—she needed to adjust to the darkness if she wanted to survive the next few minutes—and scanned her surroundings. She thought she knew where she was, but everything felt foreign now, even trees she'd played near her whole life. If she was right, then there was a creek a little farther down the hill. There was no water left, hadn't been since the drought started, but there might be some cover there.

She moved slowly, pausing every few steps to listen for approaching laughter. Every leaf broken under her shoe sounded like a gunshot. Behind her, the fire seemed to be getting brighter. At first, she thought she might have misjudged where on their property she was, but after a few aching moments, the ground opened up to a dry rocky creek bed. It was hard to tell in the dark, but Sadie thought she remembered the drop being only a few feet.

"Anybody see her?" The voice came from her right and much closer than she expected.

"I can't see anything out here." That one was from her left and a little farther away. They had her surrounded. "I don't know how long Kyle expects us to stumble around in the dark. I can't even see my own hand."

"He sounds pissed," said the first one. Sadie heard a branch break under his foot.

"He always sounds pissed."

"He sounds worse than usual."

"Just keep looking."

The Laughing Boys' demons snickered. Sadie held her breath until her lungs burned. Her heartbeat throbbed in her busted ankle. She heard more steps from the closest Laughing Boy; he was getting nearer. There was no time and nowhere to run. As silently as she could, she eased down into the dry creek. A rock tumbled and she froze.

"You hear that?"

"*Oh, yes. I heard it. I heard it!*"

The other Laughing Boy answered from back up the hill. "I didn't hear anything."

Sadie let her hand move slowly down to her jeans pocket. She hadn't lost everything, not yet. Her pocketknife was still there, the only thing left she had of her mother's. She slid it out. Another step, some muted swearing, more laughter. She eased the blade free from the handle.

I'll kill you. The thought scared Sadie, but she held onto it, hard and sharp like the knife. She didn't want their long fingers on her and she'd do what she had to. She could see his outline now, a black space that blotted out the stars beyond. He wasn't looking at her. Her hand tightened around the knife.

"She's long gone," the Laughing Boy muttered. He kicked some loose rocks over the edge into the old creek. A few hit Sadie's face and shoulders, but she stayed crouched. "Let's get out of here before someone sees the fire and calls the cops."

Sadie waited. The shadow disappeared, but still she waited. The sounds of his footsteps faded, but still she waited.

"I know you're out there!" Kyle called out. "If you'd been nice, you could have just walked away. But now I'm going to find you. You can hide, but I'm going to find you."

Go to hell, Kyle, Sadie thought.

"I've got your precious books," Kyle shouted. "Come and get them!"

The ledgers. As desperately as she needed it, the cash could be replaced. But her ledger was part of her now. She'd just gained this power, and now it had slipped through her fingers. And the other ledgers were a link to her past that might be lost forever. She couldn't lose them. Not to these bastards.

But she wasn't about to go back up that hill. She was exhausted, in pain, and furious. But she wasn't stupid.

She moved down the creek bed, careful to stay low, to step in the dirt, to stay away from the rocks. She heard more shouting, more laughter. She saw only darkness, the barest of outlines of the land ahead of her. In that darkness she saw the flames consuming her home and the terrible red eyes in the cavern. She saw the deputy lose his fingers, and the King's Man cut apart by gunfire. She saw Graciela's averted gaze, hands drumming on the steering wheel. And she saw her mom, pristine and full of cancer, lying in a hospital bed. She saw her chest rise, and fall. Rise, and fall. And go still.

Eventually the creek leveled out and ran under a small bridge. Sadie huddled underneath, her head nearly scraping the top. The road above her would lead to town, miles away. She had no choice; she had to walk it. But for now, she waited. The Laughing Boys would come this way, when they ran out of patience, and she didn't want to be found limping on the side of the road. So she would wait.

She kept the knife out and in her palm. It wouldn't do much, if it came to that, but she wanted to do all she could. They might take her, but they'd regret it. Every day for the rest of their miserable lives, they'd think back and regret coming for her. The rules of Red Valley said not to trust the Liar. Well, Sadie was going to amend that rule: *Don't fuck with the Liar.* Don't come to her home and burn down her memories and steal her family's past. Don't take away everything she has in this world. Because then she has nothing to lose.

Her head drooped, her eyes closed, and she slept.

THE FIRE BURNED. Even when the house shuddered and fell in on itself, the fire grew. Ash and embers blew glowing into the air. But not all ashes came from this fire. Other ashes, blown north on the wind, ashes that had come from far off, ashes that came with a purpose, settled among these flames. Fed them. Breathed life into them.

The color of the fire changed. If you looked closely, with eyes to see, you might see the shadows of faces waiting among the flames.

Power does not come from nothing. Life comes from life. The truest fires are not fueled by wood or grass, but by the end of one life and the start of another. Nothing burned like a soul.

Those who waited behind the flames knew this well.

They knew this very well.

The fire on the hill grew. The night fled.

Men were gathered around the fire, men… and something more, hiding within them. Blue dead light gleamed in their eyes. Those who waited behind the flames recognized the things that had taken over these men, knew from where they came, to whom they swore allegiance. But they did not care. One of these corrupted men stood close to the fire and those who waited behind the flames sang their burning song to him. His demon sensed the danger, but too late. They pulled him into the inferno. His screams brought the rest of his brothers, but they could do nothing for him. These small devils recognized that they were in the presence of something vast, something they should fear, and they fled into the night.

Those who waited behind the flames savored the burnt offering. They would be stronger now. Strong enough, if the whispers could be believed. And they would be stronger still before they reached the King. There was much yet to consume.

If there was a breeze that summer night, it blew off to the west, away from Red Valley. But the fire did not follow the wind, as it should. It came south, straight for the town, as if driven by a mind of its own.

SADIE JOLTED AWAKE when a car ran over the bridge. She brought the knife up in front of her, but she was alone. The car drove on, fading into the distance. There was just one, so it was probably not the Laughing Boys. Hopefully they were long gone.

She looked out from under the bridge and saw a world lit with orange dawn light. Her whole body hurt and she smelled smoke. Her ankle was stiff and swollen, but the pain had dulled somewhat. The road was empty. The sky back toward her house was full of black billowing smoke. The fire hadn't gone out. In fact, she could see the angry flicker of flames at the crest of the hill. There was nothing between here and Red Valley but dried grass. It would all burn so easily.

Sadie folded up the knife and put it away. It couldn't help her now. She put some more weight on her ankle and felt the jolting pain start up again. It didn't matter. She needed to walk, so that's what she was going to do.

One foot, and then the other. She hobbled along the edge of the road. She felt exposed, but she'd never get to town if she tried to go off-road. Some risks just couldn't be avoided.

I'll make them pay.

I will find them. I will take back what is mine. And then I will make them pay.

Sadie wasn't sure who she was making this vow to. Her lost ancestors, the authors of the books she'd lost? Her mom, whose house had just been destroyed? Or herself, to combat the guilt she felt for losing it all? It didn't matter. What mattered was this next step, and then the next.

She walked. The sun rose, and the smoke rose with it.

I'm coming for you.

Lost in these thoughts, she didn't hear the sheriff's car until it pulled up right beside her.

CHAPTER NINETEEN

SHE RODE IN the back. The deputy didn't say much, but he hadn't tried to handcuff her, so Sadie didn't mind. She'd told him about the Laughing Boys; maybe he believed her, maybe not. At this point, she didn't care. She was just grateful for the ride into town, even if it was behind hardened glass and wire and smelled like old cigarettes.

The radio chattered as they drove. She barely understood what was being said, but it didn't sound good. Fire engines roared past them, lights and sirens ablaze, heading toward what had once been her home. Out the back window, the smoke rose ever higher.

The Sheriff's Department was an imposing chunk of sandstone that sat right in the middle of Red Valley, next to the county courthouse and across from the library. Its windows were small, like eyes squinting in the too bright sun, and hatched with metal bars. An American flag hung lifeless from a pole jutting from one corner.

The deputy escorted her inside. Their arrival raised

some eyebrows. It lowered some, as well. She ignored the scowls from jowly middle-aged men. What did they matter, after a night of hiding from blue-lit eyes hunting for her blood in the dark?

"I want to see the sheriff," Sadie demanded to the deputy.

He said nothing, but led her to a room with a metal door.

"Am I under arrest?"

"We'd like to ask you a few questions," he said.

"Do I need a lawyer?"

"Do you have one?"

He opened the door and brought her inside. The walls were painted concrete. There were two plastic chairs on either side of a heavy steel table. She sat only because of her ankle.

"I can let you make a phone call," the deputy offered.

Who could she call? Not Graciela, not after what had happened. Even if she still had the King's Man's card, she doubted he'd appreciate a call from the Sheriff's Department. No, Sadie was on her own now, more like her mother every day.

"No, thanks," she said.

The deputy stepped out into the hall. A moment later, he returned and gave her a foam cup with lukewarm black coffee. Then he disappeared, closing the door behind him.

She was supposed to feel safe here. That's what the deputies were for: protecting the people of Red Valley. That's what they'd sworn to do when they put on their badges. But those illusions had cracked at the crossroads, and been blown away entirely at the base of the King's hill. The deputies were just men, with all the crap that came along with that. They wanted power and control, and they had the means to enforce it.

Or so they'd thought, until the King opened the very ground up under them.

A few minutes later, a man with a suit and tie came into the room. He asked Sadie questions about what happened at her house. He asked about the Laughing Boys. He asked why they wanted to harm her. Sadie— of course—lied. The sheriffs didn't need to know her business. He wrote down her answers, the truthful ones and the rest, and then offered a weak smile, and left. Her coffee went cold.

Two men came the next time. One was old, the other even older. They asked the same questions. She gave them the same answers and tried not to laugh at their comb-overs. She asked to see the sheriff. They smiled and thanked her. And left.

Eventually, the door opened again. Undersheriff Hassler stood in the doorway.

"I asked to speak to your boss," Sadie said when he settled his bulk into the chair opposite. "I've got nothing to say to you."

"He's been detained," Hassler said. He offered her no smile, no feigned warmth. "So you're stuck with me. The world's gone a bit to hell out there, if you haven't noticed."

"Have they put the fire out yet?"

"No," he said. "And that's only one of my headaches today. *Things*"—he said the word with a measure of disgust—"are making trouble all over. Testing the King's Peace."

"And whose fault is that?"

"We're more than up to the task."

"You have no idea what's coming," Sadie said. She sat back and crossed her arms over her chest. "This is only the start. It just gets worse from here."

"The King tell you that?" Hassler asked. "Did he also tell you when he was going to start helping out with all this mess?"

Sadie didn't reply.

Hassler sighed and deflated a little. He spread his hands on the table. "You and I got off on the wrong foot."

"You had your men beat my friend and threatened to send him to prison."

"*Back* to prison," Hassler said. "And he's not your friend."

"You get to decide who my friends are now?"

"You know why he went to prison in the first place? He tell you that, since you're such good friends and all?"

Sadie's mouth tightened. Hassler stared at her expectantly, so after a long tense silence, she said, "No."

"Well then let me enlighten you. We knew he was selling drugs. That much was obvious. We'd see him all the time making his rounds at the apartments on the far side of the River. Everyone there is using or selling, trust me. But that wasn't enough, not for Roberto. We get a call one day. Someone's been stabbed. Deal gone bad, we suspect. Stabbed four times in the chest. DOA. Takes a hard man to do that. Shooting's easy. But a knife? That's a real killer's weapon."

"Beto served eighteen months," Sadie said. "That's what you get for killing someone?"

The creases around Hassler's mouth deepened. The muscles on his jaw flexed. "Never found the weapon. Probably tossed it in the River. Found him on the bridge afterward."

"Walking home," Sadie offered. "In broad daylight. After murdering someone."

"He got a fair trial. Due process. More than he gave that guy he killed."

"Whatever he did," Sadie said, her voice gone cold, "he served his time. What you and your men did out there was unprovoked. It was illegal. And it was evil."

Hassler didn't respond immediately. Sadie didn't care; she was tired of these conversations with the undersheriff. Nothing he could say would matter to her. Still, when he spoke, he did surprise her. "You might be right," he said. "I won't pretend I don't have regrets. But it was done in the service of a greater good."

"You really going to pull the 'the ends justify the means' shit?"

"The ends *inspired* the means," he said. "But maybe we were a bit overzealous."

"Is that your idea of an apology?"

"It's closer than you'll ever get from the King," Hassler said. He sat back and mirrored Sadie's pose. "This isn't some power grab. Hell, this is Red Valley we're talking about here. Being boss of this little town isn't something people dream about at night. I was born here. Lived my whole life here. I know the rules. But I've also seen the way the King runs this place. I've picked up the pieces after he administers his 'justice' and his 'peace.' I've scrubbed the blood from the asphalt. The people here deserve better."

Sadie let out a breath and swirled the tepid black liquid in the coffee cup. "My mom died." She laughed a little when she said it, a mirthless sound. "Just a few days ago. Hard to even remember it, after everything that's happened since.

"My mom died. My only friend hates me because of what *you* did to her brother. I got to watch one of the King's Men maim one of your deputies, then watch your deputies murder one of the King's Men. And then last night a bunch of junkies burned my house down and stole the only precious things I have left in the world. But please, tell me more about your holy crusade to rid Red Valley of evil. I'm riveted."

They sat in concrete-muffled silence for a long time. Sadie could only guess at the calculations running behind the undersheriff's hard eyes. He seemed to want something from her that she wasn't willing to give. Understanding? Approval? He obviously believed firmly in his own righteousness, but maybe he needed others to believe in it too. Easier to do the messy things when you knew someone was on your side.

"Thank you for providing your statements to my colleagues," Hassler said at last. "Our investigation will be on-going. We will let you know if we require anything further from you."

"That's it? The Laughing Boys come to my house to kill me and that's it?"

Hassler's mouth twitched. "I've got a whole list of problems on my hands today. These are eventful times." He stood up and held the door open for her. "Be safe out there."

Sadie rolled her eyes, but got to her feet and made for the door. Her ankle hurt, but she wasn't about to limp in front of the undersheriff. But as she passed him, one of his big hands caught her arm and stopped her.

"If I did have the manpower, which I don't," he said in a much quieter voice, "but if I did, I'd start my investigation at the old Sierra Nevada Lumber Mill. The place is abandoned, but that's where the Laughing Boys all hang out. I'd wager anything stolen by them would end up there sooner or later."

Sadie stared at him with suspicion. "Are you trying to help me, or get me killed?"

Now he offered the glimmer of an unreadable smile. "Be safe out there," he said again.

THE COLUMN OF gray smoke rose high over the buildings of Red Valley when Sadie stepped outside. The air tasted like ash. The summer heat baked the sidewalk that ran in front of the Sheriff's Department. It came off the stonework of the building in vengeful waves, as though willing Sadie to get away. She was more than happy to oblige.

Across the street in the county library, she was welcomed by air conditioning and the smell of aging books. She found an empty computer near the back and quickly looked up the Sierra Nevada Lumber Mill. It had apparently been closed down for decades, after the lumber stopped coming down from the mountains. She looked it up on a map. The mill was next to the River. They used to send the logs downriver to be processed here in Red Valley, but that was before the forests thinned out and the River turned mean. Most of the good paying jobs in Red Valley vanished with that lumber, never to be seen again.

She clicked another link and found a picture. It was black-and-white and more than a little grainy. A group of twenty or so frowning men with drooping mustaches were gathered on a dirt road, under a sign with the mill's name. Sadie could just make out the mill's main building behind them. Stacks of wood filled the yard, most twice as tall as any of the men. Business was booming then. Not anymore.

Sadie printed the map, waved to the librarian, and went out to brave the heat and smoke again.

And stepped into a warzone.

CHAPTER TWENTY

AT FIRST IT just looked like a bad car accident. Two cars sat at odd angles in the intersection next to the library. The front bumper on the smaller car had been completely smashed. The larger car—a blue SUV—fared better, but steam was still rising from its crumpled hood. The road was littered with broken glass and scarred by curving tire marks. Then Sadie heard the screaming.

A thing jumped up onto the SUV and made an awful sound that was somehow both a shriek and a roar. The vehicle shook under its weight. The thing looked like a huge dog, its slick gray skin covered in cruel-looking spines. Its paws were bigger than Sadie's head and ended in talons. Its mouth was long like a crocodile and full of glistening sharp teeth, and its black eyes were wide and hungry.

"Oh, fuck," Sadie whispered. *A bear-killer.* People in town told stories about these things, and they never ended well. They were supposed to hunt around the foothills far from town and never crossed the line of the King's Peace. Not until today.

A couple deputies had come outside to investigate the noise; they immediately opened fire on the beast. The pedestrians unlucky enough to be close by scrambled for cover as the bullets started to fly. The bear-killer roared, but it sounded more pissed off than wounded.

There was nowhere for Sadie to run that didn't bring her closer to the creature, so she ducked behind a big metal box where patrons returned borrowed books. One man—the driver of the SUV—didn't get away fast enough. The bear-killer sunk low on powerful legs, then exploded into the air and onto the terrified man. They slammed into the road with a wet smack and the man's screams turned to silence.

More sheriff's deputies poured out of the building across the street. The bear-killer ignored them as it began to feed, even when they started shooting. Stray bullets kicked up off the asphalt and whined around Sadie as she cowered behind the metal box. More shouting echoed down the street.

Eventually the bear-killer decided it had had enough. It raised its bloody head from its kill and eyed the arc of deputies, a low rumble in its throat. Then it struck.

Two men went down with yelps of pain. The others scattered. With the creature distracted, Sadie spun around to run toward the library to hide inside, but before she made it two steps, the doors opened. The librarian stood there, squinting in the sunlight, looking confused. When she saw the bear-killer, she screamed.

The bear-killer turned.

Shit. Sadie sprinted from her hiding place. Out of the corner of her eye, she could see the gray creature start to charge. It had a lot farther to go than she did, but its massive paws propelled it forward at unnatural speeds. Sadie tackled the poor librarian and they tumbled together through the doors. She just flipped the deadbolt as the bear-killer hit. The doors shuddered but didn't break. The thing's claws gouged long white scratches in the glass.

"Get back!" Sadie shouted. The librarian didn't need to be told twice. The doors bowed inward under the creature's weight. They wouldn't last long.

Sadie didn't even have time to run before the glass exploded.

The bear-killer's claws ripped up the carpet inside the library's doors as it let out another of its horrible cries. Sadie scrambled back, but knew it wouldn't matter. Even at a full sprint, she couldn't outpace this thing, and it still looked hungry.

But then, just as it was about to lunge for her, it stopped. A strange sound came from outside. It wouldn't resolve in Sadie's ear—was it a voice, or music, or something in pain?—but the bear-killer had heard it clearly. A moment later, it was gone. The broken doorway stood empty.

Sadie didn't risk going to the doors, but hurried over to a window looking out onto the street. A new car had pulled up next to the wrecked ones: a teal-green 1971 Dodge Challenger. The driver—a broad-shouldered man in a Hawaiian shirt wearing mirrored sunglasses—had stepped out and now stood in the middle of the road, facing off the slowly approaching bear-killer. Sadie could see a few deputies on the far side of the street behind the newly-arrived King's Man, but they stood as still as statues.

The bear-killer tore at the ground. The King's Man didn't move. The bear-killer let out a roar so loud and strange and painful that Sadie winced and shoved her fingers in her ears. The King's Man didn't even flinch.

Then it was all over in a blood-soaked instant. The bear-killer's roar ended in a gurgle. The King's Man had barely seemed to move. One moment, he was standing still in the road, the next he was back in the same place, holding a red meaty hunk of flesh in one hand. When Sadie looked closer at the dying monster, she realized it was the thing's throat.

She crept slowly over the broken glass and stepped outside. Other onlookers who had been hiding began to emerge. So too did the deputies, their guns still drawn, but clearly unsure who to point them at.

"The King has a message for his people," the King's Man said, his voice surprisingly loud. He dropped the bear-killer's windpipe onto the road and let his bloody hand hang loose as he turned to address the growing crowd. "Despite what you may have heard, you are protected. You are safe. The things outside might try to harm you, but the King will take care of his own. This is his vow."

The onlookers murmured at this. The deputies exchanged glances.

"The King asks that you not lose hope," the King's Man said. "Every one of you is precious to him. Your continued faith in the King sustains him, strengthens him. We face real threats, but together we will overcome them all."

A woman broke through the crowd and ran to the body

of the man who had been mauled by the bear-killer. She let out a wail and slumped to her knees when she saw what was left of him.

"What about him?" someone in the crowd shouted. "The King didn't protect him."

The King's Man absorbed this question for a long moment. It was a pretty *good* question, in Sadie's opinion: it was hard to convince everybody that the King was strong enough to save them when one of their own lay dead in the street.

"The King mourns this man's death, but he does not accept blame for it," the King's Man said. "There are others who claim to protect you. Others who believe they can take care of Red Valley better than the King." He raised a hand and pointed a bloody finger at the dumbfounded deputies. "Blame these false protectors. What good was their protection this day? Turn your questions on those who spread lies about the King and assault his servants. Ask them what power they have to turn back the darkness when it comes."

The murmurs were stronger now. In the faces of the assembled, shock was being replaced by anger. Sadie marveled at it. She expected the King would retaliate for the attack on the King's Man by causing another chasm to open up under the Sheriff's Department, or setting their heads on fire or something. But this was subtle. And effective.

"The King has made Red Valley a special place," the King's Man said. "Have faith. You will be cared for."

With that, the King's Man retreated to his car and drove away. The deputies did nothing to stop him.

*　　*　　*

THE WOMAN'S CAR died just outside of Salt Lake City. Some vestigial part of her brain—some tiny bit of her humanity that hadn't been burned away—understood that she'd run out of gas, but she did not concern herself with these details. It was expected, after all. Everything these mortals created—even their own foul, sloshing bodies—was fragile. Disposable. Their singular obsession was for the momentary, not the eternal, so all their toil never amounted to anything that could last. And yet they were not without value. Like any pestilence, they were numerous, so as one failed, another would appear.

This land was unfamiliar to the woman and to the presence that had hollowed her out and taken her place. It was desolate and full of dead things. Bright lights shimmered in the distance. More mortal folly. Did they ever tire of their meaningless little lives? Did they ever have a single moment of clarity, staring up at the endless sky and realizing, even briefly, that they were so shockingly insignificant as to invite madness?

The woman left the car on the side of the road and started walking toward the bright lights. Beyond the city, beyond the black mountains to the west, the woman could feel her destination nearing. That land, too, was strange and unknown, but even this far off, she could sense the King.

A large white pickup truck slowed as it passed the woman. The passenger side window rolled down and the driver leaned toward her. "What you doing out here all by yourself, sweet cheeks? Long way from town."

She examined the driver and found him wanting. She

could hear a wheeze in his lungs, feel his heart struggling to shift the blood in his calcifying veins. No, he would not be a suitable vessel. His vehicle, however, would shorten the woman's journey, and she was now more eager than ever to reach her destination. A compromise, then.

When she was finished, she slid in behind the wheel. There was blood on the windshield and on the seat, but that did not concern her. Only the destination mattered. And who waited there.

Do you know that I am coming? Are you prepared for our reunion? Have you anticipated it all these ages, as I have?

The truck rumbled westward down the highway.

SADIE HURT. HER ankle throbbed and her head felt like she'd been hit by a hammer, the result of a terrible night's sleep. She needed to rest. She needed to heal. But what she really needed was to find the lost ledgers before they were gone forever. And for that, she needed to wait for nightfall. Yet even with very few options, she still wasn't sure this was a good idea.

Thomas Gray answered the door when she knocked.

"You again," he said flatly.

"Miss me?"

Thomas said nothing.

"I need a place to lie low for a bit," Sadie said. "Just a few hours. You won't even notice I'm here."

"And why, pray tell, are you seeking refuge?"

She glanced back over her shoulder. "It isn't really safe for me out here."

"And you think it is safer to bring your troubles into my home?"

"Maybe you noticed the blood on my face? The tree branches sticking out of my hair? The cloud of smoke and death hanging over my head? Let's just say I'm desperate."

Thomas almost laughed at that, and Sadie took it as a victory. He stepped aside and let her in. He directed her to a backroom with a basin of clean water. "You can wash up in here," he said. "We can't seem to do anything about your manners, but maybe we can at least make your countenance less ghastly."

The water was cold enough to feel like a slap, but Sadie welcomed it. Using a clean cloth, she washed the dirt and blood from her neck and face and hands. When she was done, the water in the basin was brown, but she felt somewhat human again.

She found Charles waiting in the same book-lined sitting room where they'd met on her previous visit. He, at least, looked pleased to see her, though his skin was paler today, dotted with sweat.

"I'm so glad you came back," he said. His voice was a bit strained, but he tried not to let it show. He motioned for her to sit in the leather chair across from him. "I must know if you were able to speak to Mary."

"I did," she said, shivering a little at the memory.

"Remarkable," Charles said. "Truly remarkable. Tell me everything."

Sadie related the events at the crossroads. Her description of the bleak road Mary now walked did not seem to faze him, leaving Sadie to wonder what mysteries this man had seen in his strange life. When she told him about the ambush by the sheriffs, however, his expression darkened for the first time. There was a true, hot fury behind his eyes now; his hands hardened to fists.

"It never changes," he said, his usually cheerful tone bitter. "No matter what advances we make in science or medicine or what-have-you, the strong always use their strength against the weak. Give a man a badge and you'll see his true worth. And in my experience, few are worthy of that test."

"So the sheriffs were dicks in your time, too?"

This brought a laugh and a return of his cheer. "Yes," Charles said. The laughter turned to a brief but deep cough that he waved off. "Well said."

Thomas appeared at the doorway with a wicker basket. "Do not overtax yourself."

Charles gave him a mocking scowl. "I am far from overtaxed. All I do is sit around inside these dreary walls, reading books and waiting for something remarkable to happen. And here she is."

"You'll not impress me with this performance," Thomas said.

"Are you alright?" Sadie asked Charles. His breathing had become labored. More sweat had appeared on his face.

"Quite," he said. "We have our good days. Today... is not one of them." He shrugged. To Thomas, he said, "Stop worrying over me and tend to our guest. She, at least, you can aid."

Thomas approached Sadie and knelt at her feet. "Let us remove that shoe and see your ankle."

"No, no," Sadie said. "It's fine, really."

"Your limp and pained face say otherwise."

"It's all right," Charles said. "Trust him. He knows what he's doing. And he's gentler than he acts."

"You're a doctor?" she asked Thomas.

"I'm not anything anymore, but I can help."

Sadie looked at both men, then sighed and relented. When she got her shoe off, she could see that her ankle was swollen and bruised black. Thomas cradled it in careful hands and made his examination. He probed and flexed, noting when she hissed in sharp pain.

"The bone is not broken," he said when he was done. "But it will hurt for a time. You should rest."

"Rest sounds great," Sadie said. "If you could just tell everybody in Red Valley to cut me some slack, that would be wonderful."

"You are not responsible for Red Valley," Thomas said as he began to unpack the basket. He had a few glass bottles and some long strips of cloth. "You don't owe them anything, and trying to solve the problems of this town will drive you mad."

"Is that the voice of experience?" Sadie asked.

Thomas said nothing, continuing his ministrations in silence.

"What troubles is Red Valley facing?" Charles asked. "Something is clearly amiss, but details here are scarce."

Sadie leaned back in the chair. The wood creaked softly. Despite the occasional pang as Thomas cleaned and wrapped her ankle, it was the most comfortable she'd been in ages. "Are you sure you want to know?"

"No," Charles said. "It would be much easier not to. But please, go on."

So Sadie told them everything, including the secret Mary kept in her ledger. There was little use hiding it now; that damage had already been done. She told them about her audience with the King, the coming of his enemies, and his request for her help. She told them about the Laughing Boys and about the fire burning toward town. And she told them about the ledgers she had lost and had sworn to get back.

"So, yeah," she said when she was done. "Things aren't great out there."

The two men exchanged a long look. Sadie couldn't guess at the thoughts they shared in the silence, but something about it broke her heart.

"These are not the first trials Red Valley has faced," Charles said. He was smiling again, but it was different now: forced, pained.

"Were they anything like this?" Sadie asked.

"Enemies of the King have come before," Thomas said.

"And?"

"And he destroyed them," Thomas said. "Or chased them off."

"So you think he can do it again, this time?"

"He is powerful," Thomas said as he tightened the wrapping. "But he is not all-powerful. And considering Mary's Lie, perhaps his power is waning."

Sadie had heard the King's concern over the coming of his great foes. But she had also seen the unspeakable fire in his eyes, felt the ground shake with the power of his voice. How could anything defeat a monster as vast and everlasting as a mountain?

Thomas shook a few white pills out into his palm and

handed them to Sadie with a cup of water. "Take these. Then you need to rest."

She eyed them carefully. "And these are...?"

"Opium, of course," Thomas said flatly. But before Sadie could react, Charles let out a little chuckle and Thomas allowed himself a slightly upturned lip. "Ibuprofen," Thomas corrected. "For the pain and swelling. Or if you would prefer, I can see if I can drum up some leeches. No? We may dress like we're still in the Victorian era, but we did leave that time for a reason."

Sadie took the pills and looked to Charles. "He made a joke," she said in disbelief.

"Wonders never cease," Charles replied.

She let herself be led to a small guest room with a narrow bed. An intricate quilt lay across the mattress and soft afternoon light filtered in through white curtains.

"You should sleep," Thomas said. "You look exhausted."

"I don't want to impose," Sadie said, though her body ached to lie down.

"You came to my door because you had nowhere else to go," he said softly. "That is a feeling I have known, all too well. I can't save Red Valley and I can't do much to ease the road ahead of you, but I can give you a place to rest until nightfall."

"Thank you," Sadie said.

Thomas nodded, and closed the door. Sadie was asleep before his footsteps fully faded.

CHAPTER TWENTY-ONE

THE TOWN STANK of fire and of men's fear. The hunter soared above it, disgusted. It had been a long time since it had come this close to a human settlement, but now it had come in search of an old, old enemy. And now it could see it was not alone.

The humans scurried about below. Some tried to combat the creeping flames, to little avail. They were so ignorant of things that mattered, humans. Ignorance was perhaps their most defining quality, and none more so than these unfortunates. If they knew anything of the world—of the true world—how could they live out their little lives so close to something like the King?

The hunter passed over the black ribbon of the River. That too was curious. There was an anger there, a shifting, consuming fury. Did the King know the River's true nature? He must. Curious. Unexpected. The hunter stayed well away.

On the far side of the water, other things waited.

The hunter saw them all, even those who thought they were hidden in night's shadow. They were hungry, but afraid. They smelled the King's blood, but did not want to be the first to try to taste it. Even a dying animal could be dangerous; the hunter knew this. Only fools underestimated their enemies. Dead fools.

It folded its wings and landed in a forest clearing beyond the town's light. The trees around it were dead or dying, starved by a ground drained of life. The hunter crouched low and extended a single long claw. It marked a circle in the ashy dirt, which singed at its touch. It marked one, and then another, then more. It drew other symbols long forgotten, heavy words from languages never heard by man. There was precious little power to draw on from the earth, but the hunter's own strength would be enough. They would come.

When it was finished, the hunter was satisfied. The markings in the dust began to pulse with a faint, sickly glow. The hunter settled back into the shadows, and waited.

The first to arrive were small things, inconsequential. But then others came, some the hunter knew, some it did not. Its eyes watched them all closely. One of them would try, but which? It did not matter; the hunter feared none of them. Most wore the forms of men, a shameful illusion. Why would gods pretend to be animals?

When enough had assembled, the hunter spread its wings and revealed itself. The attack came almost instantly, one of the things shedding its glamor as it came. It was nearly of a size with the hunter, powered by six massive legs that churned the ground as it charged. It had a mouth full of poison and a dozen eyes full of malice. Something this strong would have been useful in the work to come, but it would be useful in this, too—as a warning.

It died just as it reached the hunter. Shock replaced the hate in its eyes, and then oblivion. The hunter withdrew its claws from the thing's skull and it collapsed.

"Some of you know me," the hunter said in a tongue that was ancient when the world was new. It pointed to the dead thing in a heap at its feet. "Now, *all* of you know me."

The strange and monstrous gathering said nothing, but there were no more attacks. They knew now. They feared. Good.

"You are all here because you want to kill the King," the hunter said. "Or you want to feast on the people who have grown fat at his table. The whispers tell you the King is dying, so you turn your eyes over the River and dream.

"Yet here you all are, waiting. Cowering."

Something stepped forward. It looked mostly human, though its skin was gray like a corpse and its eyes black and open like a grave. "The King's power is strong yet," he said in the old tongue. "Others have tried to defy the King's Peace, and now they are as dead as the thing at your feet."

"Because they were fools," the hunter said. "And fools deserve death. What of you? Are you a fool?"

The human-looking thing shook its head. "I am patient. I will wait."

"And the rest of you? Are you all fools?" The gathering said nothing. "Patience is wise. Waiting is prudent. But the time for waiting is over. I am here."

"You can kill the King?" the human-thing asked.

"*We* can kill the King," the hunter in the darkness replied. "I will show you how. You will feast on his flesh. You will gorge on his flock. You will cast aside these petty illusions that let you dwell among these bleating sheep and regain your true, glorious forms."

And the hunter told them of its plan. When it had finished, the gathering roared its approval. They looked far less human now.

The hunter had its army. Now it needed a war. Luckily, wars were always easy to find.

It dispatched the others and they fled its presence, eager for victory but still rank with fear. It hoped they would serve their purpose, but had its doubts. It had been disappointed in the past, yet sometimes even a solitary hunter needed a pack. The hunger flexed its wings, ready to take to the air, when it sensed it was not alone.

"Show yourself," it said to the night.

Shadows crept along the lifeless ground and gathered before the hunter. They took shape and form, arms that were not arms, bodies that were not bodies. These had no substance at all, yet carried a weight few of the others in the gathering had. The hunter was glad that it had not been these who tried to test its strength. It was not certain who would have prevailed.

"*You are known to us from of old*," the shadows said.

"And you to me," the hunter said to the Long Shadows.

"*The whispers spoke to us as well*," said the Long Shadows. "*We wondered who their curious tale would bring to this place.*"

"Do you doubt them?"

"*Truth or lie, it is of no concern to us.*"

"So you will not join in the battle to bring down the King?"

"*This mouth has too many teeth already,*" said the Long Shadows. "*We are not needed in your ranks. Though we do wonder: this offer of alliance, of common cause against the King. Will you take it also to those who wait behind the flames?*"

The hunter narrowed its predator eyes. "They have come as well?"

"*That fire in the hills burns too bright, too fast,*" said the Long Shadows. "*It does not burn alone.*"

The hunter was not surprised. The whispers would have told others, many others—the King's enemies, and his offenses, were legion—but it had hoped to arrive before some of them. It could dominate or destroy the petty beasts that glowered on the River's shore, but some of the King's enemies would complicate the hunt.

"What else has come to finish off the King?"

"*It is not our place to say.*"

"It is when *I* ask."

They did not speak.

The hunter's anger flared. Its wings filled the clearing and the trees groaned under the weight of its fury. "You have come to mock me?" the hunter demanded. "To see if I am afraid?"

The Long Shadows laughed softly. "*This is not our fight,*" they said. "*We will do as we have always done. We will accrue debts, and we will collect them.*" The shadows shifted, coming closer to the hunter, making its skin crawl at their nearness, their lack of fear. "*We know more than we have said. There are players in this hunt that you have not guessed. We could speak of these things, but not without recompense.*"

The hunter clawed the earth. It had no fear of the Long Shadows, but neither would it be in their debt. "Be gone," it said. "I will strike the foul old King down with my own strength. I have no need of you or your secrets."

"*Very well,*" said the Long Shadows. "*But we believe this battle will not end as you expect.*"

The hunter had heard enough. With a churn of its great wings, it was in the air, away from meddlesome, dangerous things. The high darkness welcomed it. From this vantage, it stole a single glance toward the fire burning above the town. If those who waited behind the flames had come... no. It had not lived this long—hunted this long—to be outdone on this last great effort. This was just another challenge. And the hunter would face them all.

WHEN SADIE WOKE, it was dark outside. At first, her body flatly refused orders to move. Finally comfortable, it seemed content to remain stationary until all of Red Valley's problems had vanished.

If only it were that simple. A slight whiff of smoke came through the open window, a reminder that Red Valley's problems weren't going anywhere.

Sliding out of the bed, she put some weight on her ankle and was pleased at the result. It took some struggle and some loosened laces, but eventually she got her shoe on over the wrapping and felt like she could walk again.

In the hall, she followed the only light on in the house to a formal dining room. A long mahogany table filled the center of the room and a dozen chairs flanked it on either side. A candelabra flickered brightly, its glow dancing in the gleam of polished silver and crystal. Charles and Thomas sat together at the far end of the table, a greasy cardboard box between them, large slices of pepperoni pizza hanging off the sides of white china plates.

"She lives!" Charles cried in mock victory. He looked much improved.

"Come," Thomas said. "Join us."

They pulled out a chair and filled her plate. She briefly considered turning down the offer, but then the smell reached her brain and she devoured her first slice in four quick, generous bites.

"Pizza, huh?" she asked when her mouth was empty enough to make reasonable words. "I would have thought you guys just ate stuffed pheasant or blood pudding or something."

"We had stuffed pheasant for lunch," Charles said.

"This is a rare indulgence," Thomas said as he dabbed his mouth with a cloth napkin.

"We discovered it when we came back during the 1960's," Charles said. "I thought I'd died and gone to heaven. The 60's were frankly not a great time for Red Valley, but pizza almost made up for the rest. It's sort of a tradition for us now, our last meal before..."

Sadie swallowed the lump of dough in her mouth as Charles went silent. "Before you leave again," she finished.

Charles looked at his lap. Thomas returned her stare, saying nothing.

"After everything I told you," Sadie said. "The world is literally on fire out there. Red Valley needs you. Look at me, I'm a damn mess. *I* need you."

"The world is on fire," Thomas said. "And there's nothing we can do about it."

"The fire is just one thing," she said. "There's a war coming. Hopefully the King can handle it, but if not, Red Valley is going to need all the help it can get to survive."

"Red Valley's survival is not our concern," Thomas replied. "We learned that long ago."

"So what?" Sadie said. "You and your magic house disappear out of time for a few years. What if there's nothing to come back to?" She thrust a finger toward the window. "What if you pop back and it's just a burned wasteland out there? What if they kill the King and everybody else?"

"We have faith in you," Thomas said. "You will stop the calamity."

Sadie slumped back in her chair. *Great. Leave it all to me.*

I don't know how to stop this, she thought. *I don't even know what* this *is.*

"Or you could come with us," Charles said. Thomas shot him a sharp look, but he waved it off. "I know you have a few friends here, but you've lost your mother and your home. Give yourself time to mourn, time to heal. Let Red Valley—and the King—resolve their own mess."

"He's right," Thomas said softly. "You don't owe them anything."

Sadie had never loved Red Valley. People in town barely acknowledged her, and most of those who did looked down on her. They were small-minded—bigoted even, as Graciela and Ashleigh had seen first-hand. They could be petty and ignorant, and as she knew from the steady influx of cars coming up to see her mother, they might praise the truth on Sunday morning, but had no problem with a useful Lie or two afterwards. Maybe Graciela had the right idea, getting out of here while she still could. Let Red Valley solve its own problems, deal with its own secrets. She hadn't volunteered to be the Liar, hadn't even been asked. Until this moment, no one had been particularly interested in what she wanted at all.

And yet, as much as she might hate Red Valley, it was also all she'd ever known. Nearly every memory she had was here. Her mom had lived her whole life here; and her mother before that. Her family was woven into the history of this town, good and bad. Sadie may not like much about Red Valley, but the place was in her blood. How could she run away now?

"No," she said. "I don't owe them. If anything, this town owes *me*. But this isn't about them. It's about me, and if there's a chance I can help stop some of what's coming, I'd never forgive myself if I didn't."

"That's admirable," Charles said with a smile.

"Foolish," Thomas said. "But admirable."

Sadie grabbed another piece of pizza.

When the food was gone, Thomas escorted Sadie to the front door. They stepped out onto the front porch. The summer night was still blistering hot. Her stomach was full and her ankle felt stronger, but still she dreaded what came next. She had to go out alone and get the ledgers back; she just wished she knew how.

"Thank you for everything," she said. "You didn't have to help me."

Thomas shared a hint of his own smile. "I'd never have forgiven myself if I hadn't."

"See?" Sadie said. "You're not a total asshole."

"You flatter me."

"When will you guys come back?"

"We are never quite sure," he said. "When we are gone, it can be hard to measure the passage of time. But I hope you will visit us when we do. You remind me a great deal of Mary."

"I believe you called her a 'dreadful woman.'"

"I did," he said. "And I'm pleased to see it runs in the family." Partially because she knew he'd hate it, and partially because she felt overwhelmed at the thought that someone was on her side, she wrapped both arms around Thomas's neck. "Thank you."

After a pause, Thomas returned the embrace. "Good luck," he said quietly. "Red Valley doesn't deserve you."

Sadie took a step back and quickly wiped the back of her hand across her eyes. "No, they don't. Nice to hear somebody acknowledge that."

"Farewell," Thomas said. "If ever you need our help, just come back here and screech like a wounded animal like you did last time. I'm sure we'll hear you, whether we want to or not."

"Goodbye," Sadie said. "I hope when you come back, the world's a better place."

"Go make it one," he said, then went inside and closed the door.

Sadie walked through the fragrant rose garden and out

the gate. The Gray House was nearly dark, but appeared larger than ever against the black sky. Sadie closed the gate and stepped back. She waited, maybe out of curiosity, maybe because she wasn't ready to leave. Her problems weren't going anywhere, after all.

She didn't have to wait long. At first she thought maybe it was a trick of her eyes in the dim street light, but then it was clear: the Gray House was fading away. The gate, the garden, the spires, all became spectral, like moonlight was shining through them.

One moment, Sadie smelled sweet summer roses, and then the next, nothing but dust.

"Until next time," Sadie said, wiping away a tear.

CHAPTER TWENTY-TWO

THE OLD SIERRA Nevada Lumber Mill sat in a rusted heap just along the River on the south side of town. There had been a few attempts over the years to improve the land near the mill, but now all that was left was an abandoned parking lot, a shuttered hardware store, and a very sketchy 7-11. A chain-link fence topped in barbed wire ran around the mill and alongside the parking lot. Though a few street lights in the lot still worked, there was no light beyond the fence, just the black hulking mass of the mill.

Sadie stood in the parking lot, far away from any of the functioning lights, and stared into the night. It had been a long walk from the Gray House, but her ankle was now much improved. What little pain remained just goaded her on, reminding her what was at stake.

Before she could convince herself what a terrible idea this was, she made her way across the parking lot, staying outside of the puddles of light dotting the wide empty asphalt. Broken glass crunched underfoot. An empty soda cup rattled along, pushed by a weak breeze. Back in high school, kids would come out here to drag race or do donuts until their tires smoked or until the sheriff's deputies showed up. Luckily tonight the lot was empty.

Sadie found a spot along the fence where the links had been snipped and she slipped inside. She stayed low as she cut through the weeds. Now that she was beyond the fence, she saw that the mill wasn't entirely dark; a fire burned in an old metal can in the empty lumber yard, and a few other lights flickered behind broken windows in the main building. The other buildings, which were smaller and surrounded the yard in a u-shaped arc, were dark.

As she neared, she heard voices.

"...didn't cost that much last time."

She crept forward, quiet and slow. Two cars were parked ahead. One was a polished SUV that was probably worth more than Sadie's house. The other was a scarred pickup truck with oversized tires and a spider-web of cracks on the windshield.

"Capitalism, my dude," said a lanky Laughing Boy with glowing blue eyes, leaning on the truck's hood. "Supply and demand. I've got the supply, so I make the demands."

Sadie got close enough to see the driver of the SUV. He looked maybe old enough to be a senior in high school, wearing fashionably ripped jeans and a polo shirt with a popped collar. His heavily-gelled hair shone in the headlights.

"That's not what that means," the kid said.

Then came that stupid fucking laughter. "*This one has spirit. Our brothers are going to have fun with him.*"

"Gross," the kid said. "I'd never let that thing stay inside my head."

The Laughing Boy let out a chuckle of his own. "Of course you wouldn't, my dude. Now, are we here to do some commerce, or are we just having a pleasant chat?"

The kid didn't look happy—he probably thought his scowl looked tough, but he mostly looked sulky—but eventually he pulled a wad of bills out of his pocket and shoved them at the Laughing Boy.

"Excellent," the Laughing Boy said. "I do love commerce."

Another Laughing Boy appeared from around the backside of the truck and handed the first one a glass jar full of what appeared to be white powder. He held it up to the light, then tossed it over to the kid, who scrambled to catch it before it broke on the dirt ground.

"Just use it to draw the summoning circle like we showed you. That should be enough for you and your buddies to have a good time. Just don't fuck up the circle, understand me, my dude? Bad things happen. Real bad things."

"Yeah, I got it, man." The kid cradled the jar and tried to look cool. "What is this stuff anyway?"

"The ground-up bones of our enemies, my dude. Now you have a nice drive back to town. Don't forget what I said about the summoning circle. And tell mommy and daddy we said hi."

The kid mumbled something, then got into his Escalade and revved the engine. As he drove off, the Laughing Boys watched him go.

"Stupid little prick," one of them said.

"Stupid little *rich* prick," the other amended.

"*Our brothers are going to take him soon,*" said one of their demons between fits of laughter. "*They are going to crawl up inside him and eat his soul.*"

Sadie waited until the Laughing Boys got in their truck and drove up closer to the mill before moving. She darted through the overgrowth and crouched at the edge of the outermost building. It was low, with a single bolted door and no windows, and made of bricks that left red-brown crumbs on her fingers when she brushed them. She inched up to the corner and looked into the yard between buildings. That's when she heard the dog, very close: low, angry barking, punctuated by a throaty threatening growl.

"Will somebody shut that thing up?" shouted a Laughing Boy who'd stepped out of the main metal building to smoke.

"He's saying hi," said the lanky Laughing Boy who had just been selling magic dust to the kid in the Escalade. "It means he likes you."

"That thing doesn't like anyone," the smoking Laughing Boy said.

"That's the whole point of a watchdog," said the other.

"*Let's kill it and wear its skull as a trophy,*" said his giggling demon.

"I'd like to see you try," the lanky Laughing Boy said before going inside.

Directed by the sound, Sadie could now see the outline of the dog in the poor light. It was tied up to the brick building, the thick rope knotted to a loop anchored into the wall just around the corner from where she was crouched. The dog was facing away from her, but she could see its broad frame and the cords of muscle in its back. It looked part Rottweiler, part pit bull, part hellbeast.

The smoking Laughing Boy picked up a rock and threw it at the dog. The rock fell short, but the dog stopped barking and instead just growled with pent-up malice.

It looked to Sadie like the Laughing Boys were mostly gathered in the main building. If they had her bag, it stood to reason that they'd keep it there, where they could keep an eye on it. But that meant she'd have to sneak in under all their noses and hope they were as dumb as they sounded. That prospect didn't thrill her. She'd rather be eaten by the guard dog than surrounded by glowing blue demon eyes. At least the dog seemed to hate the Laughing Boys as much as she did.

And that gave her an idea.

She eased her pocketknife free and slid out the blade. She was grateful her mom had always kept it so sharp. She shifted her feet very, very carefully. The watchdog was still glowering at the end of its rope, some twenty feet away, but one wrong move would bring it down on her in a flash of sharp teeth and pain. The rope's anchor point was close, only a little bit farther. Keeping her eyes on the dog, she pressed the edge of the knife into the knotted rope, and began to saw.

Nice little doggie, Sadie thought. *Just stand there and look at the mean Laughing Boy and imagine how good he'll taste.* The rope frayed a little. She kept at it.

Voices drifted out from the main building.

"Any beer left?"

"How the fuck should I know? Check the ice chest."

"You're standing right next to it, *you* check."

"I'm not the one who wants a beer."

"Come on, man. I just got comfortable."

"Piss off, Ted."

Yeah, Ted, Sadie thought as she tried not to imagine the dog's mouth reaching for her throat. *If you're old enough to get your body invaded by a blue-eyed demon from hell, then you're old enough to find your own beer.*

Then the knife was through. The rope fell slack to the dirt. Phase One, complete.

The smoking Laughing Boy had finished his cigarette and gone inside. Sadie slipped back around behind the brick building. She needed something to draw their attention, but not to her. She felt around on the dark ground and came up with a handful of decently-sized rocks. The building in the u-shape across from her looked newer, built of wood and metal instead of brick, and still had a few intact windows. That should work.

The first rock pinged off the roof. The dog took notice, its big head swinging toward the sound, but none of the Laughing Boys seemed to. The second one just disappeared into the dark, too high. Sadie swore under her breath. She never had been very good at baseball. Her mom had made her sign up to play right field one season; she'd made it through two games before quitting. But that had been a game, and this... well, this was something else entirely. She threw again. And again.

Her second-to-last rock hit the window with a satisfying smash of broken glass.

"What was that?" came a voice from the main building.

The dog growled. Sadie retreated.

Two Laughing Boys appeared at the door. At the sight of them, the dog started barking wildly.

"You see anything?"

"I can't see shit," the Laughing Boy who had come out to smoke before said. "Grab one of those flashlights."

Sadie moved around the other side of the brick building. As the Laughing Boys came out to investigate, she ran through the shadows to the next building toward the main one. There were only two out in the yard now, their flashlight stabbing through the night. She needed a bigger distraction. Hopefully—

"And for the love of God," the Laughing Boy said, "will somebody please shut this stupid dog up before I—"

Sadie heard the dog start to run, its paws kicking up dust. And she heard the Laughing Boys realize it wasn't tied down anymore. Between the buildings, she caught a brief glimpse of them trying to flee, and then the dog clamped down on the ankle of the slowest one and pulled him to the ground.

As soon as she heard the screams of pain and shouts of panic, Sadie ran. She came around the edge of the last building and crossed over to the main structure as the shouting intensified. Staring through busted windows, she saw close to a dozen Laughing Boys pour out into the yard as their unlucky companion tried to keep the dog from devouring his entire leg.

"Get it off me! Get it off me!"

"Kill it! Smash its brains!"

Under the cover of this chaos, Sadie found a low window and slipped inside.

CHAPTER TWENTY-THREE

THE MAIN BUILDING had a few sources of light: propane lamps spread around on a few tables, a big fire burning in a pit in the center of the room, and a dropped flashlight by the front doors. In the weird yellow-orange glow, Sadie could make out a little of the building's interior. The place was tall enough to be two stories, but was all one big open space broken up at regular intervals by sturdy posts that rose to the ceiling. A few makeshift rooms had been created with blue tarps, and a panoply of discarded furniture—sagging folding chairs, broke-bottom couches with stuffing spilling out of torn upholstery, a leather recliner that looked like it had been savaged by wild animals—was arrayed around the fire pit. Rotting piles of forgotten lumber filled one corner, decaying tools rusted beyond repair were stacked in another.

Most importantly, the room was empty of Laughing Boys.

The screams continued out front. Sadie ignored them, running to the nearest table, looking for her bag, her ledgers, anything she recognized. She found what looked like an alchemist's laboratory: mortars and pestles, various jars full of powders and liquids, strange words written out on scraps of paper. Tiny bones had been gathered in one vessel. Some were in the process of being pulverized.

But no sign of her bag.

"Hold still!" someone outside shouted, and then a wet scream of agony. "I said hold still!"

Closer to the fire pit, she found a collection of what looked like stolen goods: purses, boxes of groceries, a laptop with a broken screen. But nothing she recognized.

It had to be here. She couldn't have risked everything to come here for nothing. Sadie remembered Undersheriff Hassler's smug face when he'd told her where to find the Laughing Boys. Maybe he had sent her here to get killed after all. One less loose end. One step closer to a safe, normal Red Valley.

Except Red Valley was never going to be normal and was never going to be safe. And she wasn't going to give up.

The dog yelped. More shouting.

"Don't let it get away! Kill it!"

"*I want to eat its liver*!"

"My leg!"

Just as Sadie was about to turn and run for the back window before the Laughing Boys came back inside, she caught a glimpse of purple out of the corner of her eye. There, under one of the tables! She slid to her knees and pulled the backpack from under a fallen hunk of cardboard. She yanked the bag open. There was no sign of her money, but all the ledgers were there, right where she'd left them.

Sadie sighed and clutched the bag to her chest. A sob caught in her throat.

"Stop your whining," one of the Laughing Boys was saying. The voice came from just outside the main doors, and Sadie was in the very middle of the room, exposed.

She ran, the sound of her shoes on the dusty floor thundering in her ears. She just hoped they'd be distracted long enough so she could get out the back.

Only a few feet more. More voices behind, more laughter.

Where was the window? She lost it in the gloom.

There, there! Only a few more steps.

Just as she put her hands on the frame to vault through, she looked out into the night—and saw blue glowing eyes hovering in the dark. Drawn by all the sound, more Laughing Boys were coming toward the mill from the back, cutting off her only escape.

"...chewed my leg off!"

"You'll be fine. Besides, you deserve it, the way you treated the dog. You're lucky he didn't rip your face off."

"I'll rip *his* face off."

She was surrounded. And out of time.

Just as the Laughing Boys stepped into the fire pit's light, Sadie scurried around behind one of the hanging tarps. The makeshift room stank of mildew and piss. She fell onto a ratty, stained mattress and tried to hold her breath, lungs burning. Silhouettes of the Laughing Boys loomed on the tarp, backlit by the dancing flames.

"What I want to know," said one of them, "is who let the dog off his leash."

"Somebody who wanted you to get bit."

"Shut up, Ted."

"*How do you taste, Ted?*"

The scuff of shoes on the floor. New voices, more vile tittering.

"Where's Kyle?" someone asked. After a moment, Sadie recognized the voice as Danny's.

"Brooding."

"You see his burns?"

"*His skin melted.*"

"Yeah, pretty gross. That girl got him good."

"Wait until he gets his hands on her again. That ain't going to be pretty."

"Hope that was *some* secret your girlfriend wanted to stay hidden, Danny."

"Shut up," Danny said.

"Maybe the secret is that his girlfriend isn't real."

"That's no secret, that's just a fact."

"Didn't she dump you for some older dude?"

"Oh, but Danny still loves her!"

"Shut up," he said again.

Sadie's heart was out of control. Her mouth was dry, her fingers numb. When the Laughing Boys had destroyed her house, she'd vowed revenge. She was going to make them pay. But the world wasn't that simple, that neat. She was just one person against a whole gang of monsters, men driven mad by the foul things coiled up inside of them. If they caught her, they would kill her, and now she was surrounded with no chance of escape.

The tarp rustled. One of them was right outside.

I'm sorry, Mom, Sadie thought as the shadow loomed closer. *I fucked up everything. I lost our house, your car. I wish you were still here so you could tell me what to do. I wouldn't listen to you—I never listened to you—but I'd know you were right.* A tear dripped from her chin. *I wish you could have trusted me, in the end. I wish you could have told me...*

But she hadn't. Whatever was going on—her "bad Lie" as Brian had said—her mom had kept secret. She'd even hidden her cancer. Maybe they'd meet one day on the dark lonely road and Sadie could ask her why.

"Hey, where's that girl's bag? It was right here."

"You lost it? Kyle's not going to like that."

"I didn't lose it."

"Well I didn't—"

"*She's here, you miserable fools,*" hissed a demon. "*She's here! Find her!*"

Bile and panic clawed at Sadie's throat. *No, no. Not like this. They can't find me. I'm not ready for the dark road.*

A crash. The sound of a tarp tearing. Swearing, laughing, growling. Blue eyes in the dark.

Sadie eased her ledger out of her bag. Her mom had used her own blood to hide her cancer. Some things were worth the Liar's Price. She found a pen and started to write:

The Laughing Boys can't see me.

"*Tear this place apart! Don't let her get away!*"

She pulled out the knife again, but before she could fold out the blade, it jangled out of her trembling fingers and fell onto the mattress. She swore quietly, but not quietly enough.

"*I hear you, little girl...*" sang a demonic voice.

Footsteps approached, first slowly then faster. Shadows on the wall grew. Sadie grabbed the knife and dug the tip into the pad of her thumb. Blood welled.

"*We're going to hurt you so bad!*"

She smeared her blood into the ledger.

The tarp was torn aside, and Danny stood over her, lit up by the fire. His dead, hungry eyes stared right at Sadie, who fell back onto the mattress with the knife held up, blood still gleaming from its quivering point.

"You find her?" called a nearby voice.

"No," Danny said, turning away. "Just hearing things."

He'd been looking right at her. He couldn't have missed her, even in the dim gloom. The Lie had worked.

Sadie wanted to laugh. The urge was so strong that she had to clamp a hand across her mouth to keep quiet. She didn't know what that Lie had cost her and she didn't care. It had worked. She was safe. Oh, God. She was safe.

When she dared, she tucked her ledger and knife away and slowly moved off the mattress. The Laughing Boys were frantic now, their demons urging them on like hellish taskmasters. Tables were overturned, rooms smashed, bags and boxes emptied and scattered. Yet even as she stood up, bathed in the orange light, they took no notice of her. They screamed and roared at her, threatened her with all manner of violence, but never once even glanced in her direction.

I guess being the Liar has some benefits after all, Sadie thought.

Then the room fell completely silent. Even the laughing stopped.

"Where is she?" The voice was familiar but different. There was something human in it, but only a trace. The rest of the Laughing Boys had two separate voices: their own, and the demon who had crawled inside. But this one spoke with both at once, the two intertwined in a horrible, grating rasp.

"We're looking, Kyle," one of the others said, his word tinged with fear.

The thing that had been the Laughing Boy Kyle stepped into the doorway. The others had taken on some features of the parasites riding inside of them, but beyond the blue eyes and sharp teeth, still looked mostly like any other strung-out addict on the street. But the shape filling the doorway would never pass for human. His arms hung down nearly to his knees, with clawed fingers splayed out. Other appendages had sprouted around his arms, some short, some long. A few of them ended in more hands, others in razor-sharp spurs and spikes. One of his eyes was gone, lost in a red mass of burned flesh that covered the entire right side of his face. The other had grown to double its normal size, and now burned with icy, unholy rage.

Kyle moved into the room and the others shrank back. His head swiveled on an elongated neck thickened by burns and scar tissue, taking in everything. The terrible eye pierced through each Laughing Boy in turn with a blinding light, like some desecrated lighthouse. Until it stopped on Sadie.

The sound that came out of Kyle then was no laugh. It

started soft, then grew quickly to a wail of anguish and sorrow that made her insides twist and her legs go weak. He wasn't a Laughing Boy anymore, but a Crying Boy; and that was much, much worse.

And her Lie had been too specific.

One of the Crying Boy's gnarled hands rose, a crooked finger pointed at Sadie's heart. His mouth opened, revealing row after row of yellow teeth. "She's right there, you idiots!" he snarled in his double voice. The Laughing Boys looked around in confusion.

"Umm, Kyle, are you sure you're—"

The Laughing Boy who had spoken gasped in wide-eyed shock as a tentacle whipped out from Kyle's shoulder blade and ripped through his throat. Blood bubbled from his mouth and onto his filthy shirt.

"Shut up, Ted," the Crying Boy said with a curled, cracked lip.

All her elation at tricking the Laughing Boys curdled and her thoughts scrambled inside her head as she fought to swallow a scream. But as the Crying Boy shifted his weight low like an animal about to pounce, they coalesced into a single, terrified word: *Run.*

The building's detritus exploded behind her in the Crying Boy's wake as she ran. She was aiming for the broken window she thought she came in by, but as she reached it, she realized the pane was still intact. Too late now; she ducked her head, led with her shoulder and smashed through the glass. She hit the ground outside hard, but tucked and rolled out of the fall. Her ankle gave a quick jolt of pain, but Sadie wasn't listening. She ran.

The metal wall groaned and screamed and then was

torn apart. The Crying Boy burst through the hole, his many terrible hands churning the dirt.

She couldn't go back toward the other buildings for fear of being stuck between them, or caught by a lucky Laughing Boy. So she ran into the field behind the mill, kicking through weeds and tripping over gopher hills. She hoped to lose the Crying Boy in the dark, but his bright blue eye found her in an instant, and then he was coming again.

Sadie saw the rusty chute and ducked under it only a moment before her forehead would have collided with it. To the left, it ran all the way back up to the mill. To the right, down into darkness. The way ahead was blocked by the barbed wire fence, so instead she followed the chute downhill. The Crying Boy leapt up onto the chute only a dozen feet behind her.

"You should have played nicely, little girl," he roared.

The ground sloped down, then leveled off. Sadie heard moving water. *Oh, fuck.*

It could be hard to stay alive in a town like Red Valley. It wasn't *safe*. That's why there were rules. Every kid knew them; every kid followed them. Or else.

Do not cross the King.

Don't trust the Liar.

Never, ever go in the River.

The chute ended in a short wooden dock. When the mill had been operational and the lumber had been coming down from the mountains on the water, they'd catch it here and run it up the chute to the mill for processing. But now the forests were empty and the River was far less accommodating.

"Nowhere to run," the Crying Boy said as he crept forward on the swaying chute. "Nowhere to hide."

At Sadie's feet, the River's black water rushed by. It looked cold. It looked endless. She pulled back, sickened by the dark depths that seemed to call out to her. There was still blood on her thumb; did she have time to write another Lie, one that would hide her from the Crying Boy as well?

The dock shuddered as Kyle's bulk landed on it. No, it was too late. The horrible, deformed thing—and its glistening, needle-sharp claws—was only a few feet away. The space of a heartbeat. A final heartbeat. The Crying Boy's wail rose high, running out over the water and high into the starry sky.

"You don't know what suffering is yet, little girl," he said as he took another step toward her. "But I will show you. I will—"

But Sadie had heard enough. Maybe she was going to die tonight. The Liars never last long, Mary had said. Maybe this strange, ugly life she'd inherited wasn't meant to last. But even if that were true, she knew one thing for certain: she wasn't going to let herself get killed by some douchebag named Kyle. She took a step backward, toward the edge. The Crying Boy hesitated, surprised she'd voluntarily get closer to the River. Then just as his claws shot out for her, she moved back, over the edge, into the deeps.

CHAPTER TWENTY-FOUR

SADIE FELL. AND kept falling.

She tried to swim, tried to move, but the water held her fast. Held her tight.

She saw nothing. Not the surface, not the bottom, not the receding lights from the mill. Not the Crying Boy's single awful eye. Just the blackness.

Her lungs burned. But still she fell, away from air, away from life. The water latched onto her like hands, like chains, and pulled her down, down, down.

No! Sadie fought. She kicked her legs, rising. The water pulled, but she pushed back. *Don't stop, don't stop!* Just a little bit more. Her hand felt air and she kicked even harder. So close now. But just as her head was about to rise above the water, the River pulled her under.

As the last of her air died in her chest, suddenly she could see; and what she saw nearly drove her mad. *Things* moving in the dark water, older than time, harder than death. Eyes watching her, eyes all around her, eyes that could see through her, eyes that could consume her. A hundred thousand mouths, hungry, bottomless. Fingers probing, grasping, tearing, taking. Stuff of nightmares, beyond nightmares, beyond imagining.

And the bones. She saw the River's bottom and it was littered with bones, like a mass grave, like a killing field. They rushed past her as the River bore her downstream, human bones and other things, unknowable things. They were never-ending, always more, the dead heaped upon the dead, skulls grinning amidst the silt.

Sadie thought of Nick, the boy who had been taken by the River, whose mother had asked Sadie to Lie to make the pain go away. *Is this what you saw before the end, Nick?*

Then the black again, but not a nothingness: a presence, bigger than the sky, bigger than the world. All around her, pressing down on her, crushing her. Devouring her. Sadie screamed. The eager water rushed in, filling her up, weighing her down. But still she fought, still she screamed, soundless in the void, but angry. Defiant. Unbroken.

You are not like the others. The voice wasn't booming like the King's, but it was everywhere, like the water, in the water, *of* the water: liquid, cold, black. Inhuman.

Suddenly Sadie wasn't moving anymore, just floating. The water rushed onward, but it parted around her, enough to let air in from the surface. Sadie choked and breathed and vomited and breathed.

We have tasted many of your kind, the voice said again. *Ground them to dust on our rocks. Broken them. Buried them. But you... what are* you?

Sadie could still see nothing, just the dark water all

around her. "I am the Liar of Red Valley," she said when she had enough air to speak.

A pause. *Should that mean something to us?*

"I... don't know," Sadie said, uncertain. "Who are you?"

Red Valley, said the voice. *That is what your kind calls this place. Such a meaningless name. A valley is nothing. A long hole in the earth. Emptiness. Why name yourself after nothing? What created that valley, what carved the earth? Your kind is disappointing.*

The crush of the water returned. It forced the air out of Sadie's lungs. The opening began to close. "You are the River?" Sadie asked quickly, before she could be pulled under again.

I was, we are, they will be, said the River. *You have power. Who created you?*

"The Liar's power was given to my family by the King."

Something like annoyance crept into the River's voice. *The King? You dare speak of that pretender to us? The King has nothing to give that he has not taken. Oh, you are tiresome, creature of the King. We will let you join the others in the deep.*

Pressure built up in Sadie's ears as the water began to close in. "Please, I'm no friend to the King! He used my family because he needed to hide his secret."

The water was up to Sadie's chin, but it stopped. The voice came again, this time like a whisper coming from inside her ears. *A secret? Ah, secrets are worth knowing. We would hear it. Tell us the King's secret.*

Sadie opened her mouth to speak. The whispers seemed to have told everyone except the River the secret, so there was little use in hoarding it now. What did she have to lose? But then she realized: that was the wrong question entirely. She should be asking what she had to *gain*. She remembered her negotiation with Beto. A business transaction, he'd called it.

"My family has guarded that secret for generations," Sadie said. "Why should I give it up now?"

Would you like to drown with it?

The bones along the riverbed flashed in Sadie's mind. "You can swallow me, as you have countless others. But then you'll learn nothing. And there is no other Liar left, so the secret truly will die with me. If that's what you want..."

Water crashed into Sadie's face and she was pulled down, down, down. But then she was rising and the River split again and she could breathe.

You would bargain with eternity, said the River. *We have stood here before wind and time. We have run this course since the world was new. We are the current and the flood, we are unending, ever-changing, unstoppable, unknowable. Your forebears would give us their firstborn as a sacrifice and beg us not to overrun our banks and take more. They worshipped us with offerings of blood and treasure. They feared us. And now you would bargain when you should grovel?"

Sadie wondered if all ancient beings had these speeches prepared for when they met with defiance from puny mortals like herself, or if they were usually improvised. They did seem to like to hear themselves speak.

"I'm still alive," Sadie said. "So I must have something worth bargaining for."

The water rose. Sadie tilted her head back but it still reached her mouth. The River's voice was soft and liquid in her ears. *We could make you beg for death*.

"Let me go," Sadie said, spitting dirty water, "and I'll tell you the King's secret, and what he fears."

Done, said the River, and the water receded. *Now, tell us*.

"I have your word?"

With every moment that passes, we change, said the River. *The currents do not stop. I was, now we are. We are always new. We could give you our word and it would mean nothing, for I would already be gone and we would already be reborn*.

"So, I shouldn't trust you?"

We know not what one of your kind should do, said the River. *But you are in our deeps, held fast by our current. What other choice do you have?*

Sadie's body trembled as the water's chill seeped in under her skin. It was all around her, a wall of inky dark ready to fall on her. There were no other choices. So through chattering teeth, she told the River of the King's Lie, of his wound received long ago, and of his enemies who descended upon Red Valley. The River made no interruption, but did not loosen its grip.

When she was done, the water around her filled with a strange, musical sound. It was the strangest, most beautiful thing Sadie had ever heard. After a moment, she realized it was the River's laughter.

We are so pleased I did not devour you, said the River when the laughter faded. *This is a story we will cherish for some time*.

"So you hate the King, too?" Sadie was beginning to wonder if *anyone* liked him. The people of Red Valley feared him and everyone else seemed to despise him.

You claim you are a keeper of secrets, said the River. *But there is much you do not know. Your kind has always been foolish and quick to trust, quick to believe. You make terrible alliances and it will be the end of you.*

"What is it that I don't know? Tell me."

But you have nothing left to bargain with, said the River. *And we grow tired of you.*

Sadie decided not to press her luck. "So you'll let me go?"

In truth, we were *going to drown you even after you told us his secret*, the River admitted. *You are all the King's creatures, whether you know it or not, and deserve nothing but death. But the current has moved on and I have changed my mind.*

"Umm… thanks?"

The water slammed into her again, stealing her air. She kicked and thrashed but there was nothing to thrash against. Down, down. The weight of it pressed on her bones, her ears, her brain. The dark things in the deep fled as the River vented its anger on Sadie.

But we would have you know this: What you are, the River's voice said all around her, at last. *Your power. It does not come from the King. Nothing comes from him. This place has the power.* Had *the power, before he came. Now it all drains away, sucked up by that fat tick. The land, the air, the people, the water. The King takes it all and your kind does nothing, because you are afraid, because you are ignorant. You will lose everything and you do not even know why.*

Sadie was spinning, spinning. Rushing down the River. Disappearing.

He's going to kill us all, said the River. *And it is all your fault.*

THE BEACH AT Hogsback wasn't really anything special, just a spit of sand along a bend in the River, dotted by rocks and clumps of brave grass. During the daytime, few bothered to come here; it was far from town and there wasn't much to see. But at night, headlights blazed down Old Hogsback Road and lit up the beach. Laughter and music danced out over the black water. It had become a place of tradition and ritual for the high school students of Red Valley: a first beer, a first kiss, something more in the secret dark. They danced and sang and burned brightly under the summer sky.

They knew the River was death. Maybe that's why they came here, to live so brazenly just feet away from a sudden end. They'd all grown up in Red Valley; they knew the rules. Sometimes though, being drunk, young, and stupid, they forgot the rules. Or, more likely, they convinced themselves the rules didn't apply to them. Rules were for children or for adults, not for the young rulers of the world.

"Don't be an idiot, Bryce."

"What? I'm not scared."

"Well I am."

Bryce tossed his empty beer can aside. "C'mon, Jenny. Don't you want to go skinny dipping with me?"

"In there?" Jenny crossed her arms over her chest. "Hell, no."

The sounds of the party behind them amplified a moment as someone failed spectacularly at a keg stand. The lights from their cars and the bonfire cut through the reeds, casting yellow beams and nighttime shadows out over the River. Bryce reached for Jenny's hand, but she swatted him away.

"It's just water," he said with a sloppy grin.

"No, it isn't," she said. "You know that. Remember Alejandro two years ago?"

Bryce waved that away. "Dude was a terrible swimmer."

"He was on the swim team."

"And I beat him every time."

"I'm not going in there."

Bryce stepped closer to the River's edge. Jenny took a step back.

"Don't worry, babe," Bryce said. "I'll protect you."

"I'm going to go back to the party."

"Suit yourself."

As Jenny retreated, Bryce stared out over the River. The rushing water almost drowned out the noise from the party. Gnats tickled his face. Of course he remembered Alejandro; they had been friends since the second grade. When he'd heard the news, Bryce had locked himself in his room and cried for an hour.

He never told anyone that.

At the funeral, he'd been appropriately stony-faced, just like the other guys from school. No one knew why Alejandro had gone into the River. It didn't make any sense. They all knew the rules.

Bryce's foot was only a few inches from the River's edge. It crept forward, maybe on its own, until the toe of his shoe barely touched the dark water.

"Stupid river," Bryce muttered. He started to leave, to go make it up to Jenny and find another beer, but his foot wouldn't move. It sank into the mud, deeper into the water. *What the hell?* He yanked on his leg, but now the water was up to his ankle. His sock was soaked and his foot was starting to go numb.

"Hey!" he shouted, but Jenny was gone and the others just kept laughing and shouting. "Hey, let go!"

His other foot was now wet, too, as he tried to get enough footing to pull himself free. He was in the River. How stupid could he be? You don't go in the River. Alejandro knew that; Bryce knew that. Why wouldn't his legs move? Why couldn't he get out?

Then he saw something moving under the water. His thrashing stopped; his eyes went wide. It was coming toward him. *Oh, God. Oh, God.*

The River disgorged a body onto the bank right next to him. He screamed and suddenly his legs could move. He jumped out of the water and landed on his ass in the reeds next to the dead body of a girl with a purple backpack.

"What the—?"

Then the girl raised her head and puked black water all over the River bank.

CHAPTER TWENTY-FIVE

SADIE WOKE UP in a hospital bed. She remembered some of how she got here: the panicking high schoolers, the frantic drive back into town, the nurses asking her if she was okay. But it was all obscured in a haze, like watching her memories through rushing water.

She knew she was lucky to be alive. She'd escaped a Crying Boy and convinced the River to spare her life, all in one night. She should be dead. Instead, she was grateful for the scratchy pillow under her head and the thin blanket pulled up over her legs.

"How're you feeling?" It was Nurse Abagail, who'd called her about her mom. She stood over the bed with a clipboard in one hand and a plastic cup of water in the other.

Sadie slowly sat up. "Not great," she said with a croaking voice.

"Those kids who brought you in here said they pulled you out of the River," Nurse Abagail said with a tone of parental disapproval in her voice.

"Something like that."

"You know better than that."

"Yeah," Sadie said, taking the water but not drinking it, not yet. The hospital room was small but clean. The curtains were drawn tight but she could see a sliver of morning light outside. "I guess I do."

"We don't get many people in here who came out of that River," Abagail said sternly. She thought a second, then added, "In fact, we don't get *anybody* in here who came out of that River."

"Just lucky, I guess," Sadie said. She could still feel the River's grip on her body, still hear its melodious, terrifying voice ringing in her skull.

"Was it worth it?" Abagail asked. "Whatever it was that made you jump in there?"

"I think so."

"Well I guess that's that, then," Abagail replied as she replaced Sadie's chart in the slot at the foot of the bed. "You seem to be fine, all things considered. When you passed out in the ER, we were a bit worried, but I think you're on the mend. Which is good, since we might be needing that bed soon."

Sadie's head was throbbing so she finally forced herself to down the cup of water. "Why would you need the bed?"

Abagail frowned. Deep lines appeared on her face. "It's real bad out there, my dear. We've got firefighters coming in with burns or smoke-inhalation from the fire north of town. Sounds like they can't do a thing to contain it. They've already started evacuating people.

"And then there's the attacks."

"Attacks?"

"All over town last night," Abagail said. "Horrible things crawling out of the dark, grabbing people. The sheriffs are doing their best to keep them back, though from what I heard from the victims, it sounds like the King's Men are doing most of the work." She sighed. "The whole world's gone crazy out there, or at least our little corner of it. Not sure how it's going to get set right again."

Sadie wasn't either, and after her conversation with the River, she doubted she even understood all the dangers Red Valley was facing.

Abagail lowered her voice. "People coming in here are talking about one thing out there—the worst thing—like nothing they've ever seen before. Some great monster on giant wings, hunting people in the dark and giving orders to the other beasties."

So the King's enemies had arrived. More were probably on the way.

Abagail forced a smile back onto her face and patted Sadie's leg. "I'm just glad you're safe. After what happened with your mom, well... I'm glad you're okay."

"Thanks," Sadie said. A bubble of emotion rose in her chest and she flushed. After everything she'd been through, all she'd done and all she'd dealt with, the nurse's kindly face and simple words were surprisingly comforting. "It's been a bad week."

She started crying in spite of herself. Abagail didn't hesitate but wrapped her strong arms around Sadie's shoulders and rocked her. The tears just kept coming, like they were pulled from the River's endless depths, and they drowned out her words. She tried to talk anyway but Abagail shushed her and held her tighter.

"It's okay," the nurse said. She ran a hand over Sadie's hair. "I know what Hell looks like, and you look like you've been through it. Pain like that doesn't just go away, so you got to be strong, but not right now. Nobody in this room has to be strong. You just have to heal."

When the tears ran dry and Sadie could finally speak, she thanked Abagail again.

"We all need to cry now and then," the nurse said. She handed Sadie a box of Kleenex. "You take as long as you need, but you can go whenever you're ready." She pointed to a chair in the corner of the room. Sadie's backpack sat on it. "Your things are in there."

Sadie suddenly remembered the ledgers. "My books?"

"All fine," the nurse said. "You were wet to the bone, but those books were bone dry. Something special about them, I'd wager, but you don't have to tell me a thing. Your mom was pretty protective of her book, too."

The nurse turned to go. Sadie's brain was still waterlogged and took a moment to catch up. "Wait," she said. "My mom had a book with her? In the hospital? Before she died?"

Abagail nodded. "Never let it out of her sight. Wasn't it in the package I left for you at your house?" She thought a second. "No, no, I guess it wasn't. Huh. Sorry, I don't know what happened to it, then."

Things in Sadie's mind began to sharpen. Her mom had had her ledger with her at the hospital, her ledger with all the Lies she'd ever told. But then it had disappeared somehow before the nurses could collect it. Who would want to take her mom's ledger? And who had the chance to?

A realization began to prickle the back of her neck; a fire, sparking in her chest and spreading to her limbs. Like a window smashing in reverse, broken shards of memory began to knit themselves together. She swung out of the bed.

"I think I do," she said.

THE OFFICE WAS nicer than Sadie had expected. The chairs—both in front of and behind the big mahogany desk—were dark leather. One wall was covered by a floor-to-ceiling bookshelf, filled with Bibles of all translations, gilt-spined commentaries by Spurgeon and MacArthur, books on Revelation and predestination and effective evangelism in a post-modern age. The other wall was festooned with posters touting the armor of God from Ephesians 6 or the movie *Braveheart* or the Beatles. A window in the back looked out over the church grounds. The lawn was still mostly green despite the drought, though the parking lot was empty.

She didn't have to wait long. Pastor Steve came in, a well-practiced smile mostly hiding his confusion at finding her in his office, sitting in his chair. "I'm so sorry," he said as he came in. "If we had an appointment, it must have just slipped my mind."

Sadie flashed a smile of her own. "That's okay," she said. "I didn't have an appointment. I just woke up this morning and felt I needed to talk to someone. About God."

His smile shifted a little, became a bit more genuine. "That's wonderful. I'm glad you came. Let's talk." He still seemed somewhat annoyed that she was in his chair, but he did his best not to let it show. Instead he sat on the opposite side of the desk and said, "Tell me what's been going on."

"I've been having a hard time lately," Sadie said. "My mom died recently, but you knew that, you were at the hospital that night."

Pastor Steve nodded. "Losing a loved one is always a difficult trial."

"And since then, things have been tough. Real tough. It's left me wondering if maybe I need a little help."

"God is always ready and willing to help us," Pastor Steve said. "We just have to be willing to ask."

"I do want to ask for help," Sadie said. "But first I had some questions. I was hoping you could help me with them. Little things that just don't make sense. I'm sure you hear this stuff all the time."

He steepled his fingers and nodded. "I can try."

"So Jesus could do miracles? Like, heal people and stuff? Magically?"

"Well, it wasn't magic," Pastor Steve said. "His miracles were an expression of His Father's power. They were meant to show us that Jesus was who He said He was: the Son of God."

"What about the Liar's power?" Sadie asked. "You know my mom was the Liar of Red Valley, right? Now I'm the Liar. I've got power. Where do you think that comes from?"

He winced a little. *Oh, you didn't like that question, did you?* Sadie thought. *Good.*

"I couldn't say," he said after a thoughtful pause. "I'm not certain where the Liar's power comes from, but it does seem very different than Jesus's miracles. It is possible that it is not a gift God meant for you to use. The world is full of temptation, but it is how we react to that temptation that defines us."

"So if I was a member of your church, I couldn't use the Liar's power?"

"That would be between you and the Holy Spirit."

"I had another question." Sadie leaned forward in her chair and put her elbows on the smooth desk. "If God is all-powerful, then why do so many bad things happen? The world is pretty rough out there. Couldn't He just stop that fire that's coming down on Red Valley, if He wanted to?"

"The Lord works in mysterious ways, I'm afraid," Steve said. Now they were on more familiar ground, so this answer came easily. "I wish I knew why He allowed good people to suffer. If I were Him, I'd put out that fire and cure everyone's cancer and make sure everyone had enough food to eat." He spread his hands. "But He has a bigger plan, one we can only guess at."

"So that fire," Sadie said, her lips tightening as her feigned civility started to crumble, "and cancer, are part of His plan."

"I know that's hard," he said. "Especially losing your mother like you did. But He can make beauty from ashes. He can redeem our suffering. I don't understand it entirely myself, but He asks us to trust Him. That's what faith is for."

"Faith," Sadie repeated. The word tasted sour on her tongue. "God creates us and puts us in a world full of suffering because somehow that suffering is useful to some secret plan of His. And then if we say that that seems like a real dick thing to do, He tells us we just need to have faith that He's really on our side."

Pastor Steve wasn't smiling anymore. The conversation wasn't going how he'd hoped, and now his patience at her intrusion was waning.

"These are hard truths," he said. "Mankind has struggled with them for hundreds of years. I doubt we'll resolve them this morning."

"I just had one more question," Sadie said, shoving her anger down, at least for a moment. "And then I'll let you go on about your day. I'm sure you're very busy."

"Please," he said. "Go on."

"The virgin birth," she said. A muscle under his right eye twitched slightly. "That one just seems so weird to me."

"Well," he said, "it is weird to us, because it is unprecedented. God wanted the world to know that Jesus was the real deal, so He broke the rules just once to tell everyone that this was important."

Sadie tilted her head slightly. "So a miracle like this hasn't happened before or since?"

"No," Pastor Steve said. His eyes narrowed slightly. "Not that I'm aware of."

"So if a girl is pregnant, then that's because some dude did his thing." He reddened slightly at that and she didn't give him a chance to respond. "Say, for instance, a girl in this church, who grew up in your youth group, then started volunteering at the church during the week when no one else was around. Pretty girl, nice girl. If a girl like that got pregnant, then that wouldn't be a miraculous event, right? That would be very explainable, though very inconvenient."

The leather creaked as his hands tightened on the arms of his chair. "I'm not sure I know where these questions are coming from."

"Then let me spell it out for you, Steve," Sadie said. "I think you had sex with Courtney Barber. Like some idiot sophomore, I think you got her pregnant. That was a real problem, you being her pastor and all. I think you told her it would be best for everyone if she aborted the pregnancy, but Courtney had been in this church her whole life, listening to you talk about how sinful that sort of thing was, so she didn't want to go along with it. The problem is, pregnancy can only be secret for so long. So I think you took her to see my mom. I think you made Courtney put her blood in my mom's book to hide the pregnancy—just for now, I'm sure you said. Just until we can work this out."

The pastor's face hardened. But Sadie's face had hardened too, and she was just getting started.

"That's the thing, right? With the Liar's Price. If you told the Lie about her baby bump, that would have cost you a lot, because it is harder to tell a Lie about someone else. So you made her do it. How many sermons had you preached on the evils of witchcraft and sorcery? And then you made her come see the witch. But that wasn't the worst of it. The Lie hid the pregnancy, but it wasn't going to hide the baby. So after all that, you finally convinced her to make it all go away."

Sadie pictured Courtney's face when she'd seen her outside of the diner, the emptiness behind her eyes.

"But it didn't all go away," she said. "There was still a Lie written down, in a book, that my mom had in her hospital room."

"I think it's time for you to leave," Pastor Steve said, in a very unpastoral voice.

"No, that's not how this is going to work. I know you're probably used to telling women what to do and them listening," she said, "but I'm not in your flock, pastor. So now I'm going to tell *you* what to do, and you're going to do it." She interlaced her fingers and stared him down across his own desk. "Give me my mom's fucking ledger."

"What? Why would I have it?"

Sadie sighed. *So that's how we're going to do this.* She pulled her ledger out of her bag. "Do you know what I can do with this, Steve? You talk about Hell on Sunday morning, but you don't know what Hell is, not yet. But I'll show you. Eagerly. I didn't always like Courtney, but she deserved better than you."

A long, hard silence gripped the pastor's office. He glared at Sadie with a new-found and remarkable fury, but she was pleased to discover she didn't care. She'd stared down the King and faced the River; who the fuck did Pastor Steve think he was, next to that?

"I didn't mean for..." he started, before trailing off. "I just..."

"Please, go on," Sadie said. "Tell me all about your good intentions."

Without saying another word, Steve stood up and walked over to his bookshelves. He removed a red-leather-bound commentary on the Book of Romans and then reached through the gap it left. After a moment, he held up a book that Sadie knew very well. Sadie got up and reached for it, but at the last moment he pulled it back.

"You won't say a word about this to anyone," he said in a low, angry voice. "Not a word."

Sadie smiled, then snatched it out of his hand. "I'm the Liar of Red Valley," she said sweetly. "Keeping secrets is my job."

"I was only thinking of Courtney," he said. "She's been through enough already."

She made for the door as he went behind his desk. "Danny," she said. "He was in your youth group too. He used to be Courtney's boyfriend."

Steve slumped into his chair. His face had lost all semblance of color. "So?"

"So his family is probably on your prayer chain," she said. "He knew when my mom died." He'd known where they lived, what her mom's ledger had looked like. Now Sadie understood. Danny had been there, offering moral support, when his ex-girlfriend had to go see the Liar. A shoulder to cry on. And then he'd seen a chance to make her shameful secret go away.

"Sure," he said. "So what?"

"Don't worry about it," Sadie said as she opened the door. The air in the office had become a little stuffy, so the cooler air outside felt good on her face. So did the feeling of her mom's ledger in her hand.

"Oh," she said as she was halfway out the door. "You can probably hang up your phone now."

Steve shot up and stared at the phone on his desk. The red light indicating the speaker phone was lit up.

"Who...?"

Sadie smiled one last time. "We just left a very long voicemail message for your wife. I wonder what she'll think of it. Anyway, have a great day, Pastor Steve. God bless."

SADIE WALKED DOWN from the First Church of the Risen Christ to a little park she remembered her mom taking her to when she was little. She sat at one of the picnic tables under the shade of an old cottonwood tree. In the nearby playground, toddlers chased each other around under the watchful eye of exhausted-looking mothers. Sadie placed her ledger on the table, and her mom's next to it.

Okay, Mom, she thought. *Sorry it took me this long. It's been a bit of a week, so I hope you understand.*

She wasn't sure what she'd find in the ledger. Probably more questions than answers. But whatever was in there, it just felt good to have it, like some small part of her mom had been restored. Like some part of *herself* had been restored.

She opened the ledger and flipped through the pages. There were hundreds of Lies in there, spanning decades. So many words, so many marks of blood. Her flipping stopped when her eyes caught on something. The entry was from about six months ago, and unlike most of the others, it spanned multiple lines.

I don't have cancer.
I don't have cancer.
I don't have cancer.
I don't have fucking cancer!

The words blurred behind Sadie's tears. Her mom's pen had been pressed so deeply into the page that the paper had nearly torn. These weren't the words of someone trying to hide her affliction because of vanity or pride; her mom just wished she could tell a Lie to make it go away. But the Liar's gift had its limits. To all the world she looked healthy, but inside she knew that wasn't true. Inside she was slowly, painfully dying. Alone.

I'm so sorry, Mom.

Sadie flipped the page. And there found a Lie that made the world start to spin.

It was dated a few months ago. The blood that sealed it was darker than the rest, almost black. And she had to read the words a dozen times before her brain would agree to let them in.

The King of Red Valley is alive.

Sadie's heart pounded. Her skin crackled and was somehow hot and cold at the same time. The King of Red Valley is alive, her mom had written. Which meant that the King was really dead. Then what was that thing she'd talked to, the thing they were hoping would save them? A Lie.

Well, holy shit.

She was about to close the ledger when she noticed some folded papers tucked in the back. She turned to that page, where her mom's Lies stopped. She recognized her mom's handwriting on the papers, so she pulled them out and started to unfold them, but then her eye caught on something and the papers fell from numb fingers.

It was her mom's final Lie, dated the day she'd died.

I have a daughter and her name is Sadie.

CHAPTER TWENTY-SIX

ON THE NORTH side of Red Valley, the fire reached the first buildings. They had long been evacuated and the firefighters fought hard to save them, but the flames couldn't be stopped. The houses blackened, then lit up in orange and red. Smoke and ash rose high over town.

THE HUNTER WAITED. They had accomplished much through the night. Many of the King's people had been taken, consumed. The hunter could feel the new power in its veins; it had fed well. But the night was only so long and the King was not without fight yet. Caution was necessary. So it would wait, patient in the hunt, for the sun to go down again. And when it did, the hunter would hunt again. And the King would fall.

* * *

A HEAVILY LADEN semi-truck crested the Sierra Nevadas just outside Donner Pass. A woman sat behind the wheel, unblinking eyes staring down into the valley below. Not far now.

SADIE THOUGHT SHE was going to puke. There was a ringing in her ears that was only getting louder. And the corners of her vision were going black, hiding away everything except the impossible words on the page in front of her.

I have a daughter and her name is Sadie.

It wasn't possible. It made no sense. It was fucking insane.

I have a daughter...

Her mom's final Lie.

No. No.

I'm real. I'm alive. I'm not a Lie. I'm...

She had memories. Friends. A life. A job. A place in this world.

But as she reached for those memories, the proof of a long, real childhood, they slipped away, suddenly elusive. Had she really gone to Disneyland? Had she really played in the trees around their house? Or were those someone else's memories? She had a friend, true, but not many. Most people in Red Valley had ignored her, at least until she became the Liar. And the Treehouse Diner seemed to be getting along fine without her on the schedule. She pictured her bedroom, before the flames had burned it away. That had been hers, right? But there were no posters on the walls. Her old toys and drawings had been thrown out. What about that place had really been Sadie's?

Sadie... even seeing her name written down was jarring, like the spelling was weird or she hadn't ever seen it before, only heard it in her own mind.

No, she thought. *This can't be true.*

But the Lie was there. Unmistakable. No, no.

The pages that had been inserted into the ledger fluttered in the breeze. Sadie caught them before they could slip away. Her mom's handwriting called to her. Not knowing what else to do, she picked them up and began to read.

To Sadie:

Man, I can't tell you how weird it is to write that. I'm writing a letter to my daughter. Who doesn't exist yet. And who I'll never meet. Life is such a fucking trip sometimes. I can't even imagine what this is going to be like for you. I guess that's why I'm writing this, to give you the best shot at not going insane. Let's see how I do.

Hi. My name is Emma, and I'm the Liar of Red Valley. And, I guess, your mom?

I honestly don't know how much of this you'll already know. I've never told a Lie like you before. I tried to imagine you with everything that you'd need to be successful, but like any parent, I'm guessing I've screwed you up more than a little.

I'm not making much sense. Sorry, I don't have a lot of experience with kids. I guess that's how I should start.

I've lived in Red Valley my whole life. I've left a few times, but it never stuck. Gravity always pulled me back here. After my mom was gone and I took over as the Liar, it wasn't so bad a place, I guess. People hated me because

I knew their secrets, but they paid me, and money sure is easier to spend than respect. So I stayed. Never had many friends, never needed them. Never wanted to have kids. Yet here we are.

Mostly the Liar is asked to tell little Lies that really don't matter much. The pettiest little shit. You'll see. But that's not why the Liar exists, why the King gave us this power. He created us to tell big Lies. His big Lies. You'll find some in the older ledgers. I've left them with Brian. If I've done this Lie right, you'll remember him and know where to find him. He's mostly useless and mostly harmless.

But there's also a big Lie in my ledger. A very stupid Lie.

My life was mostly unremarkable, or what passes for it in this town. I did what I wanted, when I wanted. I told the Lies Red Valley wanted, and otherwise was left alone. And then my life started to unravel. First, what I thought was just the aches and pains of growing old was diagnosed as lymphoma. Then, one of the King's Men came to see me. The King wanted an audience. Immediately.

I knew the King's secret already. He was dying. The very first Liar did her best to cover it up to keep all the other nasty monsters from coming to settle scores with the King. But in the end, it was just a Lie and a Lie can't stop what's coming

I stood before the King and he told me as much. He told me that he'd been dying for a long time, but now he was out of strength. He felt the end was close. Having recently been given grim news about my own mortality, I empathized, as much as one can with an unknowable monstrous being lurking in a cavern two doors down from

Hell itself. But even with his final breaths, his thoughts were about the people of Red Valley. If he died, he feared what would become of the town. All the evil he'd been holding back all these decades would flood over us. Fear of the King was the only thing keeping us safe.

So he asked me for another big Lie. To keep Red Valley safe, the world had to believe the King still lived. It was the only way. So I wrote the words, and he offered a drop of his own blood. And then he died, right in front of me. And then he was suddenly reborn. He was still weak, still wounded, but he was alive. The thing standing before me wasn't real, wasn't really real, but it was real enough. I'd saved the town. That's what the Liar was for.

I remember going back home to my empty house, feeling both elated and depressed. I'd done a good thing. But with the King now sustained by the Lie, did Red Valley still need a Liar? And even if the answer was yes, who would that be when I was gone?

It took me too long to figure out the truth. I pride myself on smelling bullshit when it is piled up at my feet, but maybe it is harder to tell when it's the King doing the shoveling. Or maybe it was the chemo. Either way, I made a dumb mistake and I trusted what the King told me.

Shortly after my big Lie, Red Valley started to change. It withered. We'd had drought before, but nothing like this. It was like the light was being drained from the sky. Some people in town didn't notice it, but some people did. Special people, people with gifts and talents like mine. Some felt their own power slipping away, bit by bit, a little more each day. But where was it all going? And why?

Then it wasn't just our powers. People got sick. People died. I know people always get sick, always die, but not like this. Retirement homes started emptying out. We had six people kill themselves in a single week. The whole town was getting drained: drained of power, of life, of the will to live.

When my chemo-addled brain finally put the pieces together, I demanded another audience with the King. It only took a glance to confirm my suspicions. He was stronger now. More real. Because he was draining life from the very land under our feet. Just like he'd always done. You see, we're taught that Red Valley is full of magic because the King is here, but that's bullshit. The King is here because Red Valley is full of magic. He needed it to recover his wounds, and it sustained him for hundreds or maybe thousands of years. But it wasn't enough, so he pulled more power from the land and made a failsafe: the Liar.

He was dead. I'd watched him die. But in his place now was a Lie that seemed as real as anything, and once he stole the rest of the power in Red Valley, he'd be real enough. And then maybe he could start settling old scores himself.

The King needed Red Valley's power, but it wasn't all in the land anymore. People are born here, live their whole lives here, die here. A lifetime of exposure to Red Valley changes you, fills you up. So the King needed that too. He didn't care if it left people as empty husks. He needed it to survive, to revive. So he took it.

That same day I figured out what was really going on, the doctors gave me a few months to get my affairs in order. I was alone and I was dying.

I'd like to use that as my excuse. Seems like a pretty good one. Hard to argue with Stage 4. But that wasn't it. Even if I'd been completely healthy, I still would have done the same thing: nothing.

Because, Sadie, I'm sad to say, your mom is a fucking coward.

I did try to think of a way out. I lost a night of sleep to it. But I came up with nothing. Once told, Lies can't be recalled. So instead I did the one thing I could think of: I got drunk. Real drunk. Stayed that way a while. I never felt good, but at least there were times I didn't feel anything. But then somewhere in that haze of booze and regret, I had an idea. A really stupid, insane idea.

I was about to die, just like the King. So why not take a page from his playbook? I didn't need to create a Lie version of myself. I'd already proven I didn't know how to stop him. But what if there was someone else who could take a shot? Someone younger, smarter, better. Someone who had everything good about me in her, and hopefully a lot more. A daughter.

A Lie like that comes at a big price. I know once my blood goes in my ledger, my body ain't going to last much longer. I'm prepared for that. I'll write the Lie today, sitting in the chapel at the hospital. When the Liar's Price is taken, the cancer will have free rein. My time will be over. Yours will just be starting. Someone could probably say something poetic about that, but not me. The only remarkable thing I ever did was to unleash a version of the King desperate to devour everything good in this town.

And maybe you.

When I think about you, I picture you as strong. Independent. And stubborn as hell. You'll know the people in town don't like you, but it won't bother you. Much.

If you're anything like me, you're going to piss some people off, but that's okay. Some people have earned it. There's only so much I can change with a single Lie, but I've thought of some friends for you. I think they might be useful. Maybe you can make some of your own once you're here. I was never much good at that myself. Maybe if I'd had more people in my life, I wouldn't be sitting here alone, full of regret. Maybe you'll have a better shot.

I used to wonder about how the Lies worked. What are they? Like, are they just really good illusions, or are they real? I don't wonder about that anymore. Real or not, the Lies work. Doesn't matter if they're real, they're real enough. You just have to look at Red Valley getting sucked dry to see that. So I guess that's what I'm hoping for you. That you're real enough to change this.

If you think this is unfair, then good—that means you've been paying attention. I created a monster and then created you to deal with it when I failed. I have no idea what you might be thinking right now. You probably hate me. That seems a reasonable response. You just found out that your whole life isn't real, and now your lying mom is asking for a favor. I'd tell me to go to hell, and I'd be disappointed if you're any nicer. So yeah, feel free to hate me, but there's still a job to do. Red Valley doesn't have much left to give.

So, Sadie, what are you going to do about it?

CHAPTER TWENTY-SEVEN

SADIE STAYED IN the park a long time. Families came and went. Birds landed in the blighted trees only to flutter away. The smoky sun rose hot overhead, and her shade gradually vanished. Sweat traced slow lines down her spine.

She'd come here with her mom. She'd played on the slide and hung from the monkey bars. Her mom had pushed her on the swings, then taught her to swing herself by pumping her legs. They had sat on the grass and eaten popsicles until the melting juice ran down their knuckles.

These were good memories, happy memories.

Fake memories.

She'd never run through the sprinklers or raced along the playground or rolled down that hill with Graciela. Sadie had never actually been to this park. She hadn't even *existed* before a few days ago, when Emma Logan, the Liar of Red Valley, had sealed one final Lie in her ledger.

Sadie looked down at her hands. They looked real. She picked up her mom's notes. She could hold them in her fake fingers. She remembered asking her mom once about the Lies she told, if they were just illusions. *Perception is reality*, her mom had said. Only, she hadn't really, or at least not to Sadie. But maybe it was true. Maybe it didn't matter what was real, only what seemed real. It certainly didn't seem to matter to Red Valley that the King was a Lie; the town was bleeding dry either way.

And so what? What did it matter if Red Valley was drained of all its magic? What did she care? She didn't know these people; they certainly didn't know her. Who cared if the King was about to cheat death at the expense of Red Valley?

But even through the pain and confusion and grief, Sadie knew she could never let that happen. She didn't have many friends, and the people in this town tolerated her to the extent that she was useful. Yet she was connected to this place, more so even than her mom or grandmother. Red Valley's magic was in them, though they'd believed it had come from the King. But Sadie *was* that magic. She was Red Valley. And if the King took that all away, there'd be nothing left of her.

She left the park and walked along mostly empty streets. Cars drove past from time to time, but she ignored them. She didn't know where she was going or why, but just let her feet carry her. She turned onto unfamiliar roads, because that was less jarring than recognizing things she now knew she'd never seen before.

Well, Mom, Sadie thought. *If I can call you that. Emma, maybe. I was mad at you for dying without saying goodbye.*

I guess I should have been mad at you for dying before saying hello. Sadie remembered the blood on her mom's fingers as she lay in the hospital bed. She hadn't thought much of it then. Now she knew. She'd sealed her ledger with that blood, and her fate. *I'm sorry you were alone, Emma. Before, and at the end. I'm sorry this town used you up. I'm sorry you had to give up the last of yourself to make me. I'm sorry that seemed like the only way.*

Even knowing the truth, Sadie really didn't feel any different. She still remembered the good times and the bad times. She remembered dozing in her desk in high school history classes and drinking beers with Graciela in her backyard after her parents had gone to sleep. She remembered her mom grounding her, and screaming at her, and teaching her how to ride a bike. Maybe these things happened, maybe not. But they felt real. They felt *real*.

She stopped walking. She knew the neighborhood she was in now, knew it very well. Graciela's house was just two blocks over. But as familiar as it was, it looked very different now, cast in red-black haze. Over the tops of the houses, an endless wall of smoke blotted out the sun and sky. Caution tape had been drawn across the road. Sheriff cars were parked, blocking the way, their cabins empty but their lights flashing. Signs had been posted on the street lights. Sadie pulled one free and read.

MANDATORY EVACUATION NOTICE.
ALL RESIDENTS MUST LEAVE THEIR HOMES IMMEDIATELY.
SHELTER IS AVAILABLE AT THE RED VALLEY COMMUNITY CENTER.
DO NOT RETURN TO YOUR HOMES.
IT IS NOT SAFE.

Even though it wasn't yet dark, Sadie could see the flames up ahead. While Sadie had been lost in thought and overwhelmed by what she'd read, Red Valley was burning. The final line of her mom's note came back to her and she turned the words over and over in her thoughts:

So, Sadie, what are you going to do about it?

THE RED VALLEY Community Center was packed. Cars overflowed the big parking lot and lined the streets, double parked in places when no more would fit. More cars were arriving all the time. A young sheriff's deputy in an orange vest directed traffic. There were fire trucks and ambulances, and more than a few sheriff's department cars. Ash dusted them all. More signs directed evacuees toward the large white building at the heart of the chaos. Sadie had been in a school play that had been held here once. Oh wait. No, no she hadn't.

She pushed her way through the crowd. She saw some people crying, some smeared with soot. A little girl kept telling her parents she wanted to go home; the look in the parents' eyes told Sadie they had no home to go back to. She knew the feeling.

Inside, the floor was covered in rows of foldable cots. Most were occupied by blank-faced people staring off into nothing. Some held a memento grabbed in haste: a picture frame, a photo book, an old stuffed animal. Something that anchored them to the life they thought they had, before the fire came. Sadie was jealous.

A television had been wheeled in and was playing Red

Valley's only local news. A reporter stood in front of an inferno. All around him were the blackened remains of homes and cars, some still burning.

"...say they've never seen a fire quite like this one, Jim," the reporter was saying.

"Where is the fire now?" asked the anchor back in the studio.

"It came down from the north, but as you can see on this map, it is now driving straight into town, and nothing seems to be able to slow it down. It really does seem to have a mind of its own."

The camera panned over and Sadie's heart skipped a beat. The building was mostly gone, half of it collapsed inward, the remaining half blackened and smoldering. The tree's limbs still reached high, but the branches were curled over, twisted, charred. The only thing left was the sign over the scorched front door: *Treehouse Diner*.

"Any reports of injuries?"

"Sadly, yes," the reporter said. Everything behind him looked like a glimpse into hell. "A number of evacuees and even some firefighters have been admitted to St. Elizabeth's due to smoke inhalation, and there is a growing count of missing persons. It might be weeks before we know the full scale of the damage here, Jim."

"Stay safe out there," the anchor said as the camera switched back to him. "Cal Fire is calling for reinforcements from all over the state to join the battle, but for those who've already lost their homes, it might be too little, too late."

Sadie found Graciela and her family tucked in the corner under one of the basketball hoops. Javier was there; he noticed Sadie first, then nudged Graciela, who ran over and lifted Sadie off the ground in a hug.

"I thought you were dead," Graciela said. "I *knew* you were dead."

"Still alive," Sadie said. "For now."

Graciela held her out at arm's length. Tears had reddened her eyes. "Don't you *ever* do that to me again. When we saw on the news where the fire had started, and then I couldn't reach you…"

"Like you said, my life is a bit shit right now." Sadie laughed a little, before a sob caught in her throat. She turned her face away as the weight of the last few days threatened to crush her. The memories may not be real, but the pain of what she'd lost was.

"Oh, chica," Graciela said.

"I'm okay," she said, sniffing, grateful that her friend didn't call out the obvious lie. Sadie nodded to Graciela's family nearby. "Everybody get out?"

"Yeah," Graciela said. "I don't think it's even reached our house yet, but all of sudden we got cops banging on our door, saying everyone has to leave. It was crazy."

Sadie scanned the nearby cots until she saw Beto. He was sitting up, his back to her. Teresa sat next to him, her head on his tattooed shoulder.

"Did they tell you how long you were going to be here?" Sadie asked.

"They didn't tell us shit," Graciela said. "Just gave us some water bottles and told us to find somewhere to camp out."

"Have you heard from Ashleigh?"

Graciela went a little stiff. "They got evacuated before

us. Haven't found her yet, though. Maybe they went to a different shelter."

"I'm sure she's fine."

"Yeah."

There was a loud screeching noise from the front of the room. There was a stage there, the one Sadie had apparently not performed *The Wizard of Oz* on. It had been mostly empty when she'd walked in, but now someone was setting up a microphone and blasting half the town with audio feedback. The technician scurried away from the heat of five hundred glares. A moment later, Undersheriff Hassler walked up to the mic.

"Hello everyone," he said. His voice boomed and he backed off the mic a little. "I'm sorry to disturb you, but we have a few announcements and then you can get back to your day." A few angry murmurs in the crowd reminded everyone that there wasn't much to get back to. "We've gotten word from the Fire Department that the fire is still at zero-percent containment." More angry words, louder this time. "They are doing all they can to save as many homes as possible, but the fire seems to be moving even faster now that it is in the structures. The mandatory evacuation order remains in effect and we expect the number of homes to be evacuated to grow overnight."

Someone in the crowd called out, "Got any *good* news?"

The undersheriff ignored it. "And that brings me to my second announcement. We are issuing a sundown to sunup curfew until further notice."

Now the crowd started to turn. Murmurs became shouts. The undersheriff stood silently for a few minutes while they vented their anger at him, before demanding silence again with his amplified voice and hard stare.

"I shouldn't have to tell you all what happened last night," he said. "People died. Those things from the other side of the River... well, you saw 'em. You know what they're capable of. We have no reason to doubt that once the sun goes down, they'll be out again. We've got patrols out on every street and watching the bridge—"

A big man with a thick gut and thinning hair thrust a finger at the undersheriff. "Your patrols don't do shit. I saw it. The only thing that kept us all from getting eaten last night were the King's Men."

Hassler's face darkened. "We're doing the best—"

"Well it ain't good enough!"

"We appreciate the support the King's Men have provided," Hassler said. "But there are only so many of them and we've got a lot of ground to cover. That's why we need everyone to stay inside, where it's safe."

Another man stood up. "Give me a break. We're not safe. What would happen if just one bear-killer got loose in here? It would be a bloodbath."

A few women gasped. A kid started crying.

"I need everyone to remain calm," the undersheriff said. He sounded right on the edge of losing his own calm.

The crowd did not heed his advice.

"Remain calm? Our houses are burning and monsters are running amok down Main Street!"

"You're supposed to protect us!"

"Just get out of the King's way. He'll keep us safe."

"The whole town's going to hell out there. What are you going to do about it?"

Sadie looked down and discovered she was moving. All around her, the people of Red Valley wallowed in fear and panic. She saw tears. She saw faces hardened by anger or terror or the effort to remain strong for those around them. The shouting voices all merged into one. She heard it, and though no words could really be discerned, she knew what it was saying. What it was asking for:

Hope.

She climbed the steps to the stage. A few people started to notice her. They pointed, raised eyebrows, whispered questions she couldn't hear. Some of the anger died away, replaced with confusion. She was halfway across the stage before Hassler saw her. His brow knitted as she approached. His mustache twitched and he moved away from the microphone to intercept her.

"What are you doing?" he growled at her in a low voice.

"You had your chance," she said. "Now I'm going to talk to them."

"This isn't the time for games."

"Good thing I'm not here to play any," she replied. "Oh, and thanks for the tip, by the way. Didn't get killed *and* I got my bag back."

He stared at her, but she just walked on by. He could have stopped her, of course; probably should have. But Hassler didn't know what to say to these people. He'd tried and failed and they'd turned on him, just like the King wanted. He needed his people to rely on him, to wait for him. The King needed them docile, passive, ready for harvest.

"Hello everyone," she said into the mic. The room fell instantly silent. Everyone was listening now. She felt the weight of every pair of eyes. "Most of you don't know me. In fact, I wonder if any of you even know my name. It's Sadie." She stared back at them; they said nothing. "But some of you know *what* I am. What I can do. I haven't been here long, but I've already told Lies for some of you. My mom told Lies for many more. My family has been telling your Lies for as long as there's been a Red Valley.

"But I'm not up here today to lie to you. I'm here to tell you the truth, a truth you may not want to hear: the King of Red Valley isn't going to save you."

The evacuees rustled on their canvas cots, but didn't interrupt.

How much to tell them? What were they ready to hear? "I've been to the King's home," she went on. "I've seen him, spoken to him. He is dying."

One of the men who'd exchanged angry words with the undersheriff piped up then, demanding, "Why should we believe you?"

"I don't care if you believe me," Sadie replied. "But he *is* dying. That's why all these things are here now, attacking us. They sense the King is vulnerable, and so they're going to try to take him down. We're just collateral damage."

Someone else spoke. "Last night, I saw the King's Men fighting for us."

"I've seen them too," Sadie said. "But they're not fighting for us. They're fighting for *him*." Over the people's heads, she saw the television, full of more images of smoke and fire consuming the town. "Red Valley is in real danger, but if we want to keep it safe, we're going to have to do it ourselves."

"How are we supposed to stop that fire?"

"And those monsters? If the King can't stop them, how can we?"

The Liar of Red Valley got all the credit, but it was really the King who'd told the best lie in town. By convincing everyone that what little power they possessed had come from him, he'd ensured they'd never doubt him, never challenge him. They were nothing without him, after all. But now Sadie wondered what they all could have been if he'd never come to Red Valley. So much potential wasted keeping an old monster alive.

"People in this town don't like to talk about it, but we're stronger than we look," Sadie said. "There's magic in Red Valley, and in the people of Red Valley. We've got a house that just disappears, and then poof, comes back. That clock tower on Main Street tells perfect time, with no weight and no spring; it just works, and nobody knows why and nobody questions it. A few days ago, a brujo helped me speak to the very first Liar of Red Valley, dead for over a hundred years. This town is *full* of it. We just hide it, because your pastors tell you it is ungodly and your leaders tell you it isn't safe. But I'm up here to tell you that the *world* isn't safe, and if you expect the King or the sheriffs or God to save you, you're going to be disappointed. The only way to protect the ones you love is if you stand up and become your own saviors."

She saw some nods in the crowd, but the angry man with the bulbous gut wasn't convinced. "You want us to go out there and get killed? That's what'll happen. I don't care if someone can shoot lasers out of their eyeballs, if they go fight those things, people are going to die."

"Yeah," Sadie said. The room fell still again. "I know.

My mom died a few days ago. I've seen more death since. It's senseless and permanent and horrible. I don't have any easy answers, trust me. I just know that if we wait for the King to save us from all the hell that he's brought down on us, we're all going to die, even if the King wins. There's only one way out for us, and that's together."

The crowd's voices started up again. Only now they seemed to ignore Sadie, and instead turned inward. Arguments broke out all across the room: some believed her, some didn't, some just wanted to be left alone. There was no great surge of support, and she wasn't carried out of the hall on anyone's shoulders. But she didn't care. She couldn't make them see, even with her ledger. If they wanted to take control of their own destiny for the first time since Red Valley had been founded, that would be up to them, not her.

She heard footsteps on the stage. She turned, ready to tell Hassler to go to hell, but it wasn't the undersheriff. It was Beto. He came up to her, limping.

"Nice speech, gringa," he said.

"Beto, I'm so sorry—"

He held up a hand. "You asked me for help, I gave it." His eyes slid over to Hassler, who stood nearby with his thumbs hooked in his belt. "I don't blame you for the sins of that son of a bitch."

"I didn't mean for anyone to get hurt."

He shrugged. "Like you said, there ain't easy answers, not in this life." He jerked his chin toward the crowd. "Let me give it a shot. White people in this town love being told what to do by a respectable brown-skinned man like myself."

Beto tapped the mic until the voices died down. "Hola," he said. "Some of you know me, some of you don't, whatever. Some of you have already decided you hate me after one look. That's your choice. I don't like some of you either.

"But I like this town."

Sadie thought Hassler might make a move, but she caught his eye and he just glared back.

"Sure, it's a bit racist," Beto said. "And poor. These days it's mostly just a few neighborhoods supporting a Walmart." That drew a muted laugh. "But I've lived here my whole life. Most of you have too. We could go somewhere else, but we don't. Because there is something special here. There's a real community. People look out for each other. When my mom got sick a few years back, a whole army of people brought my family casseroles, whatever the fuck a casserole is. You white people really love your casserole.

"But there's more than that."

He held up his hand. After a moment's concentration, blue light began to crackle off his fingertips. The crowd gasped. Hassler's hands went from his belt to his sidearm.

"I'm a brujo," Beto said proudly. "I can do some things. This Liar gringa up here can change your past, just by writing in a little book. I know a guy, real nice guy called Twenty-Twenty, lives down by the River. He's got these tarot cards and shit, can tell the future. Not some cheap trick, like real prophecy." He dismissed the light with a snap. "Some of you got some magic in you, too. Got it by living here, in this weird little town. We hide it, so the sheriffs don't get upset, but it's there."

Sadie watched the crowd. Even those who had frowned when Beto took the mic were listening now.

"I like it here," Beto said. "It's the kind of town I want to raise my kids in. And if I've got to go out there and do the things I can do to protect it, then maybe that's a fair trade. That's all I've got to say."

He went down the stairs to rejoin Teresa and his family. There was nothing left to be said. Either the people would fight or they wouldn't. Either they'd die or make it through. She'd done what she could. As Sadie started to make her way off the stage, Hassler caught her arm.

"People are going to get hurt," he said, so that only she could hear. He was facing toward the crowd so he kept his demeanor pleasant, with a smile turning up the edges of his mustache, but Sadie's arm twinged in his iron grip.

"You'd know all about that, wouldn't you?"

"So you *do* remember what happened the last time you defied me," he said. "Good. Remember also that in the end, I got what I wanted, one way or the other."

"And that's how we got in this mess to begin with."

"The King got us into this mess. I'm going to get us out of it."

Sadie shook her head. "After everything, you still think you can protect this town? No, of course, it isn't really about protection. You've probably convinced yourself that it is. You'd make a good Liar. No, what you want is *control*, and you just can't imagine a world where you are so in over your head."

The grip tightened. "You're a fool," he growled. "And you're dangerous."

Sadie looked back over her shoulder at the crowd.

Most were talking amongst themselves, debating what Sadie and Beto had said. But some were watching the undersheriff closely. "Unless you're going to arrest me in front of these fine people, let go of my arm, Mr. Hassler."

His eyes flicked to the crowd then back to her. After a pause, he released her. "I am going to protect Red Valley. I am going to clean up the King's mess. If you get in my way, you'll wish I *had* arrested you."

He stomped down the stairs and into the crowd. As she watched him go, something caught her eye. Someone had just slipped out of the community center. Sadie only got a brief glimpse before the door shut completely, so she couldn't be sure, but she thought she saw the flash of sunlight off mirrored sunglasses.

CHAPTER TWENTY-EIGHT

THEY DIDN'T HAVE long before dark, and there was still way too much to do. Graciela offered to drive. There were two other evacuation centers nearby. They weren't as full as the community center, but more and more people were arriving all the time; by late afternoon, nearly half of Red Valley had been evacuated as the fire pushed deeper into town.

Sadie spoke at each center in turn. She said mostly the same things to mostly the same reaction. She didn't wait around to see how convincing she'd been. Either the people would fight or not.

Then they drove to the bridge. Already the sheriffs were erecting barricades, but they hadn't closed the road down yet.

"Are you sure you want to drive over there?" Graciela asked.

"I don't want to do *any* of this," Sadie said. "But nobody else is going to."

The far side of the River appeared unchanged. No blood in the streets, no fires burning in gutted buildings.

"I wanted to say I'm sorry," Sadie said.

"Shut up," Graciela said. "*I'm* sorry. After everything you've been through, I drop that bomb on you about moving away. I was such a jerk."

"And I've been so wrapped up in all this mess, I was only thinking about myself." She'd been so angry that Graciela was going to have a life without her, but now she knew Graciela had lived her entire *life* without her, until a few days before, when her mom wrote a Lie in her ledger.

"Fine, we were both jerks," Graciela said. "I just don't want to fight anymore, and I don't want to lose you, whatever town we're living in."

"I certainly can't blame you for wanting to leave Red Valley now."

"Seriously, chica. This place *sucks*."

"Do you remember the day we met?" Sadie asked. She tried not to picture dark eyes watching them as they drove through town.

"We were just little babies back then," Graciela said.

"So you don't remember?"

"Huh," she said. "I guess not."

Sadie didn't either. She knew Graciela was her friend, just like she knew her favorite drink and least favorite movie. But the rest of the details were hazy, unformed. Her mom hadn't considered everything when crafting her Lie. The broad strokes were there and that had felt like enough. Before she knew.

"Why do you think we're still friends, after all this time?" Sadie asked.

"You getting all introspective on me? Just because the world is ending?"

"Just questioning some assumptions, I guess."

Graciela thought about that for a while. Sadie didn't like the silence and she didn't like being on this side of the River.

But then Graciela replied, "You know my memory is shit.

"So you start asking me about when we met, why we're friends, and I don't *know*, but I don't really *need* to know. We've been through a lot together, but this"—she waved her hand to take in the entirety of their current adventure—"this is why we're friends. Because we trust each other and do really stupid things together."

"And that's enough?"

"It is for me."

Sadie had no real past, no real memories to share with her only friend. Except for the ones they'd made in the last week: the bar, the diner, the library, even the crossroads. Those were real. Or real enough.

The parking lot at Tips was fuller than last time. That was either a really good sign, or a really bad one. Graciela unbuckled her seatbelt.

"You don't have to go inside," Sadie said.

"Like hell I don't," was the reply.

The same bartender stood behind the counter. Many of the same patrons sat across the bar.

"Don't think this is a good time to be looking for a drink on the wrong side of the River," the bartender said when they walked in.

"Don't want a drink," Sadie said. "I want help."

She grabbed a heavy mug and pounded it on the bar. Voices stopped. Eyes—feral and predatory—turned her way.

"I don't have a lot of time, so I'm going to make this quick," she said, once she had their attention. "Some of you are here because you hate the King and think you've got a shot. Some of you are here because there's something about Red Valley that draws people—and other things, things that look like people but aren't. But all of you are here in this bar because you like it. The beer is cold, the place don't stink, and the game is on." She pointed back toward town. "But there are others who've come here to burn it all down, and they aren't going to stop on that side of the River. If you want this place to be standing come sunrise, then we need your help."

A huge shape stood up. Sadie recognized it as the guy who'd cracked a mug over the other guy's skull the last time she was stupid enough to come here.

"The hunter in the darkness has come, singing a song of fire and blood," the big man said. "And the King sends you to beg for our help."

"The King didn't send me," Sadie said. "The King really *is* dying, and even if he weren't, he's only taking care of himself. I'm not asking anyone to help protect the King. I'm asking for help to protect Red Valley."

"The hunter's call has driven many of them mad. They are going to tear your town apart."

"They are going to try," she said. "I'm hoping some of us will stop them. And it's your town too."

She let them all stare blankly at her as she made her way to the back of the bar, down a dim hallway, to a door that was very out of place. She knocked, then went inside. The room was the same as before: too big, barely lit, oddly cold. The same strange, human-shaped shadows sat at the table on the far side of the room, waiting silently, like they'd been expecting her.

"You remember me?" she asked.

"*We do*," said the Long Shadows. "*Vividly. Tales of your exploits continue to amuse us.*"

"I'm thrilled," she said. "Now, how would you like the Liar of Red Valley to owe you a debt?"

THERE WAS ONE last stop they needed to make. Sadie eyed the setting sun outside the car window. They should have just enough time.

Graciela put the car into park. "Look, chica—Sadie. I know what we just did was crazy, and I know everything you are doing today is crazy, but this... this is..."

"Crazy?"

"Exactly."

Sadie stared out at the River. It looked less terrifying in the daylight, and from dry land. "We need help."

"We need a miracle."

"That too."

"I used up all my courage back at that bar," Graciela said. "I'm going to stay dry for this one."

"I don't blame you." Sadie smiled at her friend, then swung her door open. "Be right back."

The ground leading up to the River's edge was soft. Sadie's feet sunk in as she approached; it felt a little too much like she was getting pulled down.

But this time, she came of her own free will. And she came bearing gifts. She waded into the water until it was up to her ankles. It was shockingly cold on her skin, like the touch of death.

"Hello again," she said out over the water.

A distant, musical voice drifted back. *Few of your kind ever enter our currents twice.*

"I'm special."

Yes, said the echoing voice. *Perhaps we should take you, then, as a worthy offering. We are owed far more, but it would be a start.*

"Before you do, I've got an offer for you," Sadie said. "And another secret you're going to want to hear."

THE SUN DIPPED below the mountains. The hunter spread its wings. It could taste blood on the night air. Below, its thralls stirred to life, eager, hungry. Yes, this would be a glorious hunt indeed.

They had tested the enemy's strength the night before. The people in the town had put up minimal resistance, as expected. The King's creatures had been more difficult, but not terribly so. A number of the hunter's thralls had fallen in the battle, but they were expendable. The hunter had killed two of the King's minions itself, felt the King's blood drip from its claws. Tonight, it would kill more of them. Perhaps all of them.

As the hunter took to the air and surveyed the lines of battle, it saw that its rivals had not been idle. Those who waited behind the flames had pushed deep into the town. Ruin and ash had been left in their wake. The hunter had no wish to do battle with them, if it could be avoided. Its careful eyes measured the lands surrounding the King's town. It could not see them, but it felt others drawing near. Others who hated the King, and others that the hunter wished to avoid. Tonight, then. It had to be tonight.

It landed on the roof of a building near the bridge. On the far side, it saw flashing lights and barricades. Humans milled about. It could smell their fear even from here. But they did not flee. And there were more than the previous night. They would defend themselves.

It would not matter. They would wipe them all away.

The darkness grew. Soon. Very soon.

SADIE STOOD NEAR the bridge. It was hard to see what was happening on the far side, but what she could make out chilled the blood in her veins, despite the lingering summer heat. *Things* were gathering. Some still looked human. Most did not. Some were small and darted around, too fast to make out. Others were huge as trucks.

"You sure about this?" It was Beto. He joined her and stared across the River.

"Nope."

"Fair enough." He crossed his wiry, tattooed arms across his chest. "You know, my buddy Twenty-Twenty thinks we're all going to die tonight."

"That's not an encouraging prophecy," Sadie said.

Beto shrugged. "I wouldn't worry about it. He's mostly full of shit."

"But didn't you tell everybody he could see the future?"

"Yeah, well, maybe I was exaggerating to make a point," he said with a grin. He pointed back over his shoulder with a thumb. "And it worked, right?"

Sadie couldn't argue with that. Dozens of people had arrived at the bridge. Some had gifts, from living in Red Valley so long. Others just didn't want to stay idly by while their town was under siege. The sheriffs had tried to turn them all away at first, but they kept coming. And so did the things across the River.

"Thanks for that," she said. "I don't think they would have listened just to me."

Beto nodded, but didn't say anything. He was staring out at the bridge. Eventually, he nodded toward it. "That's where they arrested me. Right there, on the bridge."

Sadie winced at the edge in his voice. "Hassler told me."

"Of course he did," Beto said, spitting. "Did he tell you what they got me for?"

"He said you were selling drugs, and then something went wrong."

Beto laughed without joy. "A lot of things went wrong, but I wasn't selling drugs. They thought I was, because I was going over the River all the time. A guy like me, obviously up to no good. But I was just going to see Teresa. Then one day some deal went bad, somebody gets stabbed, so the sheriffs round up the nearest brown suspect they can find. Case closed."

"I'm sorry," Sadie said.

"Me too," he said. "Real sorry. A year and a half of my life gone, just like that. Sheriffs didn't want to hear how they'd gotten it wrong. Judge didn't want to hear it, either. Took one look at me and made up their minds. I heard later it was one of those fucking Laughing Boys who did it. Pendejos."

Sadie glanced north. The smoke was like a living mountain, churning slowly as it blotted out the sky. The flames were getting closer. She could see the red glow above the buildings and trees. *One problem at a time*, she thought.

"So," she said carefully, "why—?"

"Why am I here, fighting for this town that threw me away?" He stuck out his chin toward the sheriff deputies huddled around their squad cars. "They already tried to make me leave once. I'm not leaving again. They aren't Red Valley. We are."

A woman in her sixties with long graying hair came over to where Sadie and Beto stood. She had on a flowing white dress tied at the waist with a gold cord. Countless bracelets jangled on her wrists, and a cluster of crystals of various colors on various chains swung against her chest. In her strange dress, it took Sadie a moment to recognize her as the librarian from the County Library.

"In all my years of living in this closed-minded town, I never expected to be standing alongside the sheriffs in its defense," she said.

"Tell me about it, lady," Beto said.

She held out a bony hand. "My name is Deborah. Nice to see you again. My sisters and I thought we could offer some assistance." She motioned to a group of similarly dressed women sitting crossed-legged in a circle nearby.

"We're going to need all the help we can get," Sadie said, taking her hand.

"It seems you have inspired quite an uprising, young lady."

"I reminded people that we've got to fight for what we want to keep."

"My sisters and I are not fighters," Deborah said. "But we are students of the flow of certain natural energies present here in Red Valley, and we think we can maybe delay those... things for you, a little bit."

"For how long?" Sadie asked.

"That depends on how many of them there are," Deborah said. "And how persistent."

"That's fair," Sadie said. "But I think I can use you."

When they had finished discussing their strategies, Deborah returned to her sisters. Beto left her alone so he could prepare his own gifts for the coming assault. Sadie stood, surrounded but alone, and faced the far side of the River.

I doubt you had this in mind when you brought me into this world, Mom, Sadie thought. Though it was weird to think of Emma as her mother when they'd never truly met, she couldn't think of her any other way. *But things have gotten a little complicated. You wanted me to fix one mess, but frankly it's going to have to get in line.*

She pulled out her ledger. She could just write *Then all the monsters on the other side of the River decided to be cool and go home* and seal it with her blood. Maybe that's all it would take. Could a Lie work that way? And what would the Liar's Price be for such a Lie? Probably more than she could afford.

The sun slipped away. Though the air was still plenty hot, Sadie felt a chill. Across the bridge, perched on a sign proclaiming unleaded gas at $4.09 per gallon, a huge black thing spread its massive wings. A roar built of a hundred monstrous voices erupted.

Alright, Sadie thought. *Let's do this.*

CHAPTER TWENTY-NINE

THE HUNTER SENT the weak in first. This was not its first battle, not its first siege. Strategy would likely not be required against such an unworthy foe, but still there was no call to tempt fate. This night would be bloody and glorious; it would take no risks. The King was going to die, and his people with him.

THREE BEAR-KILLERS BOUNDED across the bridge. Sadie saw them coming and quickly ducked behind the concrete barriers the sheriffs had erected. She remembered too well how much damage just *one* of those things had done outside the library, and had no interest in facing them again.

The night suddenly filled with noise as the deputies opened fire. The bullets sparked all around the monsters as they closed. Some found their targets in brief sprays of black ichor. But still they came.

Then Beto was there. His eyes were already shimmering with power.

"Remember," Sadie said. "You don't have to kill them."

Beto nodded. "Just knock them off the bridge and let the River do the rest."

"Right."

"I hope this goes better than last time I helped you," he said. "I'm okay with not looking into the land of the dead again for a while."

"We're doing this for Teresa," Sadie said. "And your baby."

"I know why *I'm* doing this," Beto said. "You still owe me that Lie."

And then the bear-killers were on them.

The closest deputies screamed as jagged teeth sank into them. A shotgun went off and tore a chunk out of one of the horrors, but the thing barely noticed. Claws flashed in the streetlamp light and another man fell.

Then Beto was humming, his hands pressed palm down into the road. Maybe this wasn't a true crossroads, but choosing whether or not to cross the River out of Red Valley was close enough. There was power here—and spirits, maybe, too. Hopefully enough. Sadie moved back as the muscles on his arms began to quiver. One of the bear-killers noticed them and scrambled up over the barricades toward them. Its jaws opened and snapped shut.

And then unseen hands lifted it into the air. It thrashed, but the grip tightened. Sadie could see tendons in Beto's neck bulge with the strain, but the bear-killer was held fast. A moment later, it was soaring above the barricades and the parked sheriff's department cars. It didn't quite clear the bridge, smashing into the barrier instead, but then it bounced off the concrete and down into the black water. There was a splash and a cry of pain, and then nothing.

More shotgun bursts exploded as deputies and people of Red Valley converged on the remaining bear-killers. One finally collapsed and lay still. The other yelped and retreated back over the bridge.

Fire was pumping in Sadie's blood now. *Is that all you got? I thought you were supposed to be scary.*

"Something's wrong, gringa," Beto said. Sweat was running down his face and staining his shirt. His skin was ashen.

"What do you mean? That was incredible."

"It was too hard," he said, shaking his head. He stumbled a little, caught himself on the barrier. "The spirits are there, but I can barely reach them. I feel like I'm bleeding out, here."

The King, Sadie thought. That's why the King's Men weren't here. The King was too busy draining Red Valley of its magic, before his enemies got too close. They didn't have much time.

Then more of the things on the far side of the River began to move.

THE HUNTER HAD not expected the initial assault to finish them off. Even the weakest defender could fight from a position of strength. But they hadn't just used mankind's crude weapons of war. They had used magic. And it was not the King's magic. This was something else. Something unexpected.

But the hunter had other forces at its disposal. And not all were on this side of the River.

Perhaps this would be a worthy hunt after all.

THE THINGS CAME in a wave. Some looked human, but shed that skin as soon as they crossed the King's Peace. There were so many that it was hard to distinguish them one from the other. It was a wave, a flood of teeth and claws and hate.

Bullets and shot tore into them. Some fell. More came over them.

Beto knocked a few aside. The River splashed hungrily. But the flood barely slowed.

If all of that *gets into Red Valley...* Sadie didn't let herself finish that thought. They'd stop them here. There were no other options.

The deputies ran. Some of them slipped and stumbled— on the blood or ichor, or the bodies of the fallen—and didn't get away fast enough. She'd tried to warn them not to be so far out onto the bridge, but they hadn't been all that interested in tactical advice from some girl. Their screams bit into Sadie's ears.

But just before the first thing could make it off the bridge, there was a gust of cool, autumnal wind. It turned Sadie's sweat to ice and she shivered. Then a latticework of silver and gold threads began to weave itself at the end of the bridge. It came together quickly, as if knitted by a host of thousands. One of the things launched itself at a closing gap, but wasn't fast enough; it was abruptly thrown back in a crackle of magical energy. The bridge was sealed.

Sadie spared a glance back at Deborah the librarian and her sisters. They were in their circle, gently swaying, softly singing. The breeze tousled their long wispy hair. Then she ran to the edge of the bridge and leaned out over the River.

"Now!" she shouted and thought she heard the River's laughter in reply.

The black water seemed to move faster, as if a dam had been opened far upstream. It hit the pylons holding the bridge up, with renewed and growing force. The water around them churned white, and cracks began to form in the concrete.

Come on, Sadie thought. *We only need another minute...*

But then she heard the screams and the cool breeze died. Then she heard the wailing.

The sisters' circle had been smashed. A few of the women were lying face down in the road, graying hair spread wide around them like auras, mixing with blood. In the center stood the horrible shape of Kyle the Crying Boy. His twisted arms slashed the air and his horrible blue eye pierced the night.

The silver and gold began to unravel.

Oh, fuck, Sadie thought. The hunter in the darkness's influence had been wider than she'd hoped. There was a loud crack. The bridge began to sway. They were so close.

She ran toward the circle, waving her hands above her head.

"Hey, Kyle!" she shouted.

The Crying Boy stopped his thrashing and looked around.

"Remember me, dickhead?"

"You," the Crying Boy said in his horrible dual voice. He started toward her. "You are going to be swept away. This whole town is going to burn and bleed."

"You live here too, moron. You think those things are going to be your new best friends?"

The Crying Boy hesitated. "The hunter has promised us."

"Wow, Kyle," Sadie said. "I knew you were stupid—you invited a demon into your brain—but this is next level."

The sisters gathered up their wounded and retreated. Deborah made eye contact with Sadie. The older woman had blood spattered on her face. She nodded, then clutched the crystals around her neck and began to sing again. The threads stopped their unwinding.

"I am going to eat your soul!" Kyle screamed. The wail inside him grew and grew until it was the only sound in the world. And then he threw himself at Sadie, every gnarled claw and yellowed fang pointed at her heart.

Sadie did not move. She balled her hands into fists, raised her chin, and stood her ground. She did clamp her eyes shut just as the Crying Boy was about to land. Even behind her eyelids, she could see his burning blue gaze.

One moment followed another, and she realized the blow hadn't landed.

She was still alive, still in one piece.

One eye opened, then the other.

The Crying Boy was suspended in mid-air, only a few feet from her. His eye and his mouth were wide in shock. A tendril of pure shadow, shaped something like a human arm, held him aloft as his limbs went slack. The wail faded, then was gone. Then the blue light went out.

"*Your exploits remain entertaining*," said the Long Shadows.

"That was close," Sadie said when she could catch her breath. "Thank you."

"*We do not accept thanks*," the Long Shadows said. "*Only repayment.*"

"I hope I live long enough to find out what horrible thing you'll want in return."

"*Oh, so do we.*"

Panicked shouting drew Sadie's attention back toward the bridge. Though the sisters' wall was holding, some of the dark hungry things had gotten through and were wreaking havoc. Beto's spirits held a few back, but he was bending under the strain. The deputies and people of Red Valley fought back with what weapons they had, but against fang and claw they could only do so much.

Just as Beto was about to fall, there was a blur of movement and the things attacking him fell back. The big man from Tips stood over him, feet planted wide. Now, though, he looked less and less like a man. His skin had gone scaly, his eyes yellow.

"Come on, you bastards," he growled. "I live in this shithole of a town too, so if you want to tear it down, you'll have to get through me."

Other patrons from Tips appeared by his side. They were outnumbered, but they looked pissed. A bear-killer made the first move, opening its jaws wide to snap at the big man. But he caught the thing in mid-flight, his massive hands holding its jaws open. His muscles bulged, the bear-killer thrashed, and then there was an ugly *snap* and it went still.

Sadie ran past all of them toward the River. The silver and gold threads weren't going to hold much longer. Huge things crashed against the wall, eyes full of malice. If it fell… She leaned out over the railing next to the bridge.

And saw the bridge's supports start to fail.

It seemed to happen in slow motion. The concrete splintered and the causeway began to wobble. The tearing at the magic wall slowed as the ground underneath the things' feet became unsteady. A few of them understood instantly what was happening and started to run for the far side. But the bridge was too long, and too far gone.

Chunks of concrete and steel began to fall into the River. Then the whole thing bent under the current and twisted unnaturally sideways, like a broken arm. The wall was forgotten as chaos consumed the things on the bridge, but not for long. With an ear-shattering crash, the bridge fell and the things fell with it. The water rose up to meet them.

There's your offering, Sadie thought with a shudder as everything disappeared beneath the River's flow.

RAGE LIKE IT had not felt in an age bubbled up in the hunter's chest. It had sensed the threat the River could pose, but had never expected it to make common cause with the pitiful defenders of the King's town. And now the hunter's army was lost in an instant, consumed by ancient waves.

This was unexpected. This was unacceptable. Blood must be spilt.

The King *would* die this night. But first his mortal thralls would suffer.

The hunter's eyes lifted from the ruin of its careful plans and took in the far shore. There were some of the things who had resisted its call, traitors who would pay. And there were humans, some living, some dying. But there was something else. A figure burning bright with magic. Human... but not. She had stood on the front lines. She had been the one to command the River.

They all needed to die, but *she* would die slowly.

CHEERS WENT UP from the bridge's defenders, but there was no time to celebrate. People all around Sadie were hurt, needed to get to the hospital; and still the fire burned deeper into Red Valley every minute. What they needed to do now was—

Undersheriff Hassler's voice cut through the night, amplified through a patrol car's speaker. "This is an unlawful assembly. You are all in violation of curfew. Return to your homes immediately or face arrest."

"What a dick," Sadie said under her breath, rolling her eyes. As the deputies started to turn their attention to the crowd, she thought about Beto. She found him sitting on a curb. His skin was ashen, his eyes red with blood.

"We did it," he said with a weak smile.

"We did," she said. "We saved this shit town."

He held up a finger. "We saved *our* shit town."

"You need to get to the hospital."

"I... hate hospitals."

"Everyone does," Sadie said. "I'll help you up."

"I'm fine," he said, though pain creased his face. "I'll be fine. Just need a minute. Or ten."

"Come on," she said. "We can—"

But Sadie never got to finish her sentence. A charcoal 1967 Cadillac screeched its tires as it pulled up in front of them. Sadie knew the car even before a tall, gaunt man with sandy hair and a ripped leather jacket got out. Streetlights reflected in his mirrored sunglasses as he faced Sadie.

"The King requests your presence," the King's Man said. "Immediately."

CHAPTER THIRTY

BETO FORCED HIMSELF to his feet and tried to step in between them, but Sadie stopped him.

"Don't worry about me," she told him. "I'll be fine. Get somewhere safe."

"You sure?"

She looked at the King's Man, then back. "Yeah. The King and I need to have a chat."

The King's Man opened the rear door. Sadie got inside.

They drove through the abandoned streets of Red Valley a little faster than she remembered last time. The King's Man said nothing, just kept his hands on the steering wheel and his mirrored eyes fixed forward.

"We could have used your help back there," Sadie said.

"The hunter in the darkness is no real threat," said the King's Man.

"Maybe not to you, but it was to the people in this town. The people who believed *you* would protect them."

"Sacrifices must be made in war."

"From what I understand, Red Valley's been making sacrifices for you for a long time," she said as the town sped by outside the glass. The streets, the houses, everything looked empty.

"You would be wise to consider who you trust."

Sadie eased her ledger out of her bag as quietly as she could. "I've been making careful consideration of exactly that over the last few days," she said, her voice covering the sound of her pen clicking. "Finding people worthy of trust in Red Valley can be a bit... tricky."

"Things are not always as they appear," said the King's Man.

Then, with an ear-splitting screech of tearing metal, the world started to spin.

At first, Sadie thought the hunter had caught them, but she then realized it was another car. It had hit them on the side, blowing through a stop sign and moving at high speeds along wide-open streets. The King's Man's car was heavy, made of steel, but the angle of impact was just right to send it careening into a lamppost, where it came to a sudden, sharp halt.

What in the hell was that? Then she saw the flashing lights. Red and blue, red and blue.

Smoke filled the car: rank, like burning oil. Sadie reached through the broken window and opened her door from the outside. As she stumbled out, she was met by a glaring spotlight and the unmistakable voice of Undersheriff Hassler.

"Put your hands in the air," he demanded from somewhere in the flashing night. More patrol cars were quickly converging on them. "You are both under arrest."

Her head was still ringing from the impact. She must have misheard that. The town was literally burning down and Hassler was trying to arrest one of the King's Men? And *her*?

"Are you fucking kidding me?" she heard herself shout. "Put your hands up!"

"No." This was the King's Man. He didn't raise his voice, but still the word cut through all the noise like a thunderclap. "The King tires of your interference. He reminds you that his patience is vast," the King's Man said, "but not infinite."

Hassler stepped out from behind the spotlight. He ignored the King's Man and looked right at Sadie. "You're probably proud of yourself, aren't you?"

"We just saved a lot of lives," she said. "So yeah, I am."

"Do you know how much that bridge cost? How long it will take to rebuild? No, of course not. You don't care about the destruction you cause. Or did you think you could just tell a Lie that would make it all go away?"

Sadie shook her head. "You really don't see it. They would have killed you."

"I warned you not to interfere," Hassler said. "And now you have to—"

The hunter in the darkness landed with all its bulk directly on top of the undersheriff, with a sickening crunch. The force of the impact knocked Sadie off her feet. It spread its wings, blotted out the sky and the pulsing lights. Gunfire erupted all around, but the hunter did not seem to even notice it. Sadie scrambled away, her palms scratched raw on the broken pavement, until she backed into the smashed car.

The hunter said something in a language that made Sadie's bones itch, then reached for her with a bloodied black claw.

Then the King's Man struck. Sadie saw only a blur, but heard the hunter's pained roar as the King's Man tore at its eyes with his bare hands.

Sadie jumped to her feet and ran. She did not look back. The night was rent with screams and roars and the sound of the creatures' feet slapping on the road. Her heart slammed against her ribcage and her ankle began to throb. None of that mattered. She just had to run. She just had to keep going faster.

More gunshots. More screaming.

Behind her, there was a rush of wind and the sound of massive wings flapping.

I really hope this works, Sadie thought. *Only time to try it once.*

She turned onto Jefferson Avenue. Washington was just one street over. Most of the way down the block, there was an empty dirt lot with houses on both sides. But no matter how fast she ran, it was just so far away. Just keep moving. Just keep moving.

The hunter struck just before she reached the empty lot. Sadie felt the rush of air and the horrible weight of the hunter's presence as it came down from the smoky sky. But as its great hooked talons swiped for her, she dropped. The ground chewed up her hands and elbows, but the slashing claw found only the space above her head.

The hunter rose up into the air. It was already turning, coming back around. Sadie's cuts burned as she moved, but she wasn't about to stop now. She ran for the lot. Her ankle flared, but she shoved that pain aside too; there would be time to hurt later. When she couldn't wait any longer, she screamed. The words tore out of her throat and into the emptiness ahead of her. Was she close enough? Would they hear? Would they be in time? She screamed and hoped. And ran.

Dust kicked up around her. And black wings followed.

Washington Street was just ahead. She had to reach the sidewalk.

The hunter swooped low, skimming the ground as it came for her.

Almost there.

And then she smelled roses.

Just in front of her, a low stone wall and iron gate began to appear. She pushed even harder. She stumbled, but caught herself before hitting the dirt, then threw herself onto the sidewalk just as the Gray House returned to its place in time.

A massive bloodied hand splatted onto the sidewalk next to her. The rest of the hunter in the darkness—the part that had been within the boundaries of the Gray House when it returned—was gone.

The front door of the house burst open.

"Sadie?"

Thomas looked down at her, puzzled.

It worked. Holy shit, it worked. She let out a shout of pure triumph, her voice echoing to the sky. *You come to my shithole town with your stupid wings and ugly face, stirring up hate and starting a war, and this is what you get. Hunter in the darkness? More like hunter in pieces.*

"Sadie?"

"Out here," she called back.

Thomas came running. He crashed through the gate, his eyes wide with panic. He stopped when he saw her, and then noticed the severed claw. "I trust we arrived in time?"

"Your timing was impeccable, Mr. Gray," she said as he helped her to her feet. "Thank you."

"You are welcome. Though I do feel compelled to ask," he said, toeing the claw, "what in damnation is that?"

"Dead," Sadie said. "That's the important thing."

Before he could reply, they were both blinded by approaching headlights. A sheriff's patrol car slowed and stopped in front of them, blocking the road.

It was no deputy who got out, however, but the King's Man. He limped, seemingly not from pain but rather a nearly ruined leg. Deep gashes had been ripped across his neck and chest and blood pooled at his feet.

"The King really must insist," the King's Man said.

Thomas drew a revolver from his jacket and leveled it at the King's Man. "Take another step and I will decorate your windshield with the contents of your skull."

Sadie put a hand on his arm and lowered the gun. "I'll be alright," she said softly. "Trust me."

"Sadie, the King should not be—"

"There's a lot of hurt people in Red Valley tonight," she said. "They could use your help, if you're willing to give it. Don't worry about me."

Thomas stiffened. He didn't raise the gun again, but neither did he put it away. "This is madness."

"Trust me," Sadie said, "I know."

"Very well," he said through tight lips as he glowered at the King's Man. "Good luck."

"Thanks." She tightened the straps on her bag and nodded to the King's Man. "Let's go chat with the King."

CHAPTER THIRTY-ONE

FROM THE KING'S hill, Sadie could see Red Valley burn. There was no night sky, not tonight, just a solid, unending expanse of ash and smoke. The fire line stretched from one horizon to the other. The whole town—what was left—was lit up red and black. And from what she could tell, the flames were converging on the hill.

The King's Man urged her forward. He was in tatters, but she had no doubt he could still break her with his bare hands, if she gave him a reason.

The inside of the manor was as hollow as before, though it was harder to tell in the dark. Down below in the basement, she noted that most of the alcoves were empty. What had become of the other King's Men, she did not know or ask.

At the mouth of the deep well, the King's Man stopped. And so did Sadie.

"The King waits below."

"I'm not going down there unless you make me," she said firmly.

The King's Man stared at her, perfectly still.

"I'm trying to save this town, and frankly I don't need—"

The King's Man grabbed her arm and shoved her forward. They descended, Sadie only a few feet in front of her escort as they went. It took some time; neither of them were in top form and Sadie was in no hurry.

Before she was ready, the path flattened out and she was standing on the cavern floor once again.

"I sorely underestimated you during our last visit," boomed a familiar voice like thunder. Two giant red eyes began to glow in the deep. **"If I had guessed at your true nature, I suspect it would have gone very differently."**

"True nature?" Sadie asked innocently. "Whatever do you mean?"

"I was distracted," said the King. **"I sensed your magic but took it to be your powers. But now I see you are more than a Liar: you are a Lie."**

"Who knew we had so much in common?" Sadie said. "I bet you wish you had just drained me of my magic then instead of waiting to do it now, am I right?"

A chuckle, like the breaking of boulders. "Why, yes," said the King of Red Valley. The walls pulsed light and the hint of a colossal face appeared in the dark. Sadie sensed more than saw an impossibly large span of jagged teeth, jutting sharp and raw like compound fractures.

"Oh, your dear mother, or whatever she was to you. I underestimated her as well. She lived an unrelentingly pitiful life, I must tell you. A waste of power and potential. Truly, not a single moment of inspiration. Up until the end, that is. But what an end!"

"You used her."

"The Liars of Red Valley have been tools, yes," said the King. "In service of a greater good."

Sadie backed up and found the King's Man blocking her way. "That greater good being you?"

The King sighed. "You insufferable mortals are terrible at so many things, but have always excelled at ingratitude."

Sadie pointed up the shaft. "You want to take a stroll outside and see the state your town is in, mighty King? Your enemies have arrived, yet you cower here while we fight your battles for you. Tell me, what should we be most grateful for, the army of monsters trying to murder us or the demonic fire trying to incinerate us?"

"Your ignorance is a stench in my nostrils."

"I know more than most, great King," Sadie said. "I know Red Valley was full of power long before you came. I know that draining that magic is the only thing that's kept you alive all these years. And I know it wasn't enough, so my mom Lied to revive you. Now you're sucking Red Valley dry in the hope it'll make you a real boy again."

The King's burning eyes towered high above her. "What stunning arrogance! You think you have discovered a truer history, but you have existed for a week. Your head is full of lies and other people's memories. I heard your lofty speech to the people of Red Valley, rallying them to your cause. But you aren't one of them. You are an aberration, a trick."

"You're the same as me."

"No," said the King. His voice filled the cavern. "I have existed throughout the ages. I have toppled mountains. I have commanded the heavens. I am fear and I am fury and I am the sundering wind. I am mighty. I am forever. You are **nothing**."

Sadie waited for his rant to end and for the cavern to fall silent before replying. "You are an echo," she said. "And you are fading."

"I was wrong to let you live," the King said. "I thought you would be harmless. I actually thought you might prove useful. And in some ways, you have. You killed the hunter in the darkness, no small feat for any mortal. Your defense of Red Valley has given me the time I needed to gather my strength. Soon there will be nothing left for me here and I will move on. But now you bore me, so I think I will take back what I gave to your family."

Sadie felt every cell in her body suddenly seize. It was like something was reaching into her guts and *pulling*.

Pain doubled her over, and the King's eyes grew brighter.

"Perhaps I never should have given this power to anyone in Red Valley," the King went on. "You have certainly never thanked me for it. Yes, I took it from the land, but I did share it. Perhaps if I had kept it all to myself, it would have been enough to keep me from succumbing to my wounds. But that does not matter anymore, does it? I will be stronger now, truly immortal. A Lie, more truth than truth. How fitting. Though she complicated my plans at the end, I should thank your mother for that, at least."

Blotches of white and red light burst in Sadie's vision. Her muscles spasmed. Her head was suddenly too heavy, her fingers numb and cold. It felt like dying, like her blood was turning to stone in her veins. *Blood.* That word shoved the pain aside in a brief spark of clarity.

"You know, for somebody who claims to have created the Liars of Red Valley," she said as she slid her ledger out of her bag, "you're awfully cavalier about where you leave your blood lying around." Sadie stuck her finger into the puddle of black blood around the King's Man's shoes.

"What are you—?"

She smeared the blood into her ledger, next to the words she'd written earlier:

The King is good.

Nothing moved in the King's cavern for a long time. Those red eyes glared down at her, unblinking, unmoving. Sadie felt the Liar's power working, but it was different than before. Would a Lie like this even work? The Lies could do much; she knew that well. But could they change the very nature of something like the King? She couldn't know, but the terrible draining pain had subsided; *something* was happening.

The King's massive head lowered until it was level with the floor and only inches from her face. She could feel heat radiating off him, whatever he was. Sadie slowly got to her feet. The King could kill her, but at least she'd be standing.

A low rumble came from the King's throat. The ground under her feet trembled. *Don't fight it, you big ugly bastard*, she thought as she glared into his fiery eyes. *You are already a Lie. I just made you into a better one.*

"Thank you, little Liar," the King said, in a voice like the end of all things. Then it softened: "I now know what I have to do."

When the King moved, it was like watching the night sky get up and walk away. The darkness that filled the cavern shifted and rose. Ancient rocks – or maybe ancient bones, too long idle – cracked and split. Sadie scrambled back as far as she could go and pressed herself into the wall as stones fell around her like a hailstorm. Something like a huge hand – covered in craggy, lichened scales and tipped in claws – passed over her head, gripped the side of the well, and pulled upward. Her mouth filled with the taste of sulfur and decay and she screwed her eyes shut as the world around her vanished in an explosion of noise and fetid air. And then, the King was gone.

Sadie peeled herself off the cavern wall, grateful and more than a bit surprised to be in one piece. High above, where there had only been dark before, she could now see the sky.

At the base of the stairs leading up, Sadie found the wounded King's Man. He was sprawled out on the floor, covered in dust and rocks that had fallen when the King made his exit. She nudged him with the toe of her shoe, but he didn't move.

"Sorry about that," she said to the fallen King's Man. She remembered the gleam of the sheriff deputy's blood dripping from his mouth, that first night. "I hope I did the right thing. I guess I should go up and see." The stairs looked long and treacherous. Even the thought of climbing them made Sadie's legs ache, but she was eager to be free of this place. "Well, I guess I'll leave you to it. I think you've earned a break."

The climb took a while. She hoped something of Red Valley would remain by the time she got to the top.

The manor house was gone, smashed to wooden bits by the King. Sadie scrambled out of the pit and surveyed the damage. The separate garage remained untouched, though a whole swath of trees leading toward town had been flattened. Giant footprints broke the dry ground. And in the distance, she saw the last great battle for Red Valley.

The King was there, surrounded by smoke and ruin. Flames tore at his black, twisted body like they were alive. And hungry. His flanks had been scorched and burned, exposing raw, bloodied flesh. But he fought back, snapping with fang and claw. Darkness moved behind the flames, but the King slashed at it too. Sparks and gouts of flame and sprays of ichor shot up into the sky.

When it was done, the fire faded. The darkness vanished. The night went still.

And the King fell.

We got him. That was for you, Mom, Sadie thought. *I hope you felt it, wherever you are.*

A dusty car crested the hill and came to a stop at the edge of the crater that had once been the King's home. Sadie tensed, fearing that one of the King's Men had somehow survived, but it was a woman who got out. She was maybe forty, dressed in workout gear, with her hair pulled back in a tight ponytail. She looked normal enough, or as normal as anyone could, standing on the King's hill that strange night. But the moment Sadie saw her, every hair on her body stood straight up. She didn't know what this was, but she knew it was bad. Real fucking bad.

"Can I help you?" Sadie asked in an unsteady voice.

"Yes," the woman said. "I've come to see the King."

Sadie looked over her shoulder and pointed. Unless she missed her guess, the King's body had come to rest in the shattered ruins of Red Valley's Walmart. "You just missed him."

The woman looked briefly at the town in the distance, then shook her head. "That is not the King."

This is bad. Bad bad bad.

"Okay," Sadie said. "If the King still exists, he's down that hole. As I've just crawled my way out of it, I'd rather not—"

"Show me."

Sadie was tired. She hurt. She wanted to see if anything she loved had survived the night. But she wasn't stupid. Whoever this woman was—*whatever* this woman was—Sadie knew she wasn't going to ask again. So against her will and better judgement, she once again found her way to the mouth of the King's well and started down the damp stone stairs.

The bottom was dark. The bioluminescent algae had faded to a barely visible glow. Sadie was about to apologize and maybe recommend coming back in the daytime, when the woman said something Sadie didn't understand and the cavern filled with blue light. Sadie looked around but couldn't identify where it was coming from. The light stretched into the distance, exposing parts of the cavern she'd never seen during her audiences with the King.

And there, tucked away in a corner that had been filled with gloom and shadow, were the bones of the King. The real King, long dead.

The woman laughed. Sadie shivered.

"It was you, wasn't it?" Sadie asked. Her voice echoed in the nearly empty cavern. "The one who challenged the King, who gave him the wound that killed him?"

"'Challenged'? Is that what he told you?" A pause. "Did he tell you my name?"

"He said it should never be spoken."

She laughed again. It was a distressingly normal sort of laugh. "Such a convenient answer. In truth, the King was not deemed worthy to know my name. Would *you* like to hear it?"

That question terrified Sadie more than any of the monsters she'd faced in the last week. "No," she said shakily.

"A wise answer." The woman approached the King's skull. She ran a hand along bone and rotting flesh. "A long time ago, we fought. I gave him a mortal wound and he fled. And I waited."

"What are you going to do now?"

The woman turned back. "What do you mean?"

"The King is gone. There's no one here to stop you."

"Stop me from doing what? I came to make sure he was dead," the woman said. "I've no other interest here." She looked around the cavern and nodded. "Though I think I will rest a while. It would be mutually beneficial if I am not disturbed."

"I'll spread the word."

The woman smiled, then collapsed to the cavern floor like her body was suddenly made of liquid. Something moved out of her and crept out among the broken rocks, something Sadie couldn't have described even if she ever chose to, and she never would.

This time, she climbed all the steps out of the King's well at a run.

CHAPTER THIRTY-TWO

SHE BRIEFLY LOOKED at the stolen sheriff's patrol car, but the driver's seat was still slick with dark blood and it would probably draw the wrong sort of attention. So she went into the garage. The lights didn't work, but enough smoky dawn light spilled in that she could find her way around. The first few tarps she pulled revealed nothing of interest, but then she hit pay dirt. She pulled the tarp all the way off then started to smile. A 1966 Shelby GT350, shiny black, with a pair of white stripes down the center line. And the keys were in the ignition.

"Well your majesty, you were an evil, blood-sucking bastard," Sadie said as she slid inside, "but at least you had decent taste in cars."

IT TOOK A while, but eventually Sadie found Beto at the hospital. The halls were full of the wounded and the grieving. Nurses with blood-stained smocks ran around with bags of antibiotics and rolls of gauze. Shell-shocked doctors with glazed eyes stumbled from room to room. But the reports on the TV in the waiting room said that the fire was now at 100% containment, thanks to the last-minute intervention of a massive creature everyone was assuming was the King. Sadie wandered the hospital in a daze until she found the familiar face of Nurse Abagail, who directed her to Beto's room.

Graciela was sitting at her brother's side. As soon as Sadie walked in, she ran over and hugged her, lifting her off her feet.

"You've *got* to stop almost dying," she said into Sadie's shoulder. "It's killing me."

"Deal. How's Beto?"

He had tubes in his nose and arms, and his eyes were closed. His heart rate beeped weakly on the screen of an attached machine. It reminded Sadie too much of her last—and as it turned out, first—visit with her mom.

"He'll live," Graciela said. "They weren't sure, didn't know what was wrong with him, but then he started improving not too long ago, like someone flipped a switch."

Sadie hoped the same would be true for the rest of Red Valley as well, with the King finally gone.

"I told you she'd be here," said a voice from the doorway. Thomas and Charles stood there, the former looking very uncomfortable dressed in green hospital scrubs.

"Thank you," Sadie said. "I'm sorry I made you come back."

"I'm sorry we left," Charles replied. He elbowed Thomas in the ribs. "He's sorry too."

"You decided to help?" Sadie asked Thomas.

"I volunteered my services," he said. "I may not be a modern man of medicine, but I can dress a wound, and there were plenty of those to go around."

"This town is lucky to have you."

"Yes," he said with a little twitch of a smile, "they are."

"How is the Gray House?"

"It survived the carnage," Thomas said. "Barely."

"Kind of like Red Valley."

"Indeed. And how much of that survival is due to you, I wonder?"

Sadie put a hand on Beto's arm. His skin was cool to the touch. "I didn't do anything," she said softly. She'd seen people being interviewed on the news when she came through the waiting room. They spoke about the King with a kind of reverence, some with tears in their eyes. They honored him. They mourned him.

It was all a lie, a damned lie. She remembered what she tried to tell them in the community centers, when she tried to get them to fight for themselves. It had worked, hadn't it? They'd come, they'd fought. And won.

Yet here they were, prostrate at the feet of their dead god, eager for their next fix. Maybe people didn't *want* to fight for themselves. They wanted a hero, a god, a savior. Lies, but maybe lies people needed. "It was the King who saved us."

"Indeed," Thomas said. Then, quieter: "You've got the makings of a great Liar, Sadie."

BETO WOKE A few hours later, complaining about scratchy sheets and dry air. The nurses needed the bed and didn't need his attitude, so he was discharged with remarkable speed. Sadie waited with him just outside while Graciela went to pull her car around.

"I hate hospitals," he said.

"Everyone hates hospitals," Sadie said. She could still see the dark stain on the asphalt from where the King's Man had mauled the deputy.

"So you did it, huh?" Beto said. "Saved the town at the bridge, then convinced the King to come out of hiding and stop the fire, or whatever that was."

"Yeah, not gonna lie," she said. "I'm pretty amazing."

"I think you're crazy," Beto said.

"That too."

An ambulance with pulsing lights pulled into the lot and Sadie and Beto moved out of the way. The EMTs jumped out and raced their patient into the hospital, another burst of chaos, already lost in the noise.

"I saw something on the news," Sadie said when they were gone. "It said Undersheriff Hassler was killed in the fighting last night." She didn't share her memories of his final moments, or of the sound of his bones shattering.

Beto's face was impassive. "Fucker got what he deserved, then."

Sadie didn't argue.

"So what happens now, gringa?" he asked. "No King, no Peace, no bastard undersheriff. What's Red Valley look like now?"

Maybe it was the exhaustion, but for the first time in a while, Sadie was genuinely cold. It was sure to be another blazing summer day in Red Valley, but in that moment, she felt a hint of autumn.

"I guess that's for us to decide," she said.

"Yeah," Beto said. "We'll probably fuck it up."

"Yeah," Sadie said. "Hey, you still want me to write that Lie for you?"

He shook his head. "Been giving that a lot of thought. At first I thought a Lie was a way out, a way forward. Once you've been inside, life doesn't feel like it belongs to you anymore. That's for other people. But fuck that. They don't get to take that from me too. My kid is going to know where they come from. Who they are. What kind of world they live in, good, bad, ugly, all that. Maybe learn from my mistakes, do it better than me."

"That's good," Sadie said, thinking of the last time she'd visited someone in this hospital. She could remember every crease in her mother's face at the moment the life had gone out of her. And those were real memories, *her* memories. Maybe she'd only been alive a week or so, but she'd made it a memorable one. "That's all any of us can hope for."

SHE DROVE HER new car as far as the barricades would allow, then parked and walked the rest of the way. Firemen were still putting down small blazes here and there, but no one bothered to stop her as she worked her way through the ruins of Red Valley. Late afternoon sunlight fell on what was left of Main Street. The shops that she'd seen boarded up only a few days ago were now gutted. Broken glass sparkled on the sidewalk. A burned election poster fluttered by. The undersheriff's face was blackened and mostly gone. Only a few words were left:

FOR A SAFER RED VALLEY. It looked like an ending, but maybe also a new beginning.

Red Valley had been here since the days of lumber and gold coming down from the mountains, but it had lost those callings years ago. Now, for the first time in generations, it would have to decide what it wanted to be, and why. She hoped it came up with a good answer; she was stuck here, after all. The Liar's powers were limited to the land that had given them, so this was her home, like it or not.

As she stared at the charred remains of everything she'd ever known, she was surprised to discover that she didn't mind. Her house on the hill was gone, but she'd never really lived there, had she? That had been her mom's house, isolated, separated from town. Sadie thought she'd move somewhere closer. There would be a lot of work to do, now.

When she reached the Treehouse Diner, she almost walked right by. The sign was gone, as was the rest of the building. Only the tree still stood. Its trunk was black, its branches bare. It broke her heart to see it like this, even more than the homes or the storefronts.

But there was something new in the air, something she couldn't really explain. She stepped through the charred parking lot and over the burned threshold. She could see where the counter had been, and make out the melted booths along the right wall. There was even a bit of a menu that had survived, touting the daily specials that never really changed. If she closed her eyes, she could smell the grill working in the back, hear the clank of plates from the dish room and the hum of chewing and conversation. The spice of apple pie filling tasted sweet on her tongue, even as her mouth filled with ash.

She waded through the destruction until she reached the tree. It stood in the middle of the destroyed diner, leaves turned to dust, branches curled and burned, barely distinguishable from the rest of the ruin. Its crown used to stretch high above the diner's roof. Now there was no roof, no incongruous, outstretched limbs. Just a husk. A shadow. How many times had she brushed a hand along the tree's rough bark as she moved around the diner over the years? A reassuring touch, a whispered word. Like an old friend.

But those moments weren't real, were they?

They were as real as she was.

Real *enough*.

Sadie touched the charred trunk and her fingers came away black. But then she brushed harder. She wiped away the layers of soot and charcoal. She pulled back the grime and broke away what had been killed by the fire. She dug and cleaned, until she found what she'd hoped to find. Underneath it all, sustained by a land that was finally free to breathe again, it had begun to regrow.

ACKNOWLEDGEMENTS

THIS IS CALLED the "acknowledgements" section so there's something I'd like to acknowledge first: writing a book is hard, and I wouldn't want to do it alone. There's one name on the cover, but don't let that fool you. Getting a novel out of the writer's imagination and into your hands is the work of a community of mostly unsung heroes. I will enumerate some of them here. If you like this story, you can thank each of them for making it what it is. And if you don't like it, well, I did try my best.

This book wouldn't exist without Jen Udden, who convinced me to write it and then convinced me to rewrite it. I pitched it to you thinking there might not be something here; you disagreed and you were right. You gave me tough feedback; I disagreed and you were right.

Of course you wouldn't be reading this at all if not for my editor David Moore and the team at Rebellion. Thank you all for taking on this weird, gothic, genre-fluid story and giving it a platform and an audience.

A special acknowledgement is due to Velma and Gabe, who were willing to mine our collective traumas of growing up in a fading, rural California town for this book. You'll recognize some stuff in here; sorry about that.

My wife is always my first reader, and I appreciate the tight balancing act that requires. Thank you for improving every book I've written, and for ignoring my anxious, impatient glances while you're reading. Though next time maybe can you read a little faster? That'd be great, thanks. (This will be an interesting test to see if my wife reads the acknowledgements section in this book.)

And finally, Grandma—if you are reading this—I'm really sorry about all the swearing.

ABOUT THE AUTHOR

Walter Goodwater is a writer, fencer, software developer, book-lover, and dad. His work has appeared on *Tor.com*, *Crime Reads*, and *Barnes & Noble*. He is the author of the *Cold War Magic* series, the latest book of which was nominated for a Dragon Award. His newest book, *The Liar of Red Valley*, is a story of magic, monsters, and secrets in a small rural California town, much like the one he grew up in. Today he lives on the Californian coast with his family, cats, and overflowing bookshelves.

wlgoodwater.com
@wlgoodwater

FIND US ONLINE!

www.rebellionpublishing.com

/rebellionpub   /rebellionpublishing /rebellionpublishing

SIGN UP TO OUR NEWSLETTER!

rebellionpublishing.com/newsletter

YOUR REVIEWS MATTER!

Enjoy this book? Got something to say?

Leave a review on Amazon, GoodReads or with your favourite bookseller and let the world know!